Enza

Kristy K. James

ISBN: 978-1470189648

I had a little bird,
And its name was Enza.
I opened the window,
And in-flew-Enza.
~Unknown~

Chapter 1

Whoosh!

Like a cannon ball exploding from its barrel, the sled took off down the hill, runners slicing through the snow like a warm knife through soft butter as it gained speed.

Jonathon Owens, all of ten years old, felt his heart pound at the thrill of it. He knew this was as close as a boy could come to flying, soaring over Europe at the controls of a Bleriot XI, hunting the Kaiser down.

But he wasn't over there helping to win the war. By the time he was old enough it would be over, the brave soldiers hailed heroes long home and old men. So the only thing he could conquer was this trail, avoided by all but the very bravest.

His blue eyes squinted against the bright

sunshine and keen wind that stung bare flesh until it was as red as a morning glory in the middle of July, though little was actually exposed. Just a narrow strip wide enough to see through was all that had escaped his mother's determined hands. From the thick knit hat covering his head to the even thicker scarf wrapped round and round his face and neck, to the heavy woolen coat and mittens, he was well protected from the elements as he flew across the white blanket that covered the hill - and everything else in sight.

Whoosh!

He quickly guided the sled around the branches of a bare hydrangea bush and actually left the ground, careening off a steep drift and sailing through the air.

His breath caught in his throat as, for mere seconds, he found himself airborne. He would have shouted for joy, except that same breath was knocked out of him when boy and machine made contact with the hard packed snow again.

Whump!

Whew! That had been close, he thought, his grip tightening against the wood. He had, narrowly, managed to maintain his position atop the sled and knew he wouldn't be able to resist boasting of this accomplishment at school Monday morning. Not that just everyone would believe him, of course, but it didn't matter. He figured those who claimed that they didn't were, plain and simply, green with envy over the exciting life he led.

All about him children swarmed the hill, engaged in the same glorious activity, screaming and squealing with glee. Oblivious to the frigid February weather they, like Jonathon, made countless trips to the bottom, but he ignored them all. Scaredy cats. They stayed on the safe trails. Trails for sissy girls.

As he neared the bottom, and the field where he would eventually coast to a stop, the wind beat against frozen cheeks, bared after the brief flight, and subsequent jarring from the landing. No matter. He couldn't wait to do it again. And again and again!

Vaguely disappointed with the swiftness in which the ride had ended, he didn't wait for the sled to come to a complete stop but, instead, rolled off and jumped to his feet. Standing with his hands on his hips he squinted toward the top, the glare of bright sunshine against brilliant white nearly blinding him. Finally he spotted her amongst the crowd.

"Beat that, Kathleen!" he shouted triumphantly, knowing his running start had sent him a good ten yards farther than before. Farther than his sissy girl sister could ever manage. Not that she would ever come down this trail. Kathleen stuck the pink tip of her tongue out at him. Jonathon couldn't actually *see* it, but she always stuck her tongue out at him so he was sure she did now.

Shrugging his shoulders, he bent down to grasp the rope tied securely to the sled in one mittened hand and walked to the side, near a small stand of trees that was safely out of harm's way. He knew first hand that being plowed into by the unyielding missiles could have painful consequences. Absently he rubbed the leg that had been broken two years ago.

As he trudged uphill in almost knee deep snow, to where Kathleen and his two brothers waited, Jonathon's legs ached and burned with the effort. But then he'd made many such trips this morning. It truly seemed unfair that such a joyous pastime should be hindered by an equally miserable climb. Still, it was a necessary evil.

Panting as he reached the top, his breath coming out in great, steaming clouds, he couldn't resist bragging about his latest accomplishment.

"*Did you see that?*" he demanded with enthusiasm.

"I did," Richard, five years his senior and the eldest of the Owens sons, shot back. "And if you do it again, I'm telling Mother."

"You would," Jonathon muttered irritably, bristling at the adult-like tone in his brother's voice. At fifteen Richard towered over almost everyone and thought he could boss whomever he pleased.

"You're lucky you weren't hurt," Richard continued, tugging the rope from Jonathon's hand, his other holding the smaller one of Charles, youngest of the five children.

"Hey! I was gonna go again."

"*We're* going down one last time, and then we're all going home. Charles and Kathleen are getting tired and cold." Gently he sat the boy on the wooden slats and climbed on behind him.

"That's not fair," Jonathon complained, trying to adjust the scarf on his face with snow crusted mittens, a painful move against icy cheeks.

"Too bad," Richard said simply, inching the sled forward with his heels in what Jonathon knew would be a wasted trip down the hill. Everyone who knew anything knew you needed a good running start.

He glared at the back of his brother's black coat, almost identical to the one he wore. Just once it would be nice if he could come alone and stay as long as he wanted. But no, Kathleen and Charles always had to tag along and spoil his fun.

With much envy he watched his brothers begin their descent and, before he could stop himself, stuck his tongue out. Then, feeling a bit foolish, he pulled it back in again before anyone could see. Bad enough when Kathleen did it.

Babies. When he grew up he wasn't having children. They spoiled everything.

"Thanks a lot, Kathleen," he snapped angrily. "I wanted to stay all afternoon."

"I'm sorry," came the timid reply, tears welling up in her blue eyes, the same shade possessed by each member of the family.

"Oh jeez. Don't cry or Mother won't let me come out for weeks. And then the snow'll be all gone."

"I'm sorry," she repeated, wiping a fat tear from her cheek. "I won't, I promise."

"Hello, young Owens'!" came a shout from the road. Jonathon turned to look, then groaned.

"Hello, Reverend Thornton," he called back, groaning again as he waved. All he needed now was for the reverend to find out he'd made his sister cry.

~~~

Colby Thornton shivered at the sight of the
~~~

Owens' children playing out in this particularly arctic weather. Just driving his buggy to Maude Granger's house had left him chilled to the bone, his teeth chattering now as he made his way back to town. He would be glad to get home and huddle near the stove today.

Another quick wave and his young parishioners were out of sight. Shaking his head, swathed in a thick scarf, Colby realized that it had been years since he'd frolicked in the snow. He wondered how it was that, as children, the weather had little effect but, as one aged, the cold and damp got to be more - well, cold and damp. More so with every passing year.

Not that it mattered. As minister to a rather large congregation he would never let something as trivial as the weather keep him from his duty, which included visits to the ailing, his mission this particular morning. Maude had been the last stop on a list of three.

These trips always annoyed his wife to no end. He could clearly see Anna's thinned lips, her eyes narrowed into unbecoming slits, as he closed the kitchen door behind him right after breakfast. After, of course, her incessant nagging that he never spent enough time with her.

Time for *what*, he wondered, waving to Mr. Hanley, who was shoveling several inches of fresh snow from the steps at the chair factory.

Time to listen to an endless list of complaints? That she never had enough of anything, from fashionable clothing to the sweets that had rounded her once lovely figure so that she looked like the snowman in a nearby yard. He always thought it odd that she should have let herself go so, yet still worry about keeping up appearances.

The only important thing in life to Anna, he supposed, was appearances.

Colby sighed. Eighteen years. Eighteen years of listening to those complaints. To that whining voice, comparable to fingernails screeching across a blackboard. Eighteen *long* years.

Approaching the intersection of Main and Lawrence, he noted that Charlotte was bustling with activity. Citizens stocking up on provisions, he expected, as they usually did following a heavy snowfall. Even though it was unlikely that another would follow, it seemed that most residents felt safer with overflowing cupboards.

He waved, calling out greetings to most everyone hurrying along the sidewalks. Bundled snugly to protect themselves from the chill they walked, leaning slightly forward against the wind that beat relentlessly against everything in its path. It was an almost comical sight. But they had no one to blame for their misery but themselves.

He doubted any were starving, or had such pressing business that they *needed* to be out. Not when they could have easily remained at home, warm and snug instead of-

Colby gasped in disgust at himself, taken aback at the direction of his thoughts. These people weren't miserable. *He* was. And no matter that they weren't aware of it, he had no business taking that misery out on them.

It wasn't their fault that he, a minister of the

gospel, wished every day of his life that he had the power to turn back time and choose a different wife. Or no wife at all. Which would be much better than to be bound to a woman that had never spared him so much as a token of honest affection once his ring was on her finger.

Making a determined effort, he shook himself out of the irritable mood that had fallen on him and guided the horse to a hitching post near Zourdos and Spires. Perhaps some chocolates would cheer Anna so that his afternoon might be spent as peacefully as possible.

A blast of warm air hit him full in the face at the same time his nostrils were filled with the wonderful aroma coming from two long glass cases on either side of the narrow store. Each was filled with glorious, mouth-watering confections.

Removing his gloves, leather stiff from the cold, Colby walked toward the counter where Angelo Spires waited with a smile. He wasn't sure how his own might appear because his skin felt as inflexible as his gloves, and a bit numb now as well.

"Good morning, Reverend Thornton," the shopkeeper greeted jovially. "How are you today?"

"Very well, thank you. And yourself?" He hoped that, rather than sounding like the lie it felt like, his response would fall under the 'calling things that were not as though they were' category, but silently asked forgiveness just in case.

"The same, my friend, the same. Praying for an early spring and an end to this hateful weather, but I can't complain." Colby flashed him another smile, one that felt like his lips actually moved this time.

"That makes two of us. Perhaps if we pray hard enough, the good Lord might grant our request, hmm?"

"One can hope." Angelo laughed heartily and said, "What can I get for you this morning?"

Colby quickly scanned what he hoped would be a peace offering and decided a dozen bonbons might be just the ticket. He'd say they were Anna's favorites except most anything made with sugar could be considered a favorite of hers.

"Anything else?" Angelo asked, his eyes lighting on the jar of peppermint sticks about the same time Colby glanced that way.

A fairly disciplined man, he prided himself in maintaining not only excellent health but a strong physique as well. Unfortunately he'd had a weakness for peppermint since he was a boy. And the red and white striped candies standing brightly in pristine jars on the countertop seemed to be calling his name.

He didn't indulge often but was overdue for a treat, he decided, holding up one finger.

"Only one?" Angelo teased, raising a dark, bushy eyebrow.

"I'm afraid so," Colby said, chuckling. "Not that I couldn't polish off every one of them, mind you."

A few more minutes of cheerful banter and Colby left the shop, his mood much improved. Even the thought of spending the rest of the day in the company of his wife didn't seem as daunting as it had a short while ago.

For a man of thirty – eight, he climbed back into his buggy with surprising agility and wasted little time in urging the horse along. Somehow, after the warmth of the store, the air seemed even colder.

Turning east on Seminary he saw that while the Sanitorium on his left was quietly peaceful, the Owens' home across the street was anything but. Jonathon was bounding up the steps, followed at a more leisurely pace by three of his siblings. He and Richard seemed to be quarreling. Again he called a greeting and waved at the bickering fellows.

~~~

Startled by the sudden crash of the door opening, Elliot Owens was momentarily distracted from another ongoing, wearisome argument. He glanced up, as did his wife, who was standing before their eldest daughter, hands on her hips, as Jonathon burst inside, fairly flying up the stairway in the hall.

"Jonathon Andrew Owens!" Margaret admonished at once. "You're tracking snow all over the house!"

"I'll clean it up when I'm done," came the muffled reply from somewhere overhead.

"You'll clean it up this instant," his wife was saying, though it would have taken a miracle for Jonathon to hear her as the hall filled with the rest of his brood. Elliot watched, for a moment, as Richard began to help the youngest children remove their boots and outerwear before turning his attention back to his wife and daughter.

As golden haired as her mother was dark, Elizabeth sat rigidly in one of the overstuffed chairs
~~~

flanking the stone fireplace across the room, glaring at Margaret defiantly.

"I fail to see why I should be forced to endure something I don't believe in simply because you do," she snapped irritably.

Elliot sat as calmly as he could on the sofa, poised to act as mediator should the need arise. Which it did more often than not with this contrary child. Since her involvement with the Women's Suffrage Movement, there had been little peace in the house. He had hoped that, in time, the situation would calm but as months passed, it only continued to escalate.

"As long as you live under this roof, you *will* obey our rules," Margaret said firmly, glancing toward the hall again as Jonathon's footsteps pounded back down the stairs and carried him outside. Muttering something about the Lord having mercy, she turned back to Elizabeth, who was saying,

"How can you possibly believe in something you can't see, touch or hear? It's one more way you let others control your life, Mother. Only in this instance, it's your invisible God instead of a man." Elliot sighed.

"That's quite enough, young lady," he told her, fixing her with a parental stare that any of the other children would have wilted under. But not Elizabeth.

"Enough for *whom*, Father? You've had enough of my opinions and expect me to bow to your wishes? Aren't I, too, entitled to have had enough of your antiquated fantasies of God?"

"*Elizabeth!*" Margaret's face actually paled at that. "I will not allow such blasphemy in this house! Our family *will* attend church. And as *you* are a member, whether you like it or not, you will go as well."

"Of course, *Mother*. Whatever you say, *Mother*," she said sarcastically, coming quickly to her feet, her gaze not wavering from her mother's face. "Why should I be entitled to a feeling or thought you haven't forced on me?"

Elliot braced himself. He'd known Margaret long enough to know that the girl was coming perilously close to crossing the line with her.

But before catastrophe could strike, Elizabeth flounced from the room, stepping carefully around the puddles of melting snow covering the hall floor and stairs. Richard, from where he stood helping Charles hang his coat, scowled at his sister.

Elliot looked back at Margaret, noting that she hadn't moved so much an inch, still standing before the now empty chair.

"Papa?" Kathleen had crept over to where he sat, fat tears ready to spill down her cheeks, still rosy from the trip to the hill. Elliot lifted her onto his lap and held her close, stroking her soft brown hair. Sweet child.

Like Richard, Kathleen possessed a very gentle spirit but, while Richard tried to fix problems, she was deeply hurt and confused by them. He knew that Kathleen viewed Elizabeth's recent rebelliousness as a threat to her family and his heart ached for her.

"Mother?" Richard said hesitantly. "Charles

would like some hot cocoa. Should I make it?"

Elliot saw his wife inhale slowly, deeply, and relax the slender hands that had curled into fists at some point during the argument.

"I'll do it," she murmured, a stiff smile at their son as she turned toward the hall. "Would you mop up the snow before someone slips and hurts themselves please? I'll see to it that Jonathon does one of your chores when he comes back inside."

"It's all right, Mother. I don't mind."

"I'll see to it, Richard," she repeated, disappearing in the direction of the kitchen.

While Richard followed her to get the mop, Charles headed for a small box in the corner, flashing a dimpled grin at his father.

"We went swidin', Papa," he said happily, dumping a small mountain of wooden blocks on the rug that covered most of the honey colored floor.

"I know you did," Elliot told him, continuing to stroke Kathleen's hair. She had relaxed to the point he suspected she'd fallen asleep.

"Jonafon was mad 'cause Wichad made us go home."

"I'm sure he was. And what about you, young man? Were you also angry about having to come home?"

"No, sir. I was co'd."

Elliot smiled, watching his youngest child as he built- Well, only Charles knew what he was building, but he took great pride in the effort.

"Wichad was mad, too."

"Goodness," Elliot exclaimed dramatically. "And I thought sledding was supposed to make children happy."

"Jonafon slided down the dangewas pawt of the hill an' Wichad said he was gonna bweak his neck."

This time Elliot couldn't suppress a chuckle. His oldest son had long ago appointed himself caretaker to everyone, and between Elizabeth and her current attitude, and Jonathon's adventuresome spirit, poor Richard was turning into a nervous wreck.

"Is that why you had to come home? Because your brothers were fighting?"

"No. Me an' Kafleen was co'd," he said simply then, seemingly done talking, concentrated on his blocks.

Not for the first time did Elliot marvel at the differences in his children. Raised by the very same parents each possessed uniquely individual personalities and, with them, their own peculiarities. Especially Jonathon.

No one need ask where his middle son had hurried off to, first to his room to retrieve his journal and pencil, and then to a 'safe' place to take detailed notes on old Mr. Mertz again.

Jonathon was sure the poor man was a German spy, and had followed his movements relentlessly since America had entered the war. All Mr. Mertz had to do was sneeze wrong and he was under suspicion for some imagined infraction.

Elliot knew full well that the old man was innocent of any crimes but, much to Margaret's dismay, did nothing to discourage Jonathon. Truth be told, he probably *encouraged* him because the boy's enthusiasm and unwavering belief that he would, by war's end, be hailed a hero, tickled Elliot to no end.

Richard, finished with the task of cleaning up after his brother, walked wearily to the chair so recently abandoned by his sister. He lowered himself slowly into it, as though he were very tired, and stared vacantly into space.

Elliot wished he could ease the young man's burdens but was powerless to do so. No matter that he'd tried time and again to convince Richard that the problems the family faced were for him to deal with, Richard couldn't seem to help taking them on anyway.

Within moments of Margaret striding into the hall, announcing the cocoa was ready, the telephone rang. With an exasperated sigh she lifted the receiver.

"Hello?" she said quietly into the mouthpiece. Elliot saw her roll her eyes heavenward and grinned.

Anna Thornton.

Had the entire family, save Elizabeth for the moment, not thought so highly of Colby Thornton, they would long ago have found a new church. Except for other gossipy busybodies like herself, no one particularly liked the preacher's wife. Margaret was among those who couldn't bear to think about, much less speak, to the woman.

~~~

"...and the things spewing from the woman's mouth! Lord have mercy, Margaret," Colby heard his wife saying as he opened the front door to their
~~~

parlor. “I can’t even repeat the words!”

He managed to avoid the expected glare, slinking over to set the small Zourdos and Spires box on the round, polished table in front of her before quietly slipping out of his coat. He hung it in the closet beneath the stairway and hurried out to the kitchen.

There he poured a cup of scalding coffee, dragged a worn chair before the stove, and sat down as close as he dared to absorb the warmth radiating from its iron jacket. It seemed, for a few moments, that he was actually colder than he’d been outside as his body adjusted to the drastic temperature change. Shivering just a bit, he raised the heavy cup to his lips and took a cautious sip. The hot liquid burned a path all the way to his belly and he thought nothing had ever felt better.

Absently, the quiet drone of Anna’s voice reaching his ears, Colby took the small bag containing his peppermint stick from the pocket of his suit coat. In a moment of sheer defiance, he dipped the tip of the candy into his coffee and stirred it gently. Anna thoroughly disapproved of the practice, complaining that it was childish, but he thought it added a very pleasant flavor to the brew.

And there wasn’t much that was pleasant here at home. Instead of enjoying the coziness of the kitchen with a woman who could appreciate it as much as he did, he sat alone, aching for the companionship most people took for granted.

A sigh that seemed to originate from the soles of his feet escaped him and, finally warming up, he slumped back, staring moodily out the window.

Thick crystals of ice that had built up around the edges of the glass during the night cast a rainbow of colors across the room as rays of brilliant sunlight shone through them.

Though he'd momentarily shaken the gloomy feelings that had assaulted him as soon as his eyes had opened shortly before six, they'd returned with a vengeance as soon as he'd set eyes on Anna again.

Another sip of the newly, and *strongly*, minted coffee surprised him, and he looked down to see that almost an inch of the stick had melted. He sat the cup on the sideboard and popped the candy into his mouth, his lips curling around the end with the same anticipation one usually saw displayed in children.

Count your blessings, he commanded himself sternly.

A thriving church. A congregation who loved him nearly as much as he loved them. Good, no, *wonderful* friends.

Life could be much worse. He could be bound to Anna without those things. And then life wouldn't be worth living. Not at all. As it was, nearly every moment away from her was heaven on earth. Surely he deserved a bit of heaven before actually making the trip there. Without a doubt Anna provided insight into what hell must be like.

His thoughts were interrupted by a light tap at the back door. Glancing up he saw that the frost was too thick to see who the visitor was. But he knew. A grin lit his face as he got to his feet and strode to the door.

"Good morning, Marcus," Colby greeted, a fresh blast of cold air chilling him.

"Good morning," came the quiet reply. The man stood about a head shorter than Colby on a good day. In the frigid temperatures, huddled against the wind, Marcus McClelland appeared even smaller. "I saw the missus in the hall and took a chance that you might be out here."

"And you were right," Colby said, his grin broader. Though he tried to hide it, he knew that Marcus would rather kiss a hog than spend even a minute in Anna's company. "Come on in. The stove is hot."

"No. I can't. I just came to return your book." He reached into a massive pocket and pulled out Tom Sawyer. "I hadn't read it since school. I'd forgotten what a good author Mark Twain was."

"So you enjoyed it?"

"Immensely. Thank you, Colby."

"Sure you won't come in for a while? You owe me a game of chess. As I recall, you beat me quite badly last time."

"I wish I could," Marcus sighed. "But I got word last night that Mr. Taylor wasn't doing very well. I'm expecting a call for arrangements any time now."

"I'm sorry to hear that."

"So was I." Marcus scuffed his foot in the snow. "Well, I'd best be going."

"Come again when you can stay longer."

"I will. Soon."

"I'll look forward to it."

~~~
~~~

Marcus made his way back to the road, shivering uncontrollably. He hated winter. It seemed like he could never get warm, as though the chill permeated his bones the moment the last leaves fell from autumn trees and setting in until the spring thaw. Why he remained in Michigan was a mystery because he longed for the warmer climate of, say, Florida or Arizona.

Pulling the collar of his coat close around his neck against the brisk wind, he quickened his pace. If he didn't hurry, he'd be frozen through before he got home.

And he had to stop at Waddell & Boyer's if he intended to eat something other than oatmeal for supper. There was no one to blame but himself. They would have sent a delivery boy if he'd remembered to phone them first thing this morning. But he hadn't.

Oh well. He'd survived it before and would this time, too.

As he walked, he mentally went through his inventory. The Taylor's weren't well off at all. And as he refused to stock the ugly pine boxes, he would be taking a loss on one of the finer caskets stacked in the shed attached to the back of his house. Mr. Taylor's son, Clive, was a friend of his. Or as close a friend as Marcus allowed himself.

An undertaker, Marcus had a problem with handling funeral arrangements for anyone he knew well so he refused to allow himself to get close to anyone. It led to a fairly lonely life but at least it was a life free from grief.

And it wasn't that he was *alone* alone. He was involved in many community activities and meetings for the businessmen's association. But, he had to admit, he was a little lonelier than usual today. A game of chess had been on his mind when he started out for Colby's a short while ago. But the expression on Anna Thornton's face when he caught a glimpse of her through the etched glass in the front door had quickly put that thought to rest. Better to leave the book and head for the safety of anywhere but there.

Poor Colby. Life wouldn't be worth living, in his opinion, if one were saddled with a wife like that. Thank goodness he wasn't the one who was stuck with her. It was just too bad that Colby was. He didn't deserve that.

Suddenly he wasn't as lonely as he had been. Amazing what the trials of others did to show you that you didn't have it so bad after all.

Marcus turned right when he reached Main Street and he was thankful that the bricked sidewalks had been shoveled by conscientious shopkeepers, making his trek a bit easier.

The weather never seemed to hinder people, he thought wryly, observing the crowded street. Nothing, with the exception of rain (and then even that was debatable) kept the kind folks of Charlotte home when there was shopping or socializing to be done. Marcus realized he was no different, about the same time he realized he'd reached the door of the meat market.

He grimaced and glared at the door handle as though it might bite him then, taking a huge gulp of air, and stealing himself for what he knew awaited him, he reached for the knob and reluctantly stepped inside.

The huge slabs of meat that hung from thick hooks anchored in the ceiling behind the counter turned his stomach and he stared at the floor as he approached it. But it wasn't the meat hanging all around him that made the bile rise up in his throat; it was the pungent smell of blood. An odor guaranteed to sicken him.

"Good afternoon, Mr. McClelland," Arthur Boyer greeted him, a smile in his voice. Marcus never actually saw it, but always *heard* it when he was forced to enter the establishment. He always thought it odd how one could *hear* a smile, or a frown. "What can I get for you today?"

"Steak," was all Marcus could manage as he tried his best not to breathe.

"Coming right up."

Marcus heard the sharp knife slice through bone, then paper being ripped off the roll, and soon a neatly wrapped package was being slapped down on the counter. He paid for his purchase and hurried toward the door just as fast as his feet would carry him.

Safely outside, he leaned against the window and took in huge breaths of fresh air. In a few moments his stomach settled and he felt like he could resume the trip home.

"Are you all right, Mr. McClelland?" a quiet voice asked. Marcus looked up to see Daniel Pullman standing in front of him, looking a bit worried.

"I'm fine," Marcus said quickly, straightening.

~~~

"Are you sure?" Daniel asked, concern lacing his voice. Mr. McClelland looked a little pale in his opinion.

"I'm fine, just fine," the man assured him and hurried away. Daniel just stood there and shook his head. Mr. McClelland struck him as an odd sort of fellow. Nice enough, but there was just something about him...

He shook his head again and started across the street, glad to be finished working for the day. It seemed as though half the town had letters and postcards to mail and the post office had been a beehive of activity from the moment he'd arrived that morning. Of course he preferred it when there was plenty to keep him busy. It helped the hours to pass quickly.

He glanced back at Mr. McClelland, just to assure himself that the man was all right, a grave mistake he would regret a few seconds later when he failed to see the gleaming Model T round the corner. The driver took it faster than was safe under the best of conditions, but considering his attention was on a pretty girl across the way instead of on the snow covered road ahead of him, he didn't see Daniel until it was too late.

Daniel heard the shouts from passersby just before the bumper plowed into his hip. But that pain was nothing compared to the tires rolling over his leg after he was thrown to the ground. He felt the bone break in at least two places.
~~~

Just before he lost consciousness he lamented the fact that his enlistment in the army would have to be postponed for a while.

Chapter 2

Despite the fact that someone - or something - seemed to be sitting on his leg, and though his eyes seemed to be very firmly closed, Daniel felt surprisingly good. In fact, he felt better than he had in quite a while. Happy, even. Now if he could just open his eyes.

With a great deal more effort than it should have taken, he managed to raise a hand to his face and tried to lift one lid. It helped a bit and, for a brief moment, he saw a flash of daylight.

"Hmm."

And so he concentrated a little harder – but only succeeded in pushing his fingertip across his eyeball, which was definitely not his intention. Not to mention that it hurt like blue blazes. After giving it a little thought, he decided that there really didn't seem to be any urgency in opening his eyes after all and let his hand fall back to his side.

Since there wasn't anything he could do for the moment, he wondered what he might do to pass the time. Because, even though he felt terrific, it was rather boring to simply be laying here doing nothing.

"If you would please remove yourself from my leg, I would be most appreciative," he said to whoever was sitting on his leg. No one responded. Which was probably just as well. What exactly did one say to someone who had been making themselves comfortable while using your leg for a chair?

"Mademoiselle from Armentieres, Parlez – vous," he began to sing. Or to try and sing. His lips didn't seem to be working a whole lot better than the rest of him, but he liked the song and concentrated on recalling the words.

"She hasn't been kissed for forty years." Did that sound more like, 'he hasn't been kicked for fourteen ears'? No, he was singing it right. It had to be that his ears weren't up to par either.

"Mademoiselle from Armentieres, Parlez – vous, she got the palm and the Croix de Guerre, for washin' soldiers underwear." Daniel wouldn't even consider what that part had sounded like to him.

"Mr. Pullman?"

Now he was talking to himself?

"Mr. Pullman?" No, that was definitely not his voice.

"Are you the person who has been sitting on my leg?" he asked curiously. "Because it is quite rude, you know. I would appreciate it if you removed yourself immediately."

"I assure you, sir, that I am *not* sitting on your leg."

"Then could you please demand that whoever is go and sit somewhere else now?"

"There's no one sitting on your leg, Mr. Pullman."

"I can't move it," he said reasonably.

"That's because it's in a splint." He thought about that for a moment and figured his ears were in worse shape than he'd imagined.

"No, I believe someone is sitting on my leg."

"Mr. Pullman," came the amused response. "Your leg was broken in four places when the automobile ran over you. You also have a concussion."

"An automobile ran over me?" Daniel asked clearly doubting the validity of that possibility.

"Yes, sir. Early this afternoon." Vague images of a shiny black Model T flashed through his mind.

"I think I might remember that" he murmured wondering why his memories were so unclear. "Why doesn't it hurt? *If* I broke my leg?"

"Laudanum," she answered.

"Oh, I can't take Laudanum," he told her pleasantly. "Who are you?"

"Your nurse."

"'Your nurse?' That's a very unusual name."

"I am Miss Hakes, your nurse."

"Well, Miss Hakes, your nurse. You sound very pretty. Are you? You see, I find that I am unable to open my eyes and, therefore, cannot look for myself." He heard an exasperated sigh.

"Whether I am or not makes little difference.

How are you feeling, Mr. Pullman."

"Very well, thank you."

"No pain?"

"If I were in pain I wouldn't feel very well now would I?" he asked patiently.

"Are you thirsty?"

"Not especially. Are you?"

"No. Hungry?"

"Then you should eat something."

"I beg your pardon?"

"I said if you're hungry, you should eat something."

"I'm not hungry."

"Then why did you say you were?"

"Mr. Pullman, I was asking if you were hungry."

"No. I distinctly remember you asking me if I were thirsty." He thought he heard a low growl. It seemed to him that if she were getting frustrated, then she should be a tad more clear in trying to get her point across.

"*Mr. Pullman*, are *you* hungry?"

"No, Ma'am, I am not."

"Is there anything I can do to make you more comfortable?"

"I'm perfectly comfortable, thank you."

"Then, if you'll excuse me-"

"What did you say your name was?"

"Miss Hakes."

"Miss Hakes, I don't want any more laudanum."

"You would be in a great deal of pain without it, Mr. Pullman."

"Then I suppose I shall have to live with the pain, Miss Hakes. I don't want any more." She didn't respond for several long moments.

"I'll have to speak with the doctor about that," she finally said.

"Miss Hakes?"

"Yes, sir?"

"My grandfather had a problem with laudanum after the war between the states. I don't want that kind of problem."

"I – understand."

"Miss Hakes?"

"Yes, Mr. Pullman?"

"I still think you sound pretty."

~~~

"Jonafon? Jonafon?" Jonathon felt his hand being tugged and tried in vain to stay asleep. In his dream he was an esteemed war hero, fearlessly fighting in the Great War and killing every bloody Hun he saw. And there were so many of them he could have fought them the entire night. Maybe even a week! For every one he massacred, there were a dozen to take his place.

"Go away," he mumbled into his pillow.

"Jonafon. I had a bad dweam. I'm scawed."

With a mighty sigh, Jonathon let the last remnants of the dream slip away as he rolled to his side and flung the blanket back. Charles quickly scrambled up, snuggling against him and Jonathon could feel him trembling. After he smoothed the covers over his brother he gently rubbed his back.

"What did you dream about?" he asked sleepily, then yawned.
~~~

"A monstu was unda my bed. He was gonna eat *me*!" Charles shuddered against his shoulder. Jonathon rolled his eyes in exasperation but only said,

"How could a monster fit under your bed? Monsters are *huge*. Way bigger than Pop. And Pop can't even fit under your bed."

"It was unda my bed," Charles repeated stubbornly, shuddering again. "It was big an' gween an' had big teef."

"I guess that would scare me, too," he said sympathetically, yawning once again. "*If* I thought there was a monster under my bed. But I already told you, there isn't enough room for a monster to hide."

"You sure?" came the hopeful response.

"I'm positive. But if you're still scared you can sleep with me tonight. I won't let anything hurt you."

"Okay. Fank you."

"You're welcome. Now go to sleep so we won't be too tired tomorrow."

"Okay."

Jonathon continued to pat Charles' shoulder until he was sure he was asleep, then closed his own eyes hoping the dream would come back.

Babies!

~~~

Marcus looked through the sheer curtain that covered the oval, etched glass window in his front door. As usual there were few people out at this early hour and he quickly opened the door and
~~~

hurried across the porch, shivering against the cold.

Peering up and down the street again, just to be sure that someone hadn't come out, he ran down the steps to where his newspaper lay. About five yards from his house. In approximately the same spot that it could be found every morning, day after day. Even year after year, which was surprising, given that he'd had a number of different delivery boys during that time.

Snatching it up he ran back into the house, the hem of the silk dressing gown his mother had sent at Christmas flapping about his knees. One of these days he would have to call the editor and demand that it be delivered on the porch.

Slippered feet made no sound as they padded along the oriental runner that ran the length of the hallway leading to the kitchen. Marcus tossed the paper on the table with a soft thud on his way to the stove.

Giving the pan of oatmeal a single stir, and deciding it had finally reached the proper consistency, he spooned a generous mound into a china bowl, topped it with several heaping spoonful's of brown sugar and a little ice cold cream, then carried it, and a cup of coffee, to the table.

The telephone rang as he was about to be seated but, after the briefest of hesitations he decided to ignore it. A man ought to be able to enjoy his breakfast in comfort and peace, oughtn't he? If it was important, the caller would try again.

Sighing, he opened the paper to get a better look at the picture of a new American submarine.

War officials hoped it would be powerful enough to beat the dreaded U-Boat, he read, as he alternated bites of oatmeal with sips of scalding coffee.

"Very impressive," he thought, as he read the dimensions of the vessel. Not that he could imagine ever setting foot on it. In fact, he doubted the sanity of each and every man who could seal themselves in that floating tomb, far beneath the ocean's surface, for days at a time.

Just the thought of being trapped in an enclosed place like that, with no means of escape, was enough to pepper his forehead and upper lip with tiny beads of sweat. It brought the memory of the worst thing that had ever happened to him immediately to mind. Back to the afternoon he'd decided to play a trick on his father.

He'd crept into the storeroom, where there were always two or three extra caskets. A family had just chosen the finest one and had gone home to prepare the body of their loved one for burial. His father was to bring it around shortly.

So Marcus snuck in and, after quite a struggle, managed to get the lid open. It had been well built, solid wood stained a rich, glossy walnut, and buffed until it gleamed. His plan had been to hide in it until his father came to load it in the wagon.

"Oh ho!" he had laughed, anticipating the surprise on his father's face when he opened the lid and Marcus sat up and shouted, "Boo!"

But the lid had come down with a bang and he worried that the sound might have given him away. When no one came running, he readied himself for the big moment. And waited. And waited.

After what felt like an eternity, Marcus decided that the idea really hadn't been such a good one after all and pushed on the lid to open it. Only it hadn't budged. So he pushed with all his might and it still wouldn't budge.

Hindsight, and the common sense that naturally comes with age, might have suggested if he couldn't easily open the lid while standing and using his body weight to help heft it up, then he certainly wouldn't have been able to open it while lying on his back, with little room to move.

But at nine years old, common sense hadn't been in great supply.

Even now, some eighteen years later, Marcus felt his heart begin to race, the panic and fear nearly as real now as it had been then.

All told, his parents decided he'd spent less than thirty minutes in his confining hiding spot, his father waylaid by a talkative neighbor. By the time he'd been set free, though, he'd screamed himself hoarse, his hands bruised and bleeding from his struggle to escape.

With a shudder, Marcus pushed the memory away. He never allowed himself to remember that incident and silently cursed the photograph that had brought it back so vividly.

He closed the paper abruptly and pushed it away, finishing his breakfast much faster than usual. Which would be for the best. He had to pick up a body and deliver it to the church in about two hours anyway.

In short order, he was walking into his small parlor, wearing one of his customary suits, this one a dark gray. Sometimes he thought it would be a pleasant change to don a pair of woolen trousers and a ratty old work shirt but he took his reputation as an undertaker quite seriously and was, therefore, never caught looking anything less than professional.

A glance at the grandfather clock that stood in the northwest corner of the room told him there was ample time until he had to leave. Enough so that he decided that it was a good time to look at the letter from Derek McGovern that had arrived in the post the day before.

Carefully sliding the silver letter opener in, he made a quick, precise cut and took out a single sheet of paper. Another baby on the way?

Since graduating from college, Derek had gone on to open a successful funeral parlor in Philadelphia. He'd also married a lovely young woman and, at last count, was the proud father of four young children, two boys and twin girls.

Sometimes Marcus owned up to an occasional twinge of jealousy when comparing his lonely, solitary life to that of his friend. Not that he had the remotest desire to saddle himself with a passel of children. But still, sometimes he wondered if he might not be missing out on something. Then again, he'd never had a conversation with a woman when he hadn't hemmed and hawed, and stammered and stuttered. So no, he probably was better off as he was. If he couldn't, at the very least, talk with a woman, it was unlikely that he would ever get around to procreating with one.

His attention back on the letter, he expected to

hear about baby number five. Perhaps even another partnership offer. Those came about as regularly as birth announcements.

But it was just another update on life in the big city, although in closing there was another offer to join him in business.

~~~

Elliot turned the sign in the window so that it said, 'CLOSED,' locked the door behind him and took off walking at a brisk pace. Time had gotten away from him and if he didn't hurry, he'd be late. That just wouldn't do at all.

As usual, Charlotte was bursting at the seams with people. Neighbors, friends, even strangers passing through town, stopping for a bite to eat or to put petrol in their automobiles. He waved to everyone who seemed on the verge of stopping him, hoping he looked like a man on a mission, because he really didn't have time to make small talk. That being the case, he made a point of glancing at his pocket watch every few seconds.

Elliot only slowed once as he crossed Lovett Street, when Burl Overmeyer commented on his closing up shop so early. He quickly replied that he was late for an appointment and kept right on going.

Fortunately that was the only thing that threatened to detain him and he rounded the corner at Seminary in good time. A few more feet and he was bounding up the stairs and letting himself in the front door.

Kathleen waited patiently in the parlor, her tea
~~~

set laid out neatly on the table. When Elliot entered the room she smiled brightly and ran over to him for a hug. He lifted her easily and held her close.

"How's my girl feeling this afternoon?"

"Much better, Papa," she said with a giggle. Kissing her forehead he was pleased to find no trace of the fever that had kept her home these past two days remained and he sighed with relief.

"Well that is *good* news," he exclaimed, sitting her down gently. He reached up to loosen his tie and remove his wool jacket before easing down to sit on the floor in front of the miniature child's table.

Kathleen was already pouring tea from a tiny pot into equally tiny cups. Very small squares of sandwiches sat on plates that matched the rest of the service, and his young daughter refused to take her place in the small chair until she'd served him first.

"I have to say that everything looks absolutely delicious, Miss Kathleen," Elliot said honestly. "I was very glad to leave the store today so I could come home and have dinner with such a lovely young lady."

"Papa!" Kathleen giggled softly as her cheeks flushed a pretty shade of pink.

"Well, it's true. Now let me taste this tea because I worked up quite a thirst on my walk, you know." He made a show of lifting the cup, far too small and dainty for his large hand, and took a sip. "Mmm. Very good. Did you make it yourself?"

"Papa, *your finger*."

"Oops." Elliot suppressed a grin as he stuck his little finger out, just as all well behaved ladies should. "I forgot."

"Well you shouldn't," she said sincerely. "You mustn't drink your tea if you can't drink it right." From the expression on her face, Elliot knew that his wife had actually prepared their repast *without* help, and Kathleen preferred to pretend that she hadn't.

"I'll try to remember that," he promised, sitting the cup down and gazing at her. "So tell me, what have you been doing today?"

"Oh lots of things!" She rattled on and on as they ate diminutive sandwiches, filled with thin slices of roast beef.

Evidently Meg had continued to confine her to bed, until it was time to prepare for their tea party. Still, Kathleen had managed to take good care of her extensive collection of dolls, rather *babies*, and she gave her father a detailed account of how each of her charges were doing. Poor Bessie had managed to catch the cold that she, herself, was finally getting over. Annie had also begun to sneeze. Harriet had fallen and bumped her head, requiring a cool cloth so she wouldn't bruise.

"My, it sounds as though you've had a busy day."

"Oh yes, Papa, I have had!" She took a sip of her tea, pinky finger pointed straight out. "And have you been busy, too?"

"My goodness, yes."

He proceeded to entertain her with a detailed description of one of his older customers. Mrs. Winfield suffered from the delusion that her wide, size nine foot would fit neatly into a slender size four. One of his challenges was to convince her that, due to the weather, her poor feet must have swelled, making it necessary to move to a larger pair.

"She sounds silly," Kathleen told him, laughing merrily when he held his hands apart to indicate how small a four was compared to a nine.

"Well, between you and me, Sweetheart, she is rather silly. But we must never say that to her."

"Oh I wouldn't, Papa. *Never.*"

"I know that. And I appreciate your discretion. We wouldn't want to hurt her feelings. Now, could I impose upon you to pour me some more of that delicious tea please?"

"What does 'scretion' mean, Papa?" she asked, carefully refilling his cup.

"Hmm. Discretion means that I can trust you to keep our conversations between just you and me."

"And you can trust me, right?"

"Of course I can trust you."

Elliot knew many men who wouldn't be caught dead having an afternoon tea party with their daughter but he thought it was great fun. Not only did it enable him to spend some special time with her, but it also made Kathleen feel special that her Papa would close up shop an hour early just to be with her.

"Are you ready for dessert, Papa?" she asked, wiping her fingers daintily on an embroidered napkin.

"Didn't you know?" he leaned close to whisper in her ear. "That's the very best part of a tea party. But don't tell your mother I said that or she'd have my head."

More giggles as Kathleen sliced a piece of devil's food cake, no more than two or three bites big, and carefully laid it on his plate. No, Elliot wouldn't trade moments like this for all the treasure in the world.

A flash of movement behind Kathleen caught his eye. From the doorway Meg stood watching them, a tender smile on her face. Elliot winked at her then turned his attention back to his hostess.

~~~

The scent of apple pie and fried chicken assaulted Colby's nose the moment he walked in the front door and he closed his eyes in anticipation. Two of his most favorite foods, and both of them on the same day. Anticipation mingled with unease over the reason behind the treats. Anna never did anything nice for him unless she wanted something. He only hoped it wasn't too extravagant because, of course, he would have to agree to whatever it was. Or bear her wrath over the coming weeks.

A glance at the grandfather clock in the parlor told him that he had about a quarter of an hour before supper would be served and so he crept quietly down the hall to his office. Putting off the inevitable, he knew, but at the moment he couldn't face her and another of her selfish requests.

A new dress, he figured, sinking into his chair and closing his eyes. She had enough dresses, skirts and blouses to clothe ten women, yet she always wanted more. Which explained the natty
~~~

clothes he, himself, wore. By the time Anna finished spending every cent he earned, there wasn't much left over for the things he needed.

"I thought I heard you come in." Colby looked up to see his wife in the doorway, the pinched smile he'd come to recognize through the years in place and he very nearly grimaced. She wanted more than simple garments.

"Just a moment ago," he said weakly.

"Have you had a difficult day?" she asked, forcing compassion into her voice. He had to stifle a groan when she rounded the desk, coming to stand behind his chair.

"Not especially," he murmured, closing his eyes when she reached out and began to rub his shoulders.

"I made fried chicken and apple pie for you," she said softly.

"I know. I could smell it when I came in. What's the occasion?"

"Does there have to be a reason for me to make a special meal for my husband?" she asked, her high pitched laugh grating on his nerves.

"Usually," he said under his breath. He let his head drop as she continued the massage. Oh but it felt good. It had been such a long time. More than three months this time. Not since this past Christmas, in fact, because she'd wanted the new buffet for the dining room. And had gotten it. He truly hoped whatever it was she wanted wasn't quite so costly this time.

"So tell me about your day, Colby." Dear Lord, he thought despondently, it was probably twice as expensive as the buffet.

"There isn't much to tell," he sighed. "Just some visits to members of the congregation who can't get out or are sick. The same thing I do every day."

"You're a good minister, Colby." He felt her kiss the top of his head and squeezed his eyes closed. "So who did you visit?"

Wishing her interest weren't contrived, he sighed and told her about his day, knowing she wouldn't let up until he did. Knowing that he would play along with her game because he lacked the control to do otherwise.

"I really don't know how you do it," she said, when he'd finished telling her about Archie Baker's broken ankle. "All those sick people. It would drive me insane. But not you. You have the patience of a saint. No wonder everyone in the church loves you."

Not everyone, he thought, as she took his hand and pulled him along to the dining room. Usually they took their meals in the kitchen, unless they had company, which was seldom. Or unless Anna wanted something, which she very obviously did.

The table was set with a pretty lace tablecloth, their best china and silver. Candles sat in the center, along with a bowl of oranges. She'd outdone herself this time, meaning that he would probably be in debt for months to come.

"You sit down and get comfortable while I bring the food in," she ordered in what he supposed she figured was a teasing manner. But she couldn't manage to pull it off as well as she thought she could. She hated buttering him up every bit as he hated her doing it. Still he sat and waited, listening to her idle chatter throughout the meal, waiting for the reason.

He'd no sooner swallowed the last bite of his slice of pie when she pounced, sliding her chair right next to his and grasping his hand in both of hers. For the first time since she'd begun the charade, her smile was genuine, her eyes lit with excitement.

"Oh, Colby! You'll never guess what I saw while I was in town today!"

"What?" he asked after a long moment of silence.

"I stopped off at the jewelers when I saw the new display. And, oh my! They were the most beautiful things I've ever seen!"

Jewelry. He shouldn't be surprised. She had a drawer full of it because, if there was one thing in life his wife treasured, it was that. He ignored her description of the necklace, bracelet and ear bobs, because it just didn't matter. They would be more than he could comfortably afford, and she would have them as soon as the store was open for business tomorrow.

And she would be nicer for a few days. Maybe this time for a week or more. Until the thrill wore off, or she stopped getting compliments from the ladies around town. Not as nice as today, of course. But life would be marginally easier for a while.

"I would be ever so grateful, Colby. *Very* grateful," she was saying softly. He closed his eyes, nodding, and she squeezed his hand with more strength than he'd guessed she possessed. "Does that mean-"

"Yes, Anna."

"Then I should expect you to come to my room tonight?" Oh, how he wanted to say no. He had prayed so often for the strength to say it but always gave in. Always.

"Yes," He whispered, opening his eyes in time to see the last traces of a grimace on her face. She quickly replaced it with another phony smile.

"That's good then. Why don't you go relax while I clean up here? I'll see you in a few hours."

As he hurried back to his office, Colby was filled with both excitement and self-loathing. For years he'd done his best to overcome this weakness, because if he could, she'd wield that much less power over him. But three or four times a year she wanted something badly enough that she would force herself to fulfill her wifely duties, and he had never been able to develop the willpower to tell her no.

Next time, he always swore to himself. The next time, he'd be strong enough. But he never was, so it was with a heavy heart that he sat back down at his desk, trying to relax as she'd commanded him.

~~~

If his grandfather hadn't died from his addiction to Laudanum long before Daniel had been born, Daniel would cheerfully have slugged him. Aspirin helped, to a minimal degree, the pain from his broken bones, but not nearly as much as the Laudanum had. Sometimes it was excruciating, making it all but impossible to sleep.

Almost as bad was the utter boredom of being
~~~

laid up in a room with no other patients to keep him company. The nurses came in to check on him and feed him several times a day but they never stayed long. He'd been given a bible, which he read fairly often. Mostly because, cover to cover, he believed it was true. Partly because there was nothing else to do.

To distract himself he gazed around the room for what must be the thousandth time. Three other unoccupied beds, one next to his and two across from them, each sat with their own little bedside table. Sheets and thin wool blankets were stretched tautly over the mattresses, a fluffed pillow lying at the headboard. Everything was sparkling clean. Even the windows were so clean you wouldn't know they were there but for the reflection of the door in the glass. A pretty painting of a flower garden graced one wall but that was the only decoration in the room.

He scowled at his leg, encased in the cloth covered splints. Three days in this hospital was two more than anyone should have to endure.

"You don't look very happy today, Mr. Pullman."

Daniel brightened instantly. Being here wasn't *all* that bad, he thought, looking at Nina Hakes appreciatively. Even the pain wasn't as bad when she paid visits to his room.

He'd known that first day, when he couldn't force his eyes to open, that she would be pretty. But he could never have imagined just how lovely she was. Dark brown hair was pulled away from her face and bound in a neat braid that fell several inches below her shoulders. He supposed it would reach her waist when it was loose. And he found he desperately wanted to see it loose.

Her skin was flawless, cheeks naturally rosy, her lips full and smooth. Big brown eyes were fringed with thick, sooty lashes and were, he had to admit, his favorite feature. All of this sat atop a slender frame which was covered in a freshly pressed nurse's uniform. A gray dress covered with a crisp, white apron. He thought the colors were quite becoming, even considering the plainness of the clothes.

Nina's small hand reached out and pressed against his forehead checking, he knew, to see if he'd developed a fever since the last time she'd looked in on him. The doctor worried about infection at the site where the bone had torn through the skin, but so far, so good.

"If I don't look happy," Daniel finally replied with a grin, "it's because I'm bored."

"Mrs. Taylor said you haven't had any visitors," Nina acknowledged quietly, her gaze filled with compassion. "Don't you have any family we could try to contact?"

"Just a couple of great aunts over in Detroit. My father died when I was eleven and my mother just last month. No brothers, sisters, cousins, or even third cousins thrice removed."

"No friends either?"

"Of course I have friends. Unfortunately most of them have enlisted in the Army and are in training as we speak."

"I'm sorry."

"Thank you."

"Is there anything I can do for you, Mr. Pullman?" she offered sweetly.

"I don't suppose you could keep me company for a while?"

"I would but we're getting ready to deliver supper to the patients. I was on my way to help prepare trays and thought I'd make sure you still didn't have a fever. I really need to be going." He hid a smile when it became obvious he'd flustered her. As she turned to leave he said,

"Miss Hakes?"

"Yes, Mr. Pullman?"

"Do you remember that first day I was here? When I said you sounded pretty?"

"I- Yes." Her cheeks flushed a darker shade of pink.

"I was wrong." A spark of annoyance flashed in her eyes and he grinned. "You're not. In fact, you're quite beautiful."

Chapter 3

Marcus sat at his desk in the somber room he called his office. Dark paneling. Dark draperies. Dark furniture. Dark wood floors. Perfect for meeting with a grieving loved one, but not exactly an atmosphere conducive for penning a cheerful response to Derek's latest letter.

He'd first met Derek McGovern when he'd gone away to college. They'd been roommates at Mrs. Shettenhelm's boarding house and being a friendly, outgoing fellow, Derek had won Marcus over after a few months of daily pestering. Sometimes hourly, it seemed. Did Marcus want to study at the library with him? Go see the newest moving picture show at the nickelodeon? Get a bite to eat at the ice cream parlor? Eventually Marcus had started giving in just to make him stop asking, figuring Derek would soon tire of his company.

But he never did and it wasn't long before they'd become almost as close as brothers. The only best friend he'd ever had.

Four years later Marcus had graduated with honors and moved back to Michigan to take over his father's funeral business. Back to a solitary life as his parents decided to move out west. Derek had returned to his home town, Philadelphia, also going into the funeral business. But he'd married and now had a large family. Every letter he sent, usually twice a month, was filled with all sorts of entertaining news.

The exploits of his friend's four children never ceased to amuse Marcus, though children weren't people he generally liked to be around. He couldn't pretend to understand them and, though it was embarrassing to admit, they rather scared him.

Still, it was hard not to chuckle when reading about Derek Junior who, at eleven years of age, had hidden one of his sister's kittens in a casket prior to a funeral. The scratching noises coming from inside had frightened the mourners nearly to death, and had gotten the boy a sound and well deserved spanking.

Reading further he heard about how Rebecca, one of the twins, who would turn five later in the summer, had stunned everyone at their church when an elderly spinster had tried to pick her up. In the honest way that children have, Rebecca requested quite bluntly to be put back down. It seemed that the girl had taken offense at the woman's breath and had, in fact, informed her that her mouth stank.

After a few more family-related stories, Derek finished up, as usual, with the invitation that Marcus come to Philadelphia. If not to join him as a partner, which he would love to see happen, then at least for a visit. Marcus had yet to see any of his children, and they were growing up quickly. Derek was nothing if not a proud father.

Marcus read through the letter a second time, and then a third, as he wracked his brain for something interesting to write back. His letters always seemed dull in comparison to Derek's, no matter how hard he tried to change them. Usually he mentioned the weekly businessmen's meeting, adding something about Colby's sermon, how he'd beaten Colby at chess yet again, and occasionally, *very* occasionally, an amusing story about how Anna Thornton had made a fool out of herself.

Usually he tried to report only the things he'd actually seen, figuring stories from someone else's lips might be considered gossip. And Marcus did not believe in gossiping. Much as he did not like the reverend's missus, he didn't really like maligning her either. It was just that his life lacked...something.

A lot of things, actually. Excitement. Happiness. Joy. The love of a family of his own. So those missing elements made his life appear somewhat, well, *dull*. Especially when he tried to put it in writing.

He wished he were more comfortable around people. But other than his folks and Derek, he'd always had trouble talking to people. The ability to take part in interesting conversations came in pretty handy if one wished to make a few friends.

Maybe he would wait until later in the week to reply to the letter. Perhaps by then, if he went out of his way to be out and about around town, he might stumble upon something of interest to write about. One could hope anyway.

He pushed the chair away from his desk and got slowly to his feet. Maybe he would get a cup of tea and try to figure out a way to add some excitement to his week. Just this once.

As he walked into the kitchen he became aware of how quiet his house was. It was a little unsettling. Probably because he'd just finished reading about all the chaos in his friend's home. He wondered if Derek ever wished for this sort of silence.

Shaking his head he figured he probably didn't.

~~~

'Dear President Wilson,' Jonathon wrote with the fountain pen he'd just borrowed from his mother.

He puffed his chest out proudly as he sat at the little desk in the bedroom he shared with Charles and stared at the words on the paper before him. 'Dear President Wilson.'

He didn't know of one other person in Charlotte who had written to the President of the United States. Actually, he didn't know of anyone anywhere who had. But *he* was. And he grinned from ear to ear because just writing the salutation made him feel important.

'Dear President Wilson,

'My name is Jonathon Owens and I live in
~~~

Charlotte, Michigan. I feel it is imperative that I tell you about Mr. Wilhelm Mertz. Mr. Mertz lives right next door to me and I've been watching him real close for months. I believe that he is a spy.

'Mr. Mertz gets several packages and letters delivered to his house each week. He buries things in his backyard. He never goes into his house without looking around to make sure no one is watching. But I am watching him, only he doesn't know that I am. At least I don't think he knows. There was that one time I was hiding behind the bush and my little sister yelled at me but I've been real careful ever since.

'You should know that he does very odd things and that he is German. He even talks with a German accent and I don't think you should trust him and, if you could, you should send someone to arrest him as soon as you possibly can.

'Sincerely, Jonathon Owens'

Jonathon reread the letter twice, then consulted the tablet where he'd been keeping his notes. He had forgotten to mention a few other important things and quickly rewrote the letter to include them. He wouldn't like President Wilson to think he hadn't been doing a good job.

Blowing on the ink to help it dry, he pushed his chair back, grabbed the pen to return it to the desk in the parlor and hurried down the stairs.

He needed to get the letter to his father down at the store so he could mail it for him today and, after a quick goodbye to his mother, he took off running.

"Jonathon Owens!" a woman exclaimed, startled as Jonathon nearly barreled into her. Only a quick lunge to his left prevented what might have been a very unfortunate accident. He might have been forced to write the letter over again.

"I'm sorry, Mrs. Applegate!" he apologized over his shoulder, continuing on his way. He was, however, careful to give other pedestrians a wider berth.

By the time he passed Zourdos and Spires, and the restaurant, Jonathon wished his mission weren't of the utmost importance. Even though it was so cold it hurt to breathe, he was soon parched and wishing he had time to stop in one of the places for a nice cold glass of lemonade.

But he pressed on, covering the three long blocks in record time, bursting breathlessly into Owens Fine Shoes.

"Hey, Pop!" he exclaimed but a warning glance from his father, kneeling at the feet of a customer silenced the rest of what he'd been about to say.

Scowling in frustration he wandered out to the back room, the smell of new leather strong in the air. Pacing restlessly, he wished his father had let him explain because surely something as magnificent as a letter to the president was more important than selling a pair of shoes to someone who probably didn't need them anyway. At the very least it wouldn't have hurt anyone to wait the few minutes it would have taken for Pop to post it for him.

Jonathon sighed deeply. Mother and Reverend Thornton might extol the virtues of patience but he figured it must be a virtue one acquired as a grown up because neither he, nor any other ten year old he knew, was very patient.

He peeked out into the other room to see his father pulling a different shoe from the shelves and resigned himself to waiting even longer. Another long-suffering sigh and he flopped down on an old chair and began swinging his feet.

He imagined President Wilson's reaction when he received the letter. Of course he'd be impressed by his superior investigative skills, especially given his age. Maybe enough so that Jonathon would receive some sort of medal. Imagine how jealous his friends would be! He grinned with pleasure just thinking about it.

He would put on his Sunday going-to-church clothes and wear the medal everywhere he went. Why, the town might even have a parade in his honor. Wouldn't that be something! The admiration and applause-

"All right, son, what was it you wanted to tell me?" Elliot Owens asked, walking into the storeroom. Jonathon shot to his feet and thrust the letter into his hands.

"I wrote a letter to the president, pop. I need you to post it for me *right now!*"

"A letter to the president?" His father looked suitably impressed and Jonathon's chest puffed out a little more.

"Can I assume that this is in regards to Mr. Mertz?" Elliot asked, his eyes twinkling.

"It sure is, Pop!" his son answered enthusiastically. "He got another package today and he looked real suspicious. Like he was making sure no one saw him get it or take it into his house. But I saw him, Pop. And I think President Wilson needs to know."

"Hmm." Elliot rubbed his fingers on his chin as he read the letter, saying 'hmm' a few more times before looking back at his son. "You know, I think you may be right, Jonathon. I can't mail it for you until Richard comes in later this afternoon, but I'll see to it that it's at the post office before the day is over."

"Gee, thanks, Pop!" Jonathon said grinning broadly. "I appreciate it. But I have to go see what he's up to today so if they send someone to talk to me, I can tell them everything I know."

~~~

Colby supposed he could get any number of women from his congregation to clean the sanctuary. Of course, if he'd married a different sort of woman, *she* might help him keep everything clean and dust – free. But he'd married Anna and so cleaning it himself seemed to be the perfect solution. It not only got the job done, but gave him an excuse to avoid going home when he didn't have anything better to do.

Truth be told, though, he really didn't mind. Strolling back and forth between the pews, wiping the seats and backs off with a damp rag was rather relaxing. The fact that he used a liberal hand with the lemon oil didn't hurt either. He thought it made the church even more inviting to his parishioners.

"Lord, it sure would help if you could give my wife a servant's heart," he prayed for what was
~~~

probably the millionth time.

Not for helping with the cleaning so much as he thought it might cause her to really care about other people. Especially her husband. What he wouldn't give for a woman who loved him as much as he loved her. One who welcomed him into her arms – and her bed, rather than just enduring him because she wanted something else she didn't need.

He thought back to the other night, still hating himself for his weakness. Almost hating Anna for using it against him. Because he was sure she knew that he'd spent the hours before going to her room fighting against his desire. Knowing he despised himself because this was the one area of his life he'd been unable to get under control. He also knew she'd been praying that he'd win, for once, and leave her alone.

Oh how he wanted to take her by the shoulders and shake her. To tell her that she was no better than the prostitutes she professed to hate. Offering her body to one man for jewelry and other costly goods rather than to countless strangers for money. If he thought it might do any good, that she might actually take his words to heart, he might just try.

But Anna would have to be willing to take a good long look at herself to see that he was right. To take her eyes off herself and her desires, and see what she'd become. Colby knew that wasn't likely to happen though. Like everyone else in the world, Anna was allowed free will. And a servant's heart would be the last thing *she'd* ever want.

Finished with the pews, he walked purposefully to the small coat closet in his equally small office, setting the cleaning rag and bottle of lemon oil on the high shelf and exchanging them for the broom and dustpan.

Sweeping, he'd discovered a number of years ago, was actually more productive than he'd ever dreamed it could be. Unless he'd been too busy during the week and was hurrying to get it done just before opening the door on Sunday morning. But today he had plenty of time and began the chore in a leisurely fashion. As was his custom, he did what he always did while he swept, and that was to meditate and pray.

After the service the day before he'd overheard a small group huddled in the corner near the stove worrying about the war. Again. It seemed that many of the residents around town were afraid. That the fighting might spread to American soil. That, perhaps, it might be one of the wars spoken of in the bible, meaning that the end of the world was near.

He supposed it could be, but seriously doubted it. Too many other things needed to occur first, and unless the newspapers were lax in their reporting what was going on around the globe, those things hadn't yet happened. He'd given the matter a great deal of thought, studied the scriptures and, was convinced that the fearful members of his church wouldn't have to worry about meeting their maker any time in the near future.

Spotting a couple of hymn books laying on the floor beneath a pew, he reached down and replaced them in the little wooden pocket on the back of the seat in front of it, still pondering the conversation he'd overheard.

Perhaps it was time to reassure everyone, and this coming Sunday seemed like as good a time as any to do it. Abandoning the broom, Colby made a beeline for his desk, opening his bible and, quill in hand, began to make some notes.

~~~

Elliot watched Jonathon run out of the store and didn't even mind when the door slammed hard enough behind him to rattle the glass. Heaven forbid anything should slow him down or get in the way of his mission to continue spying on their neighbor.

He looked down at the single sheet of paper in his hand and chuckled. He'd already read the words his son had written while the boy stood there, nervously shifting his weight from one foot to the other, waiting for his father to give his approval. Which Elliot had, wholeheartedly - if for no other reason than it would be a good experience for his Jonathon. He did, however, keep to himself the belief that the letter would soon find itself lying in the bottom of a waste basket.

Shaking his head, he reread the letter, and then paused thoughtfully before walking over to the counter. It wouldn't hurt to include a note to explain the situation. And, he had to admit, he felt a little thrill himself at the thought of writing words that someone in the White House might read. So picking up the fountain pen he began to write,

"Dear President Wilson, This letter is from my son who fancies himself another Sherlock
~~~

Holmes..."

~~~

After nearly a week on crutches, Daniel figured he should have been an old hand at using them. That, however, was not the case, especially given the icy patches here and there on the sidewalk. The fact that he was also trying to keep the small box of chocolates from becoming a mangled mess didn't help. Nor did the frigid temperatures.

The bulky splint had necessitated the ripping out of the seam in the affected side of his trousers and he had the distinct feeling he now knew what ladies braving the cold temperatures must endure. But at least they didn't have the additional burden of going around with only one shoe. Even though he'd slipped two woolen socks on, his poor foot was nearly frozen.

But he was determined to see Miss Hakes, his shy - though sometimes sassy, nurse. Three days since his release from the hospital and he found that he missed seeing her lovely face. Something he would be doing very shortly, unless there had been a schedule change. Daniel hoped not and bit his lip nervously. It had taken all the courage he could muster to come tonight.

A strong gust of wind nearly knocked him off his feet and he awkwardly reached up to tug the collar of his gray Chesterfield coat more snugly around his neck when another gust had him grabbing frantically for the crutch. He was vaguely aware of the sound of a nearby door closing as he hopped and danced
~~~

about to regain his balance.

"*Mr. Pullman!* What are you *doing?"* the startled voice of Nina Hakes demanded, as she hurried to help him right himself. Daniel grinned sheepishly as he finally found his footing. "Are you all right?"

Better now, he thought, gazing intently into her eyes. They called to mind the color of the sky just before night fell. Almost blue - black. The biggest, most beautiful eyes he'd ever seen.

"Shall I go fetch the doctor?" she asked, looking up at him, her expression much as it had been the first morning he'd been able to open his eyes. Except he didn't particularly want her looking at him as a nurse.

"I'm fine," he assured her, taking note that her hand still gripped his arm. He grinned again. "Just lost my balance for a second there."

"Mr. Pullman." Now her lips were pursed, as though she might be the slightest bit annoyed with him. "I distinctly remember Doctor Garlington telling you to go home and rest that leg. I don't believe that walking around in the cold could be, by any definition of the word, *resting*" Even annoyed, Daniel figured he could listen to her talk forever, just to hear her voice.

"I wanted to bring you this-" he began, and then realized he no longer held the candy. A quick glance showed that it rested neatly in a snow drift near the street. Nodding toward it he said, "That."

Nina's eyes followed his gaze and he saw a blush color her cheeks. As he tried to lean down to retrieve the foil wrapped package, she pulled him back and picked it up herself.

"Why? Why would you be bringing me candy?" she asked quietly, not quite meeting his eyes.

"Because you were my favorite nurse," he told her honestly. "And because I wanted an excuse to see you again."

"But your leg-"

"If I'd waited for my leg to heal, it would be nearly spring. I didn't want to wait that long." This last was said almost inaudibly.

"You didn't?" Now she was looking at him. With just a trace of yearning in her gaze. At least he hoped that's what he was seeing.

"I didn't. I got used to seeing you every day and- Well, I missed you." There. He'd gotten it out in the open. Now she would know why he was here. Though whether the admission was something she might find acceptable, he didn't know. After several long moments of silence he glanced away, feeling color rush to his cheeks.

"I missed you, too," she finally whispered. "Thank you for the present."

"You're welcome." He smiled at her and, as best he could, offered her his arm. Appearing a little dubious, she took it. "May I walk you home?"

"Mr. Pullman-"

"Daniel."

"Daniel. I live several blocks from here. Perhaps I should see *you* home so you can rest that leg."

"Miss Hakes-"

"Nina."

"Nina, my leg is fine. And, being a gentleman, I insist." He could see that she was torn, ever the nurse. "Please?"

"All right," she finally agreed with a sigh, telling him that she lived near the corner of Harris and Bostwick.

"I live two blocks west of you," he told her with a smile, heading off in that direction. "You're on my way home. Are you warm enough? Unfortunately it might take a little longer walking with me than if you were on your own."

"I don't mind. I'm fine. Warmer than you, probably."

"I'm fine, too." Better than fine, in fact. "Will your parents worry?"

"I don't have parents," she murmured, looking intently at the ground.

"I'm sorry," he apologized at once. "Have they been gone long?"

"I don't know where they are, or whether they're alive or not," Nina admitted reluctantly. "I was raised in the orphanage in Lansing."

"No brothers or sisters?"

"No one."

"Then we have something in common. I'm alone, too." She glanced up, a shy smile lighting her face. Daniel felt warm to his tips of his frozen toes.

"I guess we do."

Most of the walk was silent, but that was okay with Daniel. He was just pleased to be with her. Soon, he knew, conversation would be easier. It was just this first time, as they left the nurse/patient relationship behind and forged into new territory.

"Would you do me the honor of having supper with me before you go to work tomorrow?" he asked as they came to a stop in front of a well –

kept rooming house.

"I have tomorrow off," she told him softly.

"Then would you care to accompany me to the nickelodeon after?"

"I'd like to. Very much."

~~~

"Hey, Pop," Jonathon said, from where he stood behind Elliot and Richard in the sleigh. "How long till we get there?"

Elliot couldn't help but grin at his son's enthusiasm. Little did he know that in a few hours he'd be wishing he'd listened to his mother, who had wanted him to remain at home, safe and warm. Elliot wished *he* could have stayed there because he was as far removed from warm as the east was from the west.

But it was the extended period of frigid cold that had prompted Zeke Hatfield to check the lake yesterday and, upon finding that the ice was over two feet thick, he'd called everyone. This was proving to be a particularly good winter for ice harvesting. The first, in late December had been just as thick, and with a few days still remaining in February, they just might get in a third before April ushered in the beginnings of spring. If the weather held, and Elliot wasn't exactly sure he wanted it to.

While he could summon visions of how much he would enjoy glasses of ice cold lemonade, tea and water, how wonderful a batch of Meg's ice cream would taste, he simply dreaded the thought of a long day spent fighting the bitter winds, and the
~~~

exhaustion that would accompany all of them on the way home.

Lucille Hatfield would spend the day in the little soddy, built next to the hill that contained the ice house – a huge cavern that he and a dozen other men had labored over eight summers ago. Paul Sprague had pointed out that basements were always cooler in summer months, and he figured it had to be because they were surrounded by earth. Therefore, an ice house surrounded by dirt had to be cooler than the buildings other harvesters used. So far it seemed that his theory had been correct, and they'd all enjoyed long summers with plenty of ice. But that meant long days working hard to fill it.

As usual he knew they all would be grateful for the many pots of coffee Lucille would have ready throughout the day, along with kettles of steaming hot stew and dumplings that they would consume for both meals.

"Pop! *How long?*" Jonathon asked again.

"Just be patient, son. It's going to be a long ride," Elliot said with a chuckle. It would take at least two hours to get to Pine Lake since they had to stop to pick up five more men along the way. They would also be changing horses at the midway point. That was if the snow covering the narrow road was hard packed the entire way. If it wasn't, it could be longer. "You should sit down and try to stay as warm as you can."

"You'll have plenty of time to freeze when we get there," Richard told him, with just the barest hint of sarcasm.

Unlike his brother, who was almost giddy at the

thought of his first ice harvesting adventure, Richard was well aware of what awaited them. Cold, backbreaking work - and more of nothing but the same as the hours dragged on.

Not that it was all a misery. No one ever enjoyed the actual work, but they did enjoy one another's company and there was always lots of laughter and teasing. Although as the hours passed, exhaustion would set in and it would be a much quieter group climbing into the wagons to head home.

The next couple of miles passed in silence as the sleigh glided easily along. The very best thing about winter, Elliot was quick to admit, was that the scenery surrounding them was beautiful. Even though the sun had shone brightly for the past few days, the temperatures had hovered near zero so the snow hadn't melted off the trees yet. Sometimes he felt that if he had to choose a scene to look at for the rest of his life, it would be one much like this.

He waved at the driver of an automobile who passed by, heading for town, and wished he'd decided to drive his instead. It might have cut an hour or so from their travel time. It would have been a little more comfortable as well, protecting them from the cold more so than the sleigh. As it was, he decided to let Tom Buckley take over the driving when they picked him up, and then Elliot would wrap up in one of the quilts Meg had handed to him on his way out the door.

He just hoped that no one would have need of the extra change of clothes that everyone brought along, just in case. Though it had only happened a handful of times through the years, they'd learned to come prepared. The only thing worse than falling through the ice into the frigid water was having to endure the long, cold ride home in wet clothes. At least according to Paul Sprague who, being the first to experience that particular downside to ice harvesting, knew just exactly how miserable it was.

~~~

Jonathon had been so enthralled with the process of ice harvesting since their arrival at the lake that he didn't even mind when Richard placed a finger under his chin, pushing it up as he stood there, in open – mouthed awe.

"You'll be sorry you came along in about two hours," his older brother predicted as he, too, watched Tom Buckley and Chester St. John walking behind their horses, guiding the ice markers in lines so straight it seemed impossible that they weren't drawn with a yardstick.

Nearer to the ice house, their father worked with Zeke, Paul, Ed Fletcher and Hank Wardell, cutting a channel so they could float the massive blocks to shore, wrestle them onto the specially made sleds and then stack them deep inside the hill for use on sweltering summer days.

"I'll never be sorry," Jonathon murmured, paying little attention to Richard.

He couldn't wait until it was time for the sawing, when he would finally be able to help. But that would be awhile. First the grid had to be marked, then the ice plows would follow the same paths,
~~~

cutting even deeper grooves, and finally the fun part would begin.

Richard had been accompanying the men for five years now. Five years that Jonathon had been forbidden to come, forced to sit at home jealous and resentful that he was missing out on yet another adventure. It wasn't fair that Richard always got to do everything first. For once it would be nice if *he* got to do something important before anyone else.

He shook himself out of his thoughts and concentrated on the fact that he was here. When Mama made ice cream in August, he could remind his sisters that, but for him, they might not be enjoying their lovely treat.

"Oh I wish they'd hurry up," he muttered, his hands itching to curl around the handle of the saw. Out of the corner of his eye he saw Richard shake his head, a know – it – all smirk on his face. "I *won't* be sorry," he repeated adamantly, ignoring the snicker that followed.

~~~

Elliot sighed as he helped Chester maneuver the ice plow back into the soddy. Judging by the position of the sun, high in the sky, it was somewhere around eleven o'clock. They'd been hard at work for about three hours now, and the worst was yet to come. Still, he had to chuckle as he glanced at his middle son. Jonathon was chomping at the bit to get started on the sawing, believing this to be one of the rites of passage on his journey to becoming a man.
~~~

"That boy of yours is about as thrilled as can be, isn't he?" Chester asked, grinning as he closed the door behind him.

"He certainly is," Elliot said with a laugh. "I remember how excited Richard was the first time he came with me."

"*I* remember how glad he was to *leave*. And that he wasn't excited at all the next year. Or any year since."

"You try to tell them but I guess they have to experience it firsthand."

"Somehow I don't think Jonathon is going to be sorry he came. From what I've observed, he's enthusiastic about everything he does."

"That's certainly the truth. But he's like every other young man. Work is work, and it's rarely fun."

"If I didn't know for a fact that your wife would have your hide, I'd make a bet with you, Elliot. That boy is going to be just as happy when we leave as he was when we arrived."

"If *I* didn't know for a fact that my wife would have my hide, I'd take that bet," Elliot said, chuckling. "I'll give it another couple of hours and then Jonathon will be keeping Lucille company for the rest of the afternoon."

"Will not."

But it seemed that Chester would have won the bet, had one been made, because Jonathon's enthusiasm never waned. As the hours passed, he was as excited as he'd been when they'd begun.

"Slow and steady," Elliot warned, for the countless time since they'd brought out the saws. He was gripping one side of the handle while

Jonathon had the other. "You want to pace yourself so you don't tire out too fast. There's a lot more ice waiting when we finish this line."

"Yeah, Pop. It sure is hard work, isn't it?"

"Yes it is. Warm enough?"

"Yes, sir."

"Still like harvesting ice?"

"*I do!* This is *so* much fun. I don't know why Richard doesn't like it." Elliot could see that he truly didn't understand why. What wasn't to like? Outdoors in the fresh air, surrounded by friends. Even if they weren't actually his friends, they were friends of his father's and he seemed to enjoy listening to their laughter and stories.

"I don't actually enjoy it much myself," Elliot admitted. "But I will be thankful that we all put the time in this summer." Jonathon looked at his father, eyes wide and filled with disbelief, like he couldn't believe the words he'd just heard.

"Why don't you like it, Pop? This is the best day since- Since- I don't know when, but it is." Elliot had to chuckle at that. His son thought *every* day was the best day.

"You are really something, you know that?"

"*What?*"

"You're absolutely right, Jonathon. This *is* the best day - since I don't remember when." And suddenly it was. All he had to do was experience ice harvesting through the eyes of an optimistic ten year old, his ten year old, and what had begun as a chore to be endured was an adventure to be enjoyed.

~~~

Jonathon walked out of the soddy with the rest of the guys after having a delicious dinner of stew and biscuits, oatmeal cookies and coffee. Well, mostly milk, but Pop had allowed him have a little coffee poured in to warm it up a bit. He couldn't help but wrinkle his nose. What was so great about that stuff anyway? Even with lots of milk it still tasted kind of bitter. But it was what grownups drank so maybe it would taste better when he got older.

He rolled his shoulders a little as he stepped back on the lake, heading for the area he'd been helping with before they took their break. Everyone had warned him that this would be hard work, and they were right. His shoulders, arms and back were aching, but it was a good feeling to be out here doing a man's job.

"Jonathon, no!" he heard someone shout, just as he stepped on a nearly free block of ice. It broke loose with no warning, tilting wildly and catapulting him headfirst into the freezing lake.

Time seemed to stand still as he flailed about in the icy water, trying to find the surface. He hoped it would be soon because all of the air had been forced from his lungs on impact and he was desperate to take a breath. But he knew if he tried now, he would drown, and so he kicked harder and prayed he was heading up, instead of toward the bottom of the lake.

When he finally did surface, he sucked in a desperate, panicked breath, only to find it hurt. The water hurt, too. He hadn't known that cold could be
~~~

painful, but it was. Everywhere it touched him, and it was touching him *everywhere,* made it feel like he was on fire.

He wondered about that, how odd it was to feel like you were burning when you were actually freezing, as chaos broke out around him. Shouts to find branches or a rope. Someone demanding that he get to the edge of the ice. Even someone bellowing at Richard to stay back. But he saw that Richard ignored the command, diving chest first across the ice, then inching to the edge, holding out an arm toward his brother.

"C'mon, Jonathon, grab my hand!" Only Jonathon was still too far to reach it. "Kick your feet. *Swim!*"

He tried, with all his might, except the heavy, soaked clothes and coat made it almost impossible to move, even a little. But the thought of dying here scared him and he fought harder, slowly getting closer to his brother's outstretched hand. Finally, his fingertips touched Richard's, and then he was pulled quickly to where Richard lay on the ice.

"I've got him, Pop!"

"Thank God! Just hold onto him, Richard. Don't try to pull him out. We'll pull you. Don't let go of him."

"I won't. I promise." He looked right into Jonathon's eyes and whispered, "You hold on. Do you hear me?"

Jonathon really did try to answer, but he was shaking so hard he couldn't get the word out. Instead he nodded his head. Or tried to. It seemed like his head was shaking just as hard as the rest of him.

It felt like it took forever but he supposed it really was only a few minutes before he felt his body sliding up over the edge and onto the surface of the ice. Richard held his hands tightly as they were dragged safely away and then all the men hurried to help them both up.

"Your mother is going to kill me," his father said, holding him close. It sounded a little like he was laughing and crying at the same time. "We need to get you inside and get you warm."

Still shaking too hard to speak, Jonathon could only try to nod his head again.

Chapter 4

Daniel sat, or rather balanced, on the edge of a stool at the counter waiting on postal patrons. Almost a month since his accident and he was deeply grateful to be back at work.

Initially his boss, Ted Nelson had had him try sorting the mail but it had been too difficult with all the reaching and moving around. Then Ted suggested he fill the post office boxes. Only that presented the same problem, so they'd given him this position until the splint came off and he was free of the burden of crutches.

Thus far he'd been kept quite busy, for which he was grateful. Days when there weren't many customers seemed to pass at a snail's pace. Either way, though, he was glad to be earning money again. He couldn't wait to spend some of it when he took Nina to supper, an outing that was happening most days now. A foolish smile curved his lips when he realized he was mooning over her yet again.

"Happy to be back?" Mrs. Harold Baker asked from the lobby. Like everyone else today, her cheeks were red from the cold.

"Yes, Ma'am, I am *very* happy to be back. How are you this morning?"

"Just fine, Daniel. Yourself?" She casually removed her gloves and pulled several envelopes from her handbag, laying them on the counter along with a few coins.

"Much better, thank you."

"You did give us all a fright when that awful automobile ran over you, young man."

"I think I gave myself a fright, Mrs. Baker," he said with a chuckle. Her eyes crinkled at the corners when she smiled at him.

"In the future I trust you'll be more careful. I never did trust those contraptions."

"I already am being more careful," he assured her, affixing stamps to six envelopes then placing them in the outgoing mail bin.

"For my boys," she explained. Her boys consisted of her youngest son, two oldest grandsons and three nephews, all serving in the war.

"I'm sure they look forward to your letters, and hearing about all the news that's going on at home."

"That's what they tell me when they write back." Sadness filled her eyes. "It was hard when I first started sending them. I was afraid they would be bored because the Lord knows that not much exciting happens around here. But that's what they want to read, I guess."

"They miss you as much as you miss them," he said, hoping she drew comfort from the thought. Even though patriotism ran high, it didn't stop the loneliness or the missing of loved ones. Mrs. Baker cleared her throat and blinked hard.

"Will your leg keep you from the war?" she wanted to know.

"I'm afraid so. I'd planned on enlisting this spring and setting out for boot camp right after the graduations. But the doctor sent a report to the army and I guess they won't be able to use me now."

At first he'd been heartbroken because, like most young men, he had wanted to fight in service for his country. He'd also been discouraged to learn that he would probably always need the aid of a cane because the damage to his leg would leave him with a permanent limp. If it weren't for Nina, he would be wallowing in the depths of despair.

"I'm sorry to hear that, Daniel. But at least you're safe at home. It would be a shame if the Pullman name ended with you, so it's probably for the best." She waved her fingers at him as she headed for the door. "See you in a few days. And you be careful of that leg, young man. If you need anything, you be sure to let me know."

"Thank you, Ma'am. I'll keep that in mind."

He pondered what Mrs. Baker had said for a while after she left. He'd never given much thought to having a family of his own. If he'd gone to war and been killed, the Pullman name would have ended with him. No chance to have sons. His own father had died before any more children were born so he was the only one left to carry on the name. He smiled, thinking of Nina. Perhaps that problem could be solved sooner rather than later.

"Good morning, Daniel." He was jolted out of his daydreams and immediately looked up to give his attention to the next customer.

"Reverend Thornton. How are you, sir?"

"Couldn't be better," Colby Thornton told him with a smile, and then teased, "Grateful that I'm not the one having to use crutches." Daniel laughed as he stamped a single letter and gave the minister his change.

"I'll certainly be glad when *I* don't have to use them anymore."

"I imagine you will be." Colby glanced behind him and saw that no one was waiting. "What's this I hear about you courting one of my parishioners?" he asked bluntly. In the midst of swallowing, Daniel almost choked, causing one of the other postmen to pound him on the back.

"You okay?" Edward Hinkle asked worriedly. After being assured that he was fine, Ed continued on about his business and Daniel looked back at the reverend feeling a bit foolish.

"I- Yes, I've been seeing Miss Hakes," he said nervously.

"She's a fine young woman."

"Yes, sir, she is."

"Will we be seeing you in church then?"

"Yes, sir. This Sunday, in fact." Truth be told, Daniel hadn't been in any church since his mother had taken ill but he supposed it was time to start back.

"If it would help," Colby suggested, a twinkle in his eyes, "I could come and pick you up."

"I appreciate the offer," Daniel told him sincerely. "But I'll be able to walk. I'm getting around fairly well on these things now."

"So I've heard. I understand you're walking Nina home from the hospital every night."

"Yes I am." Daniel swallowed again, albeit more carefully this time. "I don't like the idea of her being out alone after dark."

"Good man. Wish I'd thought about it before but I'm glad someone is looking out for her. See you Sunday then?"

"Yes, sir."

Nina might not have a father watching to make sure he behaved like a gentleman, but Colby Thornton had just made it very clear that *someone* was paying attention. Not that the reverend had anything to worry about. Daniel would never, *ever* consider treating her as less than the lady she was.

She was, after all, the woman he was fast falling in love with.

~~~

Marcus sighed deeply as he lay his paper aside and pushed away from the table. One of these days he would have to break down and have the newfangled indoor facilities installed. Probably in the small room off the kitchen but, a man of the old school, running and rushing water in his house just seemed wrong. And foolhardy. The idea of a burst
~~~

pipe, and the mess it could make, was enough to make him cringe. That left him no alternative but to pay regular visits to the outhouse located in his backyard.

Creeping quietly into the parlor, making sure to avoid the spot that squeaked loudly when he wasn't paying attention and walked across it, he peered cautiously through the draperies.

Nothing.

Just as cautiously, he peeked out both of the kitchen windows. So far, so good. The yard next door seemed to be empty and, as slowly as he could, he eased the back door open. The process took several long minutes because no matter how often he oiled the hinges, opening it too fast would make some part of the door creak or squeal and that always meant trouble. Every couple of inches he looked in both directions, breathing a sigh of relief when the coast remained clear.

Keeping to the far right side of the steps because, of course, the center of each wooden plank creaked with age, he crept down to the grass, keeping a vigilant watch around him.

He was almost halfway to the outhouse, having made not so much as a peep, when he heard the angry snort off to his right. Almost immediately the sound of pounding hooves started in his direction. Marcus took off running as fast as his legs would carry him, the skirt of his dressing gown flapping wildly about him.

As he slammed the door behind him, pulling against it with all his might, he resigned himself to a good portion of the morning spent in the foul smelling four-by-four. Blasted neighbors should have the decency to keep that bad tempered horse locked up so people who minded their own business could relieve themselves in peace.

He wished he could figure out why that horse hated him, and hate him she did. Marcus knew for a fact that she didn't bother the family on the north side of the Franklin house. The Carson's had an outhouse, too, which meant that there were even more people out and about to bother the horse.

Except he was the only person the mare seemed to have a problem with. But she didn't always come after him. Sometimes she just stared, kicking one hoof in the dirt and snorting. If she'd been a human being, Marcus would have sworn she was taunting him.

After a few minutes he put his ear to the door and listened carefully. Silence. Taking a fortifying breath, he pushed it open slowly, closing his eyes in disgust when the door hit the horse and she snorted again.

~~~

The Owens family had their own pew. Not that it had their name on it or anything as lofty as that. It was just that week after week they walked to the same one. And every week it was unoccupied until the seven of them filed in and took their places. Each one of the children were always on their best behavior, except maybe Elizabeth, who hadn't been on her best behavior at all since she'd gotten involved in the suffrage movement.
~~~

The 'Owens pew' was third back from the front on the right side of the sanctuary. Close enough that a stern glance from Reverend Thornton could straighten out even the most distracted or misbehaving child, yet far enough back that they would be safe should he spit, or something equally disgusting during the sermon. Not that Reverend Thornton had ever spit or anything. Least wise not that Jonathon had ever noticed so he supposed it really didn't matter where they sat for two long, mostly boring hours every Sunday morning.

It wasn't that the reverend was boring. Not *exactly*. It was always fun to talk or fish with him. But sitting on the bank of the Battle Creek River and talking about everything from the war to the upcoming Fourth of July celebration this summer was sure different than listening to endless minutes of preaching. Sometimes Jonathon had a hard time not nodding off. Or letting his mind wander to the exciting things he *could* be doing if he weren't stuck spending a perfectly good morning sitting in the Owens pew at church.

Take today, for example. Here he was in his freshly starched knickers and jacket sitting in the stuffy, dark church on one of the warmest, sunniest days they'd seen since October. Even with snow still on the ground, it was nice enough that he would be able to take his jacket off to play. But here he sat.

The organist, Miss Ethel Harrison, an old spinster whose hair always sat about a foot high on the top of her head and looked sort of blue, had finished playing the hymns and was walking back to her pew (the one where half a dozen other spinsters sat) as Reverend Thornton stepped up to the pulpit and glanced around the room with a welcoming smile.

"Good morning," he said cheerfully. "And a fine morning it is, too. It's always a special treat when we have days like this in March, isn't it?" A hearty chorus of 'amens' sounded in agreement.

"I have just a few announcements before we begin." He looked down at his notes. "Fred Archer is in the sanitorium having had his appendix removed on Friday. Please keep him in your prayers. Also, Matthew and Martha Seymour welcomed a baby girl yesterday. Her name is Grace. Miss Ethel will be taking the names of volunteers to deliver meals to the family for the next two weeks. And since this has been such a long, cold winter, and we'll be freezing again before you know it, there will be a church social this coming Saturday at five. It's a good excuse to take advantage of the warmer weather so we can visit and catch up with one another. Please bring a dish to pass and plan on spending the evening with us.

"And now to get started." He smiled again and said, "Though I don't usually preach hellfire and brimstone, or gloom and doom, I'm going to do exactly that this morning."

Jonathon rolled his eyes and let his chin drop to his chest at that declaration. It was going to be one of *those* kinds of sermons. The kind that made the two hours feel more like twenty. Long, dull as dull could be and almost, without fail, loud. Reverend Thornton hardly ever raised his voice, but when he did, a person just wanted to hide his head under a pillow.

But wait!

His gaze shot up toward the pulpit. Had the good reverend mentioned *the war?* Any mention of the war was enough to grab his attention and grab it quick, so Jonathon decided maybe this sermon wouldn't be as bad as he thought.

As the reverend preached on, turning to the last book of the bible, he thought that maybe he would have to try and read it himself. Because that part was sure different from the little bits he'd read in the past. Beasts and horses and wars. Yes, he just might have to think about reading that book someday. Not that he thought it would be as good as Sherlock Holmes, but he supposed he could be wrong about that.

"It would be easy to misinterpret these passages to apply to what we read in the newspapers every day. The war to end all wars. A war that involves many countries. A war that is causing the death of untold thousands, and the suffering of thousands more who aren't involved in the fighting," Reverend Thornton was saying.

But then he started talking about getting saved and all the regular stuff. Stuff he'd heard almost every Sunday morning all his life. The boring stuff.

Jonathon started swinging one of his feet. A little too hard, he realized, when the toe of his shoe connected with the pew in front of him. One look from his parents, and an elbow to his arm from his brother, and he stilled the foot.

And the reverend droned on.

How, he wondered, could the man be so

interesting to talk to anywhere else, but here all he did was make Jonathon want to fall asleep? *Every week.*

Discreetly, he reached a hand into his jacket pocket and withdrew two tiny soldiers, intending to engage them in a silent fight when another well placed elbow from Richard, this time in the side, ended that plan. So he slipped the toys back into his pocket and counted the different colors in each of the stained glass windows instead.

~~~

"Though I don't usually preach hellfire and brimstone or gloom and doom, I'm going to do exactly that this morning," Colby began, noticing from his position behind the pulpit several people beginning to squirm. He hid a smile because, like most congregations, they preferred to hear all of the good things – the blessings - from the bible. And so he usually tried to work the less than pleasant parts into more optimistic messages.

"Earlier this week someone came to me with some concerns over the war. Which is not an unusual occurrence these days. However, this person had been reading out of Revelation and was troubled by one passage in particular.

"Please open your bibles to Revelation chapter six, verses seven and eight."

He waited for half a minute, the silence broken only by the sounds of pages being carefully but quickly turned. As soon as it seemed most had found it, he began to read,
~~~

'And when he had opened the fourth seal, I heard the voice of the fourth beast say, Come and see.

'And I looked, and behold a pale horse: and his name that sat on him was Death, and Hell followed with him. And power was given unto them over the fourth part of the earth, to kill with sword, and with hunger, and with death, and with the beasts of the earth.' He paused a moment to let the words sink in before continuing.

"These verses are prophecy telling us what will happen during the seven year tribulation, which we know to be the reign of the anti – Christ, following Christ's second coming.

"This will be a truly terrible time for those who did not accept Christ as their Savior prior to that event.

"It could be easy to misinterpret these passages to apply to what we read in the newspapers every day. The war to end all wars. A war that involves many countries. A war that is causing the death of untold thousands and the suffering of thousands more who aren't involved in the fighting.

"But these verses do not apply to us, church. The end of the world is not upon us. In fact, even where it tells of wars and rumors of wars as a sign of the times does not apply to our world today. One war does not the end times make.

"But make no mistake. Someday that time will come upon us, like a thief in the night. No one knows the day nor the hour. Only God knows and, in his mercy, gives us clues to discern when it's coming close.

"We have nothing to fear. And it's my humble opinion that it will be many generations to come before these things begin to occur.

"I could, however, be wrong. God tells us in his word that, to him, a day is as a thousand years and a thousand years as a day. So we need to be ready for Christ's return, church.

"Because the events foretold of in Revelation are real, and they are terrifying. Wars, earthquakes, great plagues that kill vast numbers of people. If the Lord were to come back today, those of you who are not ready would be facing these horrors over the course of the next seven years.

"If you believe that Christ died on the cross for your sins then accept Christ as your Savior and, if that time comes soon, you'll be taken up to heaven and not have to worry about the judgment that will befall the rest of the world."

~~~

"Jonathon!" Margaret whispered fiercely, as Jonathon slipped out of the pew and disappeared out the door before most everyone else had even gotten to their feet. Elliot hid a grin as he leaned down to help Charles to the floor. Not that he needed help, but if Meg saw him grin, she wouldn't be very happy with him. "That boy!"

"The sermon was long," Kathleen said softly, as though she knew that her brother needed to burn off some energy after sitting for nearly an hour and a half.

"It did seem that way, didn't it," Elliot said
~~~

quickly, sensing that his wife was about to chastise their daughter. "I guess Jonathon needed to stretch his legs even more than I do."

"Elliot-"

"I know, I know. But it *was* a long sermon, and you know he always gets antsy when Colby preaches hellfire and brimstone."

"I know," Margaret sighed, taking Kathleen's hand as they joined the line to shake the reverend's hand on their way out.

Elliot couldn't help but overhear a conversation going on behind them, though the participants kept their voices low. Apparently the sermon hadn't bothered them much as they discussed the upcoming social, what they intended to bring, what they hoped others would bring.

His mouth began to water because he knew what Meg would be making. And he would gladly pitch in to lend a hand to help peel and slice enough potatoes to fill their roasting pan. She would add to that bits of pork and butter, some onion and flour, and salt and pepper. Finally a pan of scalding hot milk would be poured over the lot and baked for a couple of hours.

It was, without a doubt, one of his favorite meals and he hoped the coming week would pass quickly.

~~~

As was the case with most of the congregation, Daniel and Nina filed out of the church almost silently, shaking hands with Colby at the door.

"It's really okay," he told them with a smile. "You
~~~

don't have anything to worry about." They smiled back, accepted a dinner invitation at one of the restaurants downtown on Wednesday and decided to take a stroll before returning to the boarding house where Nina lived.

As they turned a corner that would take them toward town, Jonathon Owens sped past them, fast as his legs could carry him. Daniel recalled being that age and how it seemed like the end of the world if he couldn't run like the wind after sitting through a sermon. Especially one as frightening as the one this morning.

"You're awfully quiet," he observed after another few minutes of silence.

"So are you," she countered with a smile. "I guess I was just thinking about the things Reverend Thornton said."

"Me, too. I guess if somebody wasn't saved already, hearing that would change their mind in a hurry."

"I wonder who asked him about the end of the world?"

"It could have been anyone. I've heard talk around town. Some people worry that the war could spread to America." Nina gasped, stopping and clutching his arm tighter.

"You don't think it could!" Her wide eyes stared at up at him and he sought to reassure her.

"No. *Of course not*, Nina. The enemy can't have near enough people to fight the war over there and have any left to spare to send here. I promise you, we're safe."

"You're sure?"

"I'm sure. I wouldn't let anything or anybody hurt you." He stroked her cheek softly. "I promise."

To his utter astonishment, Nina quickly kissed the palm of his hand, her face flushed beet red. Daniel felt the sting of tears in his eyes as he placed his lips gently against her hair.

"Would you like to stop at Zourdos and Spires for some ice cream?" he asked, reluctantly stepping back from her a bit.

Not too much, because he didn't think he could. But neither could he stand as close as he'd like to in sight of God and the rest of the world. When he married her, he would be taking her to the first home she would ever know. That meant he would have to be careful to protect her reputation, because he would never do a thing that might sully it.

"I'm glad you had that accident, Daniel," she whispered.

"What?" he asked, sure he'd heard her wrong. She squeezed his arm and rested her head against his shoulder as they continued their walk.

"I said I'm glad you were in the accident. Not that you got hurt but because we might never have met if it hadn't happened." Nina hastened to reassure him. "And if it hadn't happened, you'd be in France, fighting in the war and I'm *so* glad you're not."

Daniel wanted to kiss her again but managed, with great effort, to restrain himself.

"I'm glad, too, Nina. That I met you. That I'm here with you. And I'm going to be glad that you want ice cream, too, because I'm starving!"

She was laughing when she looked up at him

and knew he would love her, with all of his heart, for the rest of his life.

~~~

For the first time since Marcus had begun attending Colby's church, this was the very first Sunday that he hadn't been the first to leave. In fact, after the last of the surprisingly quiet congregation had gone, he was still sitting in the last pew. Colby closed the door and came to sit beside him. For quite a while neither man said a word then Colby asked,

"Is something bothering you, Marcus?"

"I was just thinking about your sermon."

"I imagine you're not the only one."

"You believe all of that?"

"Don't you?"

"Well, sure," Marcus said firmly. "If it's in the bible it has to be true. But do you really think that the part in Revelation is for some other time?"

"If it isn't, Marcus, then we're all in trouble."

"What do you mean?"

"If what's going on in the world today is directly related to those particular passages, that means Christ has already returned and not a soul on earth – or in the earth – was taken to heaven with him. And I don't believe that could happen." Marcus pondered that for a moment.

"I guess you have a point. I just hadn't ever thought about the war making people think this was the end of the world."

"War makes people think about a lot of
~~~

frightening things. Because war, in itself, is a frightening thing. I just wanted to reassure everyone that, while it might be awful, the world isn't on the verge of ending."

"You did a good job of that. But it still makes me think about it."

"That's good, Marcus. I'd hate to think that the moment my sermon was over people forgot what I said," Colby said with a chuckle. "Some weeks they probably do, but I hope they remember more often than not."

"I always remember," Marcus said quickly. Colby knew, from the expression on his face, that he was telling the truth. "Last week you talked about faith and answered prayer. The week before you preached about doing unto others."

"I'm impressed! And I appreciate the fact that you actually listen to what I'm trying to teach you."

"If you're not going to listen, there isn't a whole lot of point in coming to church is there?" Colby laughed heartily upon hearing those words.

"That's my opinion. Unfortunately there are those who come because they think they should, not because they want to, or want to learn anything. Some even come because they think it raises their social standing. Though I have to say that most of them won't find what they're looking for at our small church."

"I suppose." He shifted uncomfortably. He'd probably said more words to Colby in the past couple of minutes than the total of all the words he'd spoken to him in the last three years. The only people he talked to more were his parents and

Derek, and sometimes the families he served, but usually they just wanted a few words of comfort. And, of course, a casket. “I guess I should let you get home before the missus starts worrying and wondering where you are.”

“Yes. I guess we wouldn’t want Anna to worry about me, would we?” Colby shook his hand and they headed off in different directions. Colby turned around long enough to call out, “Chess tomorrow?”

“I’ll be there.”

Chapter 5

The mouthwatering scent of Mother's apple pie had begun to fill every corner of the house, nearly distracting Jonathon from the task at hand. It was only through a determined effort that he managed to concentrate on the lines and notes before him, his fingers flying over the ivories as he played Margaret Owens favorite hymn.

Not only had the wizened Mr. Holmes taught him the intricacies of proper investigative techniques - enough so that he would soon have all the evidence he needed to prove Mr. Mertz for the low down Kaiser spy he was, but he'd also taught Jonathon a deep appreciation for the fine art of music. Of course Mr. Holmes played the violin, but Mother had made it clear that since they already owned a piano Jonathon would learn on that first. If he proved that he could keep up with the lessons and practice, then they would discuss purchasing a violin. So far he thought he'd done a swell job of proving himself.

While it was true that he'd only begun lessons a few months ago, Miss Abernathy had given him the highest praise in regards to his progress. And Jonathon couldn't be more pleased with the quality of his performance this morning.

It was just too bad that Mother had decided to bake today. First the cookies, now the pie. His stomach growled in anticipation and, at the moment, the question of what was to be served for supper paled in light of the wonderful treats to follow.

A scowl turned the corners of his mouth down, certain that Sherlock would never be distracted from any task by something as trivial as apple pie. Not while detecting or playing the violin. But it was also likely that Sherlock had never had the privilege of eating something as heavenly as what his mother was baking either.

Again he strengthened his resolve, reaching the end of the last stanza with a strong finish and starting over for the third time. Miss Abernathy, who said practice made perfect, was sure to be pleased with his progress when she heard him Tuesday afternoon.

"Don't bother me," he muttered rudely, catching a glimpse of Kathleen's pink dress from the corner of his eye.

"I'm just watching," she protested softly.

"Just make sure you be quiet."

He ignored her as best he could, losing himself in the music as he played the song again and again.

Yes, indeed, the making of music was a most pleasant way to spend the morning. Although trench warfare was nice, too. Or baseball. Or even hide and seek. But the piano required his attention for now.

"Jonathon Owens!" Elizabeth shouted from the head of the stairway. "Would you please stop torturing us with that racket?"

"You just don't appreciate good music," he retorted loudly, banging his fingers with surprising strength against the keys beneath them.

"I always appreciate *good* music."

"Then stop complaining. You're making me mess up."

"The whole song is messed up because you can't play the piano."

"That's enough from the both of you," Margaret said firmly from the doorway. From the second floor the sound of footsteps stomping down the hall, followed by the resounding slam of a door, signaled Elizabeth's retreat from the argument.

"Thank you, Mother. She was disturbing my concentration."

"I-" He heard her clear her throat before continuing. "You've been practicing for quite a while now. Don't you think you should take a break? Get some fresh air?"

"The window is open right here, Mother. And I'm not practicing. I'm playing. Just for you. Don't you like it?" He turned to glance at her, a proud smile on his face. She smiled back. Sort of. Must be she was tired from all that baking.

"I- I've never heard anything quite like it. I'm –

speechless."

Disgustingly pleased at her praise, Jonathon felt as though he could play the rest of the day.

~~~

The faded drapes in Colby Thornton's office fluttered from time to time, as the gentle April breeze found its way through the narrow inch high opening. Any farther and Anna would have a conniption fit. While she welcomed the end of winter, it was still too early for her to enjoy the warmer air. If she truly enjoyed anything as innocent as a pleasant day. Still, Colby had long since grown weary of the stale air and decided to risk her wrath to let in some fresh.

He could hear, in the distance, the happy shouts of children playing outside and he looked forward to more of the same over the next several months. It was one of Colby's greatest pleasures. Not so for Marcus. The voices seemed to agitate him, however slightly, as he concentrated on his next move.

Colby smiled as he watched his friend bent over the old chess set, the wooden pieces faded with age, as were most of the rest of the things in this room. It was the only place in the entire house that had escaped Anna's refurbishing efforts. But sometimes a man had to put his foot down. This was his study and he liked it just this way.

A comfortable place where he felt free to relax and be himself. Free from her nagging and whining. Because Anna hated this room passionately, and studiously avoided it, claiming that it was an
~~~

embarrassment. Outdated and dusty. Still, it suited Colby. Perhaps he was outdated, too. Maybe even dusty.

"Checkmate," Marcus said suddenly, triumphantly.

"You cheat!" Colby accused, chuckling good – naturedly. He had, indeed, lost the game while his mind wandered. "Hmm."

He carefully considered his next move. Or lack thereof. One thing about Marcus was that he was one of the best players in town. He plotted his game much like Pershing must plot his attacks against the Hun. And Marcus was usually successful, unless Colby paid strict attention to his opponent. More often than not, though, he didn't pay much attention at all, so all he could do was admit defeat.

As he must do now. With another grin, Colby gently tipped his king over in a gesture of defeat.

"Another game?" Marcus asked hesitantly. After all this time he was still unsure of his welcome, which endeared him to Colby even more. A character, there was no doubt. But a man in need of a friend if ever there was one.

"Why not?" The longer he stayed holed up in here with Marcus, the longer he could avoid his wife. Because Anna didn't care overly much for Marcus. Claimed he gave her the willies. A fact that didn't stop her from trying to intimidate him whenever an opportunity arose. Poor Marcus. Colby figured he was more afraid of Anna than anyone in Charlotte.

"Change colors?"

"No, I like the black." Technically it was more

gray than black now, having faded with age. This set was still one of his prized possessions, passed down from his father on his thirteenth birthday. Before that, it had belonged to his grandfather. Colby often regretted that he didn't have a son of his own to pass it on to.

They didn't speak as they arranged their respective pieces on the board for a new game. In truth, they rarely spoke at all, regardless of what activity they might be engaged in. One of the oddest friendships Colby had ever been involved with.

No, Marcus never seemed inclined to talk much. But then he never seemed inclined to do much of anything. Instead, he appeared to be content just to have his company. Colby had known for a long time that this man led an utterly lonely life and he was happy to provide whatever diversion he could.

Outside his work, the only activity Colby knew for sure was that Marcus was involved a weekly meeting of some of the businessmen around town. Although he had also heard that Marcus always chose a seat nearest the door, never said a word, and left just as soon as the meeting was adjourned. Of course there was church every Sunday, too. But Marcus slipped in shortly after each service began, sat in the last row and slipped out almost before the final "Amen" was said.

Having met Marcus' parents on the few occasions they returned to Michigan for a visit, Colby was completely baffled by their son's demeanor. His family was outgoing and friendly. Marcus, on the other hand, was painfully shy and insecure.

An especially loud shriek from outside captured Colby's attention and he glanced out the window. A flash of white streaked past his window and giggles faded in the distance. Presumably more children in search of a tree-less field in which to fly their kites.

"You children get of my yard!" Anna could be heard to scream. Marcus winced visibly.

~~~

It was a beautiful morning, Elliot decided as he strolled home. On Saturday's he generally made sure everything got off to a smooth start before leaving the responsibility in the capable hands of Richard, who had been helping out for a number of years now. He knew the business inside and out and, unless it looked as though the day would be particularly busy, Elliot liked to spend a few hours with the rest of his family. Besides, if he were needed he was just a telephone call away and could be there in minutes.

Today, though, they were closing up shop early. After the mid-day meal Richard would lock the doors, hurry home to change his clothes, and then the entire family would leave to meet Bryant Sanderson at Bennett Park. They'd not had a family portrait taken since just after Charles' birth and Elliot thought it was time to have another done.

He enjoyed the warm spring breeze, gently ruffling the bright green buds that had appeared on the trees, seemingly overnight. It never ceased to amaze him how quickly the signs of the seasons appeared. But he especially enjoyed this one, when
~~~

the promise of the leaves that would provide cool shade during the hot summer months began to grow.

If he were forced to choose a favorite season, he'd be hard pressed to decide between spring and fall. Each had its own distinct characteristics, the way the air felt and smelled, the anticipation of season – related events and traditions, even in the vague feelings, some inner workings of the brain that proclaimed a new and exciting time had arrived.

The excitement was evidenced in the vast numbers of people milling about the sidewalks. Not that they weren't out and about in even the harshest of winter months. Not much kept the residents cooped up at home for long, they just left the warmth of their homes less frequently and stayed out for shorter periods of time. Now, though, they were able to visit, catch up on the latest news and gossip to their hearts content.

Rounding the corner, home in sight, Elliot quickened his pace. He hadn't gone but a few steps down Seminary Street when he heard it, and he had to grin. The windows of the neighbors' homes, as well as those in the sanatorium across the street, were wide open to let the fresh air in. He would have bet, were he a betting man, that more than a few pairs of ears were wishing that winter had lingered a bit longer, sparing them this particular serenade.

Enough of the right keys were being hit so that anyone familiar with the melody would recognize Amazing Grace. Unfortunately even more – *many more* – of the wrong keys made it unbearably awful to listen to.

Jonathon.

With grand delusions of possessing near genius musical abilities, no one had the heart to tell him otherwise, save Elizabeth anyway. And, as with anything else that snagged his interest, his son pursued it with a single – minded determination that both impressed and appalled those closest to him.

Margaret made no secret that she disapproved of the boy's spying habits, but readily admitted she couldn't fault him in that he'd learned enough so he was quite good at it. And while all but the stone deaf had to be wishing Jonathon weren't quite so untalented at the piano, no one could deny that he was enthusiastic in the endeavor.

Elliot grinned again as he cut across the street, bounding up the five porch steps. The scent of apple pie greeted him at the door and, sniffing appreciatively, he thanked God again for all the wonderful qualities and talents his wife possessed.

His footsteps carried him soundlessly inside where he paused in the doorway. Only Jonathon and Kathleen were about, the latter noticing him in mere seconds. Smiling broadly she hurried over and threw her arms around his waist.

"You're home, Papa!"

"That I am, Miss Kathleen." He lifted her effortlessly and held her close for a moment.

"Hiya, Pop," Jonathon said absently, barely glancing in his direction.

"Good afternoon, son." To Kathleen he asked, "Where might your mother be?" though he knew exactly where he would find her.

"In the kitchen. She made choc'late cookies this morning," Kathleen told him. One need not be an avid follower of Sherlock Holmes to detect the trace of a hint in her announcement.

"Hmm. Chocolate cookies, you say?" He raised his brows as he leaned close and whispered in her ear, "Maybe if we ask nicely, she might give us a few." Kathleen giggled as he carried her toward the waiting treat.

Margaret stood at the sink peeling a huge mound of potatoes, her movements quick and precise, a definite sign that she was agitated. Elliot suspected the source of that agitation sat at the keyboard in the other room.

It only took a moment for him to realize that she was not aware of his presence and, putting a finger to his lips, he lowered Kathleen to the floor before creeping quietly up behind Margaret and sliding his arms around her slender waist. She let out a startled scream and twisted in his arms, relieved to find that it was him.

"*Elliot Owens!* You should know better than to scare someone when they're holding a knife!"

"I shall keep that in mind for future reference, my dear." He kissed her cheek before a tug on his jacket reminded him that he was on a mission. "I told Kathleen if we asked nicely, you might let us have some of the cookies she said you baked this morning. So please, Mother, may we?"

"Oh for goodness sake," she sighed impatiently, starting to put the knife and potato down. "Let me wipe my hands-"

"I'll get them," he said quickly, kissing her again.

"And we'll eat them quietly so you can enjoy the music."

If the scowl she flashed him was anything to go by, Elliot decided that further teasing wouldn't be in his best interests. The knife she was holding, after all, was razor sharp.

Her back to him again, Eliot winked at Kathleen before withdrawing two glasses from the cupboard. Couldn't very well have cookies without milk. Soon he and his youngest daughter were seated at the table enjoying the first fruits of Margaret's labor. The pie was obviously to follow supper but that didn't stop him from savoring the delicious scent that filled the kitchen.

"It occurs to me, Miss Kathleen, that we have been remiss in sharing these cookies with your brothers and sister. Perhaps we should ask if they would like some, too?" he suggested, stealing a discreet glance at his wife.

"What a *wonderful* idea!" Margaret exclaimed, whirling around and staring at Elliot as though he were a genius. "Charles is napping and Elizabeth is sulking in her room, but Jonathon might want a few." The last was said hopefully as she hurried to the doorway.

"Jonathon! Kathleen and your father are having cookies and milk. Why don't you take a break and join them?"

"No thank you, Mother. I want to play this again."

"And again, and again and again." Elliot couldn't be sure, but he thought that might have been what she muttered on her way back to the sink. The scowl was back and he found he had to hide his smile behind his napkin lest she turn and see it. Not that he thought she would actually *use* the knife on him but, in her present state of mind, it was probably best if he didn't press his luck.

"So what is Elizabeth sulking about this time?" he asked, thinking to distract her. Jonathon had obviously learned a great deal about reading notes. Unfortunately he was reading the correct notes and hitting the wrong keys. The *same* wrong keys. *Every* time.

"She wanted to go to another suffrage meeting with that boy and I forbade her." She peered into the oven before continuing with the potatoes.

"Perhaps forbidding her isn't the best choice," Elliot suggested reasonably. "I fear it might be making the cause, and the boy, more appealing."

He could have bitten his tongue the moment the words left his mouth. He saw her back stiffen, and though she didn't respond, he knew the luck he had decided not to press was quickly running out. Between their eldest child being involved with the movement, and her infatuation with 'that boy,' life had become – interesting.

He was of a mind to allow Elizabeth a little freedom as far as the movement was concerned. As for Edgar Perkins, he felt there was little danger. Edgar was twenty – three and a strong supporter of women's rights. Elliot had observed no difference in the way he treated his daughter and the rest of the women involved. He merely encouraged all of them to let their voices be heard.

"Papa?" Kathleen interrupted his thoughts.

"Yes, Sweetheart?"

"What does 'preciate' mean?" He looked at her thoughtfully.

"Appreciate?" She nodded. "Hmm." How to explain the word when it could be used in more than one way. "Well, I could give you a better answer if I knew how you heard it spoken."

"Well, Elizabeth yelled at Jonathon 'cause he wouldn't stop playing the piano and he said she didn't 'preciate good music." She was very serious and Elliot had a hard time holding back a smile.

"In that case he meant Elizabeth didn't like his music." Kathleen glanced toward the front room then dubiously back at her father.

"I don't 'preciate good music either, Papa."

This time he couldn't stop the chuckle that escaped him. A chuckle that turned into full – fledged laughter when he heard Margaret mutter, "You, me and every neighbor in a six block radius!" It earned him another nasty scowl but he just couldn't help himself.

Now muttering low enough that he couldn't discern any words in particular, though he was sure that he was now the target of whatever she was saying, Margaret leaned down to peer into the oven. This time she opened the door completely, wiped her hands on her apron and reached in with a folded towel. Seconds later she pulled the perfectly golden pie out.

He was left in no doubt that she was ignoring him as she marched past, nose in the air, on her way to the porch, where the pie would cool until supper. He was going to have to find some way to get back into her good graces, lest she hold her grudge the rest of the day.

Moments later, to his complete and utter astonishment, Elliot heard his wife say,

"*Gracious me!* I must say I've seen Mr. Mertz do some odd things before but-"

She got no further before the music stopped abruptly and the sound of pounding feet exited the house.

At her heartfelt, "Thank the Lord!" Elliot nearly fell off his chair.

~~~

"Are you *sure?*" Nina asked, looking up at Daniel as they strolled along the edge of the river.

"Well, the limp may slow me down a little, but the other guys still say they want me on the team," he said, reaching out to push a branch out of their way. "And I do enjoy the game. I've played every summer since I was in school."

"I know, but that was before the accident."

"That is true, Nurse Hakes, but I promise you, I'll be fine." He saw that her cheeks turned pink at the reference to her profession and hugged her close. "I like that you worry about me, Nina. But I can't give up everything I enjoy doing just because of my leg. Will it ease your mind if I promise to be extra careful?"

"It would make me feel better if you'd ask Dr. Garland."

"It would?" Still blushing, she lowered her eyes and nodded. "Then ask I shall. But he's the one who
~~~

told me to do anything I was comfortable with."

"I know. But *baseball,* Daniel? It scares me to think of what might happen."

"*Nothing* is going to happen. Except the game could be even more interesting this year."

"What do you mean?"

"Alan Jenkins somehow talked Mr. McClelland into joining the team."

"*Marcus McClelland?"* Nina gasped, her eyes opening as wide as he'd ever seen them. Lord but she was beautiful.

"The very one," he said, shaking his head in wonder. "You could have knocked me over with a feather when I found out. I mean he avoids people like the plague, and can barely talk to another person, and he's going to be playing ball on *our team.*"

"It might be just the thing he needs though. I've never seen another adult as withdrawn as that poor man is."

"Well, he's definitely shy," he agreed, wondering if she was right. He liked Mr. McClelland well enough, but if he was as quiet and uncomfortable during the games as he was every other time Daniel had seen him, it could make for some pretty awkward moments.

"You might be surprised, Daniel," Nina told him, as though she'd been reading his thoughts.

"I suppose there is always that possibility," he said with a grin, kissing her forehead. "You're something else, Nina. You really are."

~~~
~~~

"I'm glad that's over," Margaret sighed, watching the children in the distance. Elliot enjoyed peaceful moments like this with his wife. They were sitting at the base of a tree, his arm wrapped securely around her, and he wished they could stay right there for the rest of the afternoon.

It hadn't taken long after Jonathon abandoned the piano for her sweet disposition to return, and it had remained so throughout the meal, and the readying of five children in their Sunday best clothing. Clothing they had been warned to keep clean and stain free during these few moments of play.

"You and me both." Elliot sighed, too. Between Jonathon's boredom while the photographer set up the shots, and Elizabeth's perpetual scowl, it would be a miracle if this photograph turned out half as well as their last one.

He turned his attention to his offspring. The boys were playing tag, Jonathon – surprisingly enough, making allowances for the fact that Charles couldn't keep up. Usually he was impatient with his brother and his heart swelled with pride every time he showed a little consideration.

Kathleen was chasing a couple of butterflies, flitting first in one direction, and then another, unsure of which one she liked best. Elizabeth, as had become her usual custom when forced to participate in family activities, was sitting off by herself looking bored.

"This is nice," he murmured, placing a kiss against Meg's temple. "Meg, I've been thinking."

She looked up at him, a tender smile curving her lips.

"And what is new about that, Mr. Owens? You're always thinking. It's one of the things I love most about you."

"And here I thought it was my charm and handsome face you loved the most." She reached up and cupped his cheek with her slender hand. He covered it with his own, holding it in place because her touch never ceased to fill him with joy.

"Actually what I loved the most," she whispered, gazing at him with adoration shining in her eyes, "was the fact that you had the good sense to recognize what a wonderful wife I'd make you."

For a startled moment Elliot could only stare at her, and then he threw his head back and laughed. Margaret laughed, too, and he wrapped his arms around her and held her tightly.

"I do love you, Mrs. Owens."

"I love you, too, Elliot. Very much."

While she had been teasing with her facetious comment, Elliot *was* more thankful than he could say that he'd recognized that she would be the perfect wife for him. Because she had been. Every wonderful day since they'd married.

"So what were you thinking?" she asked a few moments later.

"I almost forgot," he said with a chuckle. "I was thinking about the trip home we've been talking about. And I think I'd rather postpone it." He smiled during the lengthy pause that followed his announcement.

"Whatever you think best," she finally

murmured. Though she tried to hide it, he could tell that she was disappointed. They hadn't been back to Indiana for nearly five years.

"I really *do* think it's best. The timing just isn't right this summer."

"Maybe next summer."

"No, I don't want to go then either. I was thinking Christmas would be better." He felt her go completely still. She wasn't even breathing and his smile grew.

"Do you mean it?"

"I absolutely do."

"Oh, Elliot!" She was beaming, her eyes filled with tears, when she looked up at him. "It would be so wonderful to spend Christmas with our families again."

"That's what I was thinking, too."

"Are you sure though? You've never closed the store in December before."

"And I won't this year. Lucille Hatfield is going to work for me while we're gone. She mentioned that she'd like to buy Zeke a gramophone but wasn't sure she would be able to save enough between now and then. And so we struck a deal."

"*Thank you*, Elliot. You couldn't give me a nicer Christmas gift than this."

Chapter 6

The things Elliot thought he liked most about spring were the sounds and scents of warmer weather. He swore you could smell the grass as it turned a deeper shade of green. In his opinion, it didn't get any better than the soft fragrance of honeysuckle and lilacs as they perfumed the air all around them. The sound of children playing from all over the neighborhood and crickets chirping was a sure sign of winter's passing, as was the creak of the chains as he gently rocked the porch swing back and forth.

His arm around her shoulders, Margaret was mending a pair of dungarees, humming contentedly as Charles sat a few feet away building something with his blocks. Elizabeth was at another Suffrage meeting. Jonathon was, no doubt, spying on Mr.

Mertz again, while Richard studied for the tests that seemed to increase in frequency toward the end of the school year, and Kathleen played with her babies in the parlor.

He didn't think life could get any better than this, except maybe someday when the good Lord presented him with a few grandchildren. Not that he was in any rush to be a grandfather; it was just something he looked forward to when the time came.

He wished his or Margaret's parents lived closer because he knew the children were missing out on a great deal from not knowing them well. But when they'd moved here from Indiana after inheriting *his* grandfather's shoe store, it was a loss they'd been forced to bear.

"When do you think we should tell them about the trip back home," he asked, whispering softly in her ear.

"I don't know," Margaret whispered back. Her excitement came through loud and clear though. As much as they both loved Charlotte, Indianapolis would always be home. Still he knew they would never move back, even when he grew too old to run Owens Fine Shoes, because their children considered this home.

"I've thought about just telling them we can't go this summer after all, and then helping you pack all of our bags in December while they're at school. Can you imagine how surprised they would be? To just head down to the depot and catch the train?"

"Is that what you want to do then?" Margaret asked, glancing up at him with a smile, and a kiss for his cheek.

"I don't know. They're going to be so disappointed if we just tell them we're not able to go. Well, except for Elizabeth," Elliot said wryly. "She wasn't thrilled about going in the first place. Then there's Jonathon. He might feel the country will fall into ruin if he can't keep an eye on Mr. Mertz, so he'll be torn between disappointment and relief." The thought made him chuckle.

"Elliot, you have got to stop encouraging his spying," she admonished, though he noticed the corners of her lips twitching. "You and I both know that Mr. Mertz is no more guilty of being a spy than you or I."

"I can't help it," he laughed softly, knowing Charles paid more attention to the goings on around him than he let on. "It's too much fun. He's so enthusiastic, Meg. And *so* thorough. Have you taken a look at the notes he takes? They may be pure fantasy but he's absolutely meticulous."

"No, I haven't," she admitted, cutting off the thread she'd just knotted. "I don't want to encourage him." Elliot bit the inside of his cheek hard, knowing a reminder of the afternoon *she* had encouraged him would spoil the moment. "Do you have any idea how offended Mr. Mertz might be if he found out that our son has been spying on him for months?"

"I think Mr. Mertz is offended because his neighbors are breathing, Meg. He's the most unhappy person I've ever known."

"Maybe," she suggested, looking at him through her lashes, "it's because people like our son spy on him." Elliot seemed to consider that for a moment then grinned.

"And maybe he's just a bad tempered old man." Margaret sighed gustily at that, but he knew she wasn't really upset with him.

"I suppose that means you're not going to discourage Jonathon."

"Yes, I suppose that's exactly what it means," Elliot said agreeably.

She tried to hide it but his prim and proper wife wore a grin of her own.

Elliot couldn't help himself. He pulled her into his arms and kissed her soundly, right there, for all the world to see. If anyone was bothering to pay attention. But he doubted that they'd acquired an audience. Unless, perhaps, there happened to be a bored patient or employee at the sanatorium across the street.

~~~

The incessant buzzing of the flies was maddening, Jonathon thought irritably. Almost as irritating as the feather light landings against his bare flesh. It gave him the creepy crawlies, and tickled a little, too. No matter how often he waved them away, they returned in seconds, undeterred by his efforts. At least you could squash a mosquito. They, too, had swarmed him as soon as he started climbing, but he did have the satisfaction of knowing he'd rid the world of a couple dozen of those pesky insects so far. Too bad the flies moved so fast or he'd have reduced their population by a few dozen as well.
~~~

Nestled securely in the branches of the tall pine behind the Owens' house, he resented the distraction they seemed bent on causing. Between the mostly dense needles and the dim illumination of twilight, his view of Mr. Mertz's backyard wasn't the best in the first place. The added misery threatened the success of this mission.

And an important mission it was, too, if the peculiar goings on next door were any indication.

Three paces due south of the southeast corner of the house, and five west. Suspicious movements in and of themselves but then Mr. Mertz dropped to his knees. Well dropped might have been overstating the action just a little. To be accurate, it was more like he slowly lowered himself to the ground, and one thing Jonathon intended to be was accurate. The safety of the entire country might depend on it.

He could see that the old man had pulled a spade from the pocket of his jacket and began to dig in front of him.

Frogs, crickets, the faint noise of a carriage rolling along the bricks on Main Street, they all seemed to conspire against him. It was a wonder a boy could hear himself think much less anything else that might be important. Yet the sound of metal scraping against dirt and stones rang clear in the rapidly descending darkness. Again and again he scooped up small bits of earth, piling it in the grass beside the hole.

And then he stopped.

Jonathon had to squint hard to see more clearly, though it didn't help much. Too many shadows obscured the view between him and the yard next door. But there was no mistaking the fact that Mr. Mertz reached into his other pocket and pulled out – *something* – from its depths. And not a very large something. It wasn't very small either though.

Almost completely dark now, Jonathon didn't actually see him drop the object into the hole, but he must have done so because he quickly began returning the dirt from where it had come.

Ah- Ah- Ahchoo*!*

He'd tried to muffle the sneeze as best he could, wishing the fly who had just tickled his nose a swift and well deserved end. Mr. Mertz obviously heard the commotion because the pace of his movements increased and he kept looking around, as if to determine where the noise originated.

Yessiree, something very suspicious was going on over there. And one day President Wilson himself was going to award a medal to Jonathon for exposing a spy who could, at this very moment, threaten the safety and well – being of every American citizen.

With all the trouble he'd had so far this evening, it shouldn't have surprised him at all that, just as Mr. Mertz had gotten to his feet and was dusting his hands on his jacket, Elizabeth should shout irritably from the back door,

"Jonathon! Mother says you have to come in now!"

So startled was he that he lost his balance on the limb and slid several feet down the trunk, skinning his palms on the roughened bark and bumping his knee against a lower branch.

Fortunately for him he managed to wrap his arms tightly around the trunk.

Mr. Mertz couldn't have failed to hear the summons and probably knew that Jonathon had been spying on him. He'd have to be extra careful from now on, he thought crossly, making his way carefully to the ground.

He looked for Mr. Mertz when he cleared the tree but the old man must have hurried inside.

Jonathon marched across the yard, blowing on his stinging hands, muttering about how he got no respect, and wouldn't it be just wonderful if all his hard work was for naught because some of his family members couldn't comprehend the importance of what he was trying to do.

~~~

Colby sighed mightily, sinking comfortably into his wicker chair on the porch and setting a glass of tea on the low table beside it. It was evenings like this, pleasant spring evenings, with the sun resting just on the horizon, that he would have enjoyed the company of a pleasant wife. One who appreciated the simple things in life.

Simple things like the sound of the children laughing and shrieking down the block, playing some game that so obviously entertained them they couldn't contain their joy. Tag, he thought. Or hide – n – seek.

But the queen was tucked safely away in her castle, windows securely closed to shut out the 'racket from those brats.' Protected from the
~~~

possibility that a bug might attack her, even though he'd tried to explain that it was too early in the season for all but the hardiest of insects to venture out. Definitely chilly enough that he'd slipped into a warm jacket before settling in to take advantage of the warmer weather.

"Good evening, Reverend Thornton," little Tommy Sullivan panted, running up to the porch while casting quick glances behind him. "Can I hide in your bushes? "

So he'd guessed correctly. Hide – n – seek often expanded to include nearby yards, sheds and automobiles. It made him wish he were a youngster again, or that he could just throw maturity to the wind and join in anyway.

"You certainly may," he said with a chuckle.

"If you see Stuart Morgan, don't tell him I'm here please," he whispered, ducking behind a Boxwood shrub. In serious need of pruning, it would conceal the boy quite nicely.

"Mum's the word," he promised, holding his forefinger against his lips.

"But you won't tell him, right?" Colby laughed outright at that.

"No, Tommy, he won't hear a peep out of me."

He watched a few branches rustling as the boy made himself comfortable, and then all was still.

"Reverend Thornton?"

"Yes, Tommy?"

"Do you see him yet?"

Colby glanced up and down the street but could only see a couple of children off in the distance – and moving farther away. He hoped that the young man wouldn't be stuck too long in his little hiding place, but thought it a distinct possibility. Most of the children were afraid of Anna and they might not think anyone would be brave enough to risk her wrath.

"I think I'm gonna win," Tommy whispered a few minutes later. "They're all scaredy cats and-" Seeming to realize that he was about to say something that another husband might find offensive, he stopped abruptly and Colby grinned from ear – to – ear.

"I suspect you're right, young man. Mrs. Thornton may be your secret weapon in winning the game tonight."

An uncomfortable silence followed that announcement and Colby wished he could have seen the expression on Tommy's face just then. Finally he heard a low chuckle and Tommy whispered,

"You're an okay fellow, Reverend Thornton."

About a quarter of an hour later, one of the children shouted, "Olly olly oxen free!" Tommy stepped out from behind the bush, thanked him kindly, and trotted off down the street, head held high. He had, indeed, won the game.

~~~

Marcus stumbled down the stairs, barely awake, as the telephone rang for about the fiftieth time. He didn't know who might be calling at nearly half past eleven, but before he hung up, they would know *exactly* what his opinion of the practice was. A body
~~~

should have the right to sleep through the night without interruption.

The hardwood floor was cold against his bare feet and he wished he'd had the presence of mind to put his slippers on when he'd finally managed to crawl out of bed.

"Hello!" he snapped into the mouthpiece.

"Marcus? Dear, is that you?"

"Mother?" he asked in disbelief. Of course. She always forgot the three hour difference between their time zones. He tried to stifle a yawn but she heard it anyway.

"Did I wake you, son?"

"It's all right, Mother. I hadn't been in bed long." It wasn't really a lie. Not in the strictest sense of the word. Two hours *wasn't* long if one considered the entire eight hours he normally slept.

"What time is it in Michigan again? It's a little after eight here, son."

"Close to your time, Mother." Eleven-thirty wasn't that far removed from eight-thirty. "How are you and Pop doing?"

"Just fine, son. Missing you, which is the reason I called. I needed to hear your voice." He smothered another yawn and leaned against the wall, eyes closed.

"It's nice to hear your voice, too, Mother. How's the weather out there?" Much warmer than the fifty degrees they'd enjoyed in Charlotte today, he was sure.

"Just like summertime back home, son. You really ought to consider joining us. I know how much you hate winter." Marcus couldn't see himself living in Phoenix. His parents had moved out there about eight years ago because Doc Garlington thought it would help his mother's arthritis. He'd been out to visit a couple of times and hated the extreme heat of summer.

"You know I like the change of seasons here," he explained instead. And, truth be told, he did. Especially autumn.

"Have you met anyone special yet?" Ah. The real reason came out. Not that it was a big surprise. That was where each monthly telephone call wound up, although she usually managed to wait a bit longer than this to bring the subject up. His father worried incessantly that the McClelland name would die out if Marcus didn't marry and provide heirs. Never mind that he had several male McClelland cousins, it was imperative that this particular line continue on through the generations.

"Not yet," he sighed, holding on to his patience by sheer force of will. "I think everyone is more concerned with the war than anything else right now." The fleeting hope that he could steer her to a different subject died a swift death as she continued,

"What about that Monroe girl? Candace, isn't it? She always seemed sweet on you."

"Caroline. She married Robert Taylor a couple of years ago."

"Oh, that's a shame. Well, what about Leona Baker?"

"Loretta. She's married, too. In fact, she has three boys now." Marcus shook his head. The list was endless, his mother's mostly accurate memory being long. Fortunately most were married. One had even joined a convent so he was safe from that suggestion.

"Marcus, you know we only have your best interests at heart. It's not good for a for a fine young man like you to be alone. What you need is a good wife and lots of children." Heaven forbid! He shuddered at the thought of 'lots of children.' What he *needed* was a little more sleep.

"I know that, Mother. I just don't think I'm ready to settle down yet."

"Son, I know you've always been shy but it's time to take the bull by the horns and make us grandparents. " She waxed poetic about the joys of grandchildren and how lovely it would be when they visited one another, to spoil them. "But it's hard to spoil children that aren't *here* yet, Marcus. You're nearly twenty – eight. It's time to think about settling down."

Marcus figured if he were anymore settled, he'd be in a grave.

"I'll think about it, Mother," was all he said to her though. He'd learned long ago that arguing with her was futile. As long as it wasn't a lie, he told her what she wanted to hear. Whatever would make her stop nagging him to find a wife. So he would think about it – for about five seconds. Just long enough to make his promise the truth.

"That's what you always say," she complained in that whining to ne he so hated. He'd almost rather she shouted at him.

"And I always do. I just haven't met the right girl yet. When I do, you'll be the first to know."

"You promise?" He heard the excitement in her voice and felt a twinge of guilt. But it wasn't like he actually *knew* any women. Beyond their names anyway.

"I promise. Hey, is Pop around?"

"He's sleeping. The poor man spent most of the day with his cronies playing golf. You know your father loves that game more than anything else. Maybe even more than me. He's so pleased to live where he can play year round that he still hasn't gotten over the novelty." She laughed merrily. "Just this morning he said, 'Harriet, can you imagine me trying to play golf in Michigan in April?' I told him I couldn't. You probably still have some snow on the ground."

"Well there is a little left here and there, but it was actually quite warm today," Marcus mumbled, then yawned loudly. "The ground might have been a little too soggy, but you never know. Pop's determined enough that it probably wouldn't have stopped him." He yawned again.

"You really should get more sleep, son," his mother admonished and Marcus had to smile. He'd have gotten more sleep if she could remember that it was three hours later in Michigan than it was in Arizona.

"I'll work on it, Mother."

"I hope- Hang on a second. Yes, Dear, I'll be right there. Marcus, I have to go. Your father woke up and is wondering why I haven't come to bed yet. I love you, son."

"I love you, too, Mother. Give Pop my love."

As he trudged back up to his room he shook his

head and hoped it wouldn't take too long for him to fall asleep again. He wondered if the late night calls would continue if, by some miracle, he did find himself married someday. But he knew they would. She'd just have to find different reasons to make them.

~~~

Spring, it seemed, was here to stay. Of course there was always the possibility of a late season snow, but it would surprise him if it came. It just felt like winter was finally over. Daniel could feel it in the warmer air as he walked as quickly as he could to pick Nina up for church this late April morning.

As always, he could hardly wait to see her again, even though he'd walked her home from the sanatorium the night before. And it was even better since he'd been able to get rid of the crutches when the splint came off a couple of weeks ago.

The polished cane took a few days to get used to but he thought it made him look rather dapper, dressed in his wool suit and overcoat. Though he never thought he'd looked awful before, he found himself taking more pains with his appearance since that first night he'd gone to see Nina at the hospital.

And she always looked beautiful. Whether wearing her nurse's uniform, or one of only two other dresses she owned. Last Sunday she'd worn the black and yellow day dress so, he assumed, today she'd be wearing the pink one. He hoped it wouldn't be long before he could see to it that she had all the clothes she could ever want.
~~~

By the end of the summer he expected to have enough money to completely refurbish his house, the only home he'd ever known. Fortunately his parents had inherited it from his mother's parents, or they might have lost it after his father died. His mother's meager salary as a secretary to a prominent local attorney was barely enough to pay the property tax and put food on the table. It surely didn't allow for a coat of paint or nicer furniture.

But at least he'd known what it was like to have a home and parents, he thought, bounding up the stairs of the boarding house and knocking on the door. Nina had never known either. But she would what it was like to have a home. And he would move heaven and earth to make sure it would happen soon.

"Good morning," Nina said, smiling brightly as she opened the door.

"Good morning yourself. You look lovely," he complimented, as he did each time he saw her. She blushed, as she did each time he complimented her. "Ready to go?"

"Yes."

He tucked her hand in the crook of his free arm, and they began the seven block walk to church.

"I can hardly wait for summer," Nina sighed, stepping neatly around a puddle, a reminder of the recently melted snow.

"I was thinking the same thing on my way to your house. Shouldn't be too much longer. The first of May is this Thursday."

"I know. It'll be so much nicer weather to walk in."

"Except when it rains." Nina laughed softly at that and he asked, "What?"

"I love to walk in the rain. If it's warm, of course. And so long as there isn't much lightening." Not at all afraid of storms himself, Daniel wanted to hug her.

"Then I guess we can take walks in the rain," he decided, silly though they might look to passersby. "And have picnics, and sit on the dam when it gets too hot."

"I've never done that before."

"What?"

"Sit on the dam."

"Why not? There's nothing I like to do much more on a sweltering day."

"I always thought I'd feel foolish sitting there alone."

"Well, now you have me to sit with. If you want to."

"I want to," she said shyly, glancing at him from beneath her incredibly long lashes.

"I'm glad." This time he gave into temptation, wrapped his arm around her shoulders and hugged her to his side for a moment before resuming their walk. "It doesn't matter what we do, Nina. I just want to be with you."

"I feel the same way, Daniel."

He felt his chest puff out just the tiniest bit as they walked into the sanctuary and he wondered if he could find the time to work at a second job. At least part of the time. It would be nice to be able to take care of the house before the end of the summer. The only problem was, it would be at the expense of time with Nina. He wasn't sure he was willing to give that up, he thought, as they sat in a pew near the back of the church. From the pulpit, Colby Thornton smiled at them.

Chapter 7

"Oh for heaven's sake," Jonathon muttered in exasperation, taking the stick wrapped round and round with string from Charles' chubby little hand. "Didn't I tell you to run with it?"

"I did wun wif it," Charles said confidently. Unlike Kathleen, Jonathon's impatience rarely bothered him.

"Then why is the kite still on the ground?" he demanded irritably.

"Becauth it didn't go up."

"Because you didn't *run* with it. Here. I'll show you again. But this is the last time."

Jonathon wound the string so the kite only had about six feet of slack, grabbed it just beneath the bottom point and ran like the wind. It would be nice if it were his own kite he was trying to get up in the air but, as always, he was stuck helping the babies. Well, Richard was helping Kathleen, who wasn't faring much better than Charles.

Someday he would just sneak out alone and not have to worry about anyone but himself. Have fun without having one of the babies tagging along and spoiling everything.

Still, he had no choice at the moment and so he picked up his pace, letting the string glide easily through his fingers. As it drifted farther up, he uncoiled more until it soared high above the treetops.

"Do you want your kite or not?" he asked, every word laced with sarcasm as he glared at his brother. Charles hurried over, an awed expression on his round little face. Excitement glowed in his eyes as he eagerly took the stick from Jonathon, who cautioned as he demonstrated, "Tug on the string like this to keep it up."

"I will," Charles promised, tugging the way his brother had shown him.

"You better, 'cause I'm gonna go fly mine now."

Jonathon muttered to himself as he crossed the field until he was a safe distance away. It hadn't been long since the snow melted and the grass was a little sparse in some spots over here. That meant being a little careful where he stepped – unless he wanted to risk his mother's wrath when he returned home with mud covered shoes.

Jonathon picked up his kite and the stick – full of string and got his kite up in the air just as quickly as he had Charles', whom he put right out of his thoughts as he enjoyed the tautness of the string as the kite sailed through the air. He imagined himself up there, at the controls of a Bleriot, gunning for the Kaiser, killing more of the enemy than any soldier could ever dream possible. The most decorated hero any century had ever known.

He could see it now. Admirers lining the streets when he returned home – wounded, of course, from his last and most triumphant battle, whereupon he had managed to massacre a thousand bloody German's. Cheers from the crowd filled his ears, grateful citizens rushing up to shake his hand, awed at his fearless courage, thanking him for single – handedly winning the war.

A frustrated wail wiped the smile of satisfaction from his lips and, with a growl of irritation, he turned to see Charles' kite not only back on the ground, but broken and torn as well.

The boy knelt beside it, tears coursing down his face. He looked at Jonathon helplessly.

"I bwoke my kite, Jonafon."

"I told you to tug on the string, didn't I?"

"I did tug on it. But the kite falled down anyway."

"That's cause you didn't do it right." Why he had to try and teach these ninnies anything was beyond his comprehension. Charles, for one, was too young to be out here doing a man's job. Kathleen, barely older, shouldn't be either. He should be home playing with his baby blocks and she should be home content with her dolls and tea set. But no, here they were, ruining his day. Again.

"I twied," Charles said, a tremor in his voice.

Jonathon bit back his next words, sure to send the boy sobbing home. Mother wouldn't tolerate that because she didn't allow snapping at the babies. Even when they deserved it. So he kept quiet for a moment, wondering what he could do to mollify him.

"Why don't you watch me until we go home? Then when Pop gets you another one, you won't break it, all right?"

"Awight."

~~~

As was his usual custom, Marcus arrived at the monthly businessmen's luncheon a little late. He supposed the table nearest the door was left empty to accommodate him because no one was ever there to bother him. To force him into conversation he rarely wanted any part of.

Mr. Spiros was speaking about the impact the war was having on the economy in Charlotte. Which amounted to none at all because even though they complied what with the meatless and wheat-less days, their consumers made up for them with other purchases.

Per usual, the meeting was as dull as dull could be. Marcus was at the point where he let his mind wander, to such interesting things as the need to dust the caskets in his store room, when Elliot Owens slid quietly into the seat across from him. Marcus swallowed hard.

"Good afternoon, Marcus" Elliot said softly, turning his attention to Mr. Spiros.

Maybe this wouldn't be so bad. As soon as the 'speech' was over, the waitresses would bring out plates of roast pork and vegetables, roast because
~~~

today was not a meatless day, and probably why they met on Saturday's. And the businessmen's luncheons were always scheduled so they didn't coincide with Meatless Mondays or Wheat-less Wednesdays. In fact, the board even made sure that Waldorf salad and peach pie were served at every meeting, too.

There might have been a few people in town who understood how peach pits and the shells from nuts could be used in the production of filters for gas masks, but Marcus wasn't one of them.

At the moment, though, all he wanted was for the meals to be delivered quickly so he could eat and leave – with no chit-chat between now and then. Because Marcus was well aware of the fact that he'd never mastered the art of conversation. Partly because he'd been his parent's only child, and they had tended to be quiet people, largely due to working in the funeral business he was sure. But mostly because he'd always suffered from painful shyness. And, he figured it was because he spent more time than the average person with dead bodies and grieving families.

All he had to do in those situations was express sympathy for the loss, make certain that the body was embalmed and dressed nicely, arrange for one of the local ministers to perform the funeral – if the family didn't belong to a church, and deliver the casket to the cemetery. Not a lot of opportunity for long discussions about anything other than the task at hand.

Then there was the fact that he led a quiet life. Some might even call it boring. Whatever the case, he wasn't a sparkling conversationalist.

"Well I must say this looks delicious," Elliot was saying, lifting a forkful of pork to his mouth. Deep in thought, Marcus hadn't even noticed the plates placed before them. After swallowing Elliot added, "Not as good as my wife makes, but close."

"It is good," Marcus mumbled, taking a bite so he didn't have to say anything else.

"I hope I didn't disrupt the meeting too much when I came in late. I have a customer who wears a size nine shoe but is convinced she needs a four." He grinned at Marcus, who really wasn't sure what to say in response. "I have to persuade her that there must have been a mistake in the sizing of this particular delivery of shoes and it can be a long, drawn out process."

"I imagine so."

"So what did I miss?"

"Miss?"

"What did Mr. Spiros have to say about business in Charlotte before I got here?"

"I- Um. Not a whole lot," Marcus stammered. "He - just said that the war really wasn't affecting profits much."

"I suppose that's true," Elliot agreed. "I haven't noticed a drop in shoe sales at all. If anything, I'm selling more than before it started. But I guess it wouldn't really affect your business, would it?"

"No." Not even a little because his business was pretty consistent year after year. He only hoped he'd never have an increase like Elliot just reported.

"I was really sorry to hear that Robert Bodell passed last week. Very sad for his wife and children."

"Yes it was."

"It's good her parents are in a position to take them in."

"Yes. Very good of them." He couldn't imagine having seven children under the age of twelve thrust on him and shuddered at the thought.

"Cold?" Elliot asked. "It can be rather drafty sitting this close to the door."

"I'm fine." As fine as one could be considering how fast he was shoveling food in his mouth. The only person he'd shared a meal with in years was Colby, and Colby wasn't very big on conversation. A very good quality in a minister and friend.

"So," Elliot said, beginning to sound a little uncomfortable. "How have you been, Marcus?"

"I- Fine. I've been fine." He gulped a quick sip of coffee and shoved his half empty plate away. "It's been nice talking with you, Elliot. I need to go."

"It was nice talking with you, too."

Marcus pushed away from the table and hurried out the door, leaving an amused Elliot shaking his head.

~~~

Though early May was usually very pleasant and comfortable the air today was simply too hot - and far too humid. At least compared to the bitter cold of winter not too many weeks ago. Daniel knew that in a month or so he'd be longing for a day such as this. The change had just been too dramatic for anyone but children to enjoy.
~~~

Doing nothing more than guiding the horse, pulling the buggy he had borrowed a short while ago, Daniel was sweating profusely. Beside him Nina sat wearing the dress she'd sewn herself, alternately wearing her straw hat and fanning herself with it. Her long hair was coiled around her head to keep it off her neck. It wouldn't be long before they, along with many of their fellow citizens, started longing for the cool, crisp days of autumn.

By then he might know what had been troubling Nina since supper the previous afternoon. In one instant she'd been laughing and telling him about a cranky patient at the hospital, and the next she'd paled and gone very quiet. At first he thought it might be the heat, but it hadn't been especially warm yesterday so it couldn't have been that.

Today hadn't been much better. She was only answering direct questions – with as few words as possible. Finally he worked up the courage to ask,

"Have I offended you in some way, Nina?"

"Offended me?" she looked at him in such surprise he knew whatever it was didn't have anything to do with him. "No. Of course not. Why would you think such a thing?"

"Well, I couldn't help but notice that something has been bothering you since yesterday. You haven't had much to say to me since," he said self – consciously. The last way he wanted to come across was as complaining or whining but, in truth, it hurt that she wasn't talking to him.

"Daniel, I'm sorry," Nina apologized, laying a gentle hand on his arm. "It's not you, I promise."

"Then what is it, Nina? What is upsetting you so

much?" He noted that she removed her hand and looked out across a field, avoiding his eyes.

"There was a woman at the restaurant yesterday. She worked at the orphanage where I was raised."

Obviously that brought back bad memories for her and he transferred the reins to one hand and reached over for hers with the other.

"We've never really talked about our childhoods, have we?" he asked needlessly. The truth was they'd talked about everything but that. "You can tell me anything, Nina."

"Not this."

"Why?" It didn't look like she was going to answer him. "Nina, I swear that there isn't anything you could tell me that would make me feel any differently about you. *Nothing.*"

This time when she looked at him, there were tears in her eyes. He guided the horse to the roadside then took her in his arms and held her close. He could feel her trembling.

"Nina, please. What is it?"

"I never wanted you to find out, Daniel."

"What?"

"I- That woman – Mrs. Campbell, was in charge of the orphanage. I mean, she wasn't *'in charge'* in charge. Mr. Dixon was the headmaster. She was just in charge of all the orphans. She set the schedules for schooling and chores, you know."

"She was a hard task master?" he prompted.

"There was that," she admitted reluctantly.

"What else?"

"She was particularly hard on some of us. When

I was fourteen she beat one of the other girls for dropping a tray of plates. They broke. It was an unfortunate *accident,* but she beat that girl so bad I had to try to stop her. I was afraid she'd kill her. She was only ten and the tray was too heavy for her."

"Someone should have beat Mrs. Campbell!" Daniel exclaimed, hurting for the little girl who had been put in a position that must have terrified her. "Did she hit you, too?"

"No. I thought she would," Nina whispered against his neck. "She didn't hit me. She grabbed my arm and dragged me to her office and threw me into a chair." Her words came out on a sob and Daniel held her closer, wishing he'd known this yesterday.

"She shouldn't have been allowed to work with children."

"Not children like us. She could be good with some of them. Especially the smaller ones."

"What do you mean, 'children like us?'"

"After I was sitting down she stood over me. Her voice got really quiet but I could tell she was furious with me. She told me that if I ever interfered with her when she was disciplining another child she would beat me to within an inch of my life.

"She also told me that I needed to count my blessings that I had a roof over my head and food in my belly because no one would ever want me."

"She what?" Daniel exploded, angrier than he ever remembered being in his life. "What would possess someone to tell a child a lie like that?"

"Because-" He felt her swallow hard. "Because my mother wasn't married when I was born."

Daniel grasped her shoulders and held her away from him.

"Look at me, Nina." When she didn't, he put a hand under her chin and raised her face to his. "Nina."

"She was right," Nina sobbed, averting her eyes. "You don't want me now that you know."

"I'll always want you!" He told her angrily. But he was angry at Mrs. Campbell, not Nina, and he had to work hard to gentle his voice. "She was *wrong*, Nina. You aren't responsible for the circumstances that led to your birth. She doesn't even know if your mother was responsible. She had no right to tell you a lie like that."

"You – don't hate me?" she asked incredulously.

"I love you, Nina. I don't care if your parents weren't married. I don't care what that woman said. I love you and I want to marry you."

Nina did look at him then, her eyes wide and hopeful, and filled with tears that he never wanted to see again.

"I'm sorry," he apologized, drawing her close. "I was going to bring you flowers, get down on one knee and propose the way you deserve. I didn't mean to just blurt it out like that."

"You want to marry me?" she murmured.

"I do. If you'll have me."

"*Of course* I'll have you," Nina exclaimed, crying harder now. "I love you!"

~~~

"I think he did it on purpose," Marcus said
~~~

quietly, sitting at the kitchen table, hunched over a cup of coffee. Apparently he was still distressed over what had happened at the businessmen's meeting a few hours before. He looked at Colby and scowled.

"Why would you think that Elliot would sit at your table on purpose?" Colby asked, struggling not to smile. "Do you think he did it just to bother you?"

"Maybe. I don't know. There were *other* seats available. But he had to sit with me. And he kept *smiling* at me."

This time Colby couldn't help himself and chuckled. At Marcus' look of dismay, he reached out and patted his arm.

"There's no crime in smiling," he pointed out with good humor. "In fact, I much prefer it when people smile at me as opposed to scowling."

"He talked to me, Colby. Elliot Owens never talks to me." Marcus was making it sound as though Elliot had, indeed, committed some sort of crime.

"Perhaps he just wants to get to know you better."

"Why?"

"A person can never have too many friends, Marcus," was all he could think to say, sipping his own cup of coffee. In truth he suspected that Elliot *wasn't* trying to make friends. Not exactly at any rate. Elliot tended toward a wicked sense of humor and had probably delighted in throwing Marcus off balance. Not that Elliot Owens had a mean bone in his body. Just a mischievous one. Likely several of them.

"I have enough friends," Marcus protested with

a frown.

"You have me and Derek. And Derek lives in Philadelphia. It wouldn't hurt for you to make a few more here in Charlotte."

"No." He shook his head. "No, I don't need anymore."

"Don't need any more what?" Anna demanded, waltzing into the kitchen. Colby was torn between disappointment and amusement. Disappointment because she'd spoiled a perfectly comfortable conversation with his friend, and amusement because Marcus not only disliked his wife, but was also quite afraid of her, too.

A fact that Anna, whose *every* bone was mean, was well aware of. Colby hated that she took unfair advantage of that fear. At the moment she was walking over to the window near Marcus, passing as close as she dared to him. Marcus shrank back into his chair.

"Nothing," he mumbled.

"You don't need any more *'nothing?'*" Anna asked scornfully, glancing over her shoulder at Colby. "Keeping secrets?"

"I do have an obligation to keep the confidences of my parishioners," he told her with a tight smile.

"So you *do* have secrets, Marcus," she laughed, leaning down into his face. Colby could have sworn that he saw every drop of blood leave the poor man's face.

"I- No- No secrets, Ma'am," Marcus stammered, leaning back so far this time Colby feared the chair would tumble right on to its back, taking him along with it.

"You know that lying is a sin?" she pointed out, what passed for a smile curving her lips.

"I- I'm not lying. We were just talking."

"I suppose you were talking about me."

"No, Ma'am! We were not!" Now the flush that stained his cheeks spoke of more guilt than innocence, even though he was telling the gospel truth.

"I don't think I believe you, Marcus McClelland."

"We weren't talking about you, Anna," Colby said, feeling compelled to come to Marcus' defense when he observed beads of sweat forming on his friend's upper lip. "I am not at liberty to divulge the topic of our conversation but, I assure you, it didn't concern you in the least."

"Fine. If you say so." Anna turned and walked across the room and, while Marcus sagged in relief, reached up into the cupboard. Being such a large woman, she had to hoist her ample stomach up and over the counter in order to retrieve a tin of cookies.

That done, she leaned back against the counter, opened the tin and began to eat an oatmeal cookie. All the while staring at Marcus, who squirmed under her relentless gaze.

"Would you care for a cookie, Marcus?" she offered sweetly.

"No. No thank you, Ma'am."

"Colby?"

"No. But thank you for asking."

"So. How is the funeral business going, Marcus?"

"Fine. It's – fine."

"*Fine?* I heard that Mrs. Simms passed away

Tuesday. That's fine?" Marcus' eyes grew to about the size of saucers and he shook his head violently.

"No. No it's *not*."

"So what, exactly, is *fine* about the funeral business?"

"There is *nothing* fine about it, Ma'am."

"But you said it was *fine*."

"That's not what I meant, Mrs. Thornton. Not what I meant at all," Marcus assured her adamantly.

"Then what *did* you mean, Marcus?"

"I don't really know," he sighed. Colby figured he would bolt from the house in about two seconds if he didn't do something quickly.

"Did you have a nice visit with Edna McAllister this morning, Dear?" he inquired, asking the first thing that popped into his head.

"It was *fine*," she answered, wandering back to stand beside Marcus again. He flinched as though she'd struck him. "Are you sure you won't have a cookie?"

"I'm sure," he assured her.

"So you're saying you're *fine* then?" He tucked his chin to his chest.

"Yes, Ma'am."

"Yes, Ma'am what?" Anna persisted.

"Yes, Ma'am, I'm – fine."

"That's a matter of opinion," his wife muttered, turning to walk out of the kitchen, taking the tin with her. "Would you like to stay for supper, Marcus?" she invited on her way to the parlor.

"No!" Marcus exclaimed, then swallowed hard before adding. "No thank you."

Colby shook his head, wishing that just once

Marcus would stand up to Anna. She liked to bully people if she could get away with it, but ignored anyone that had even a little bit of backbone. If Marcus had simply told her it was none of her business when she asked the first question, she'd have gone away. Gone away sputtering and complaining, but gone nonetheless.

"Would you like some more coffee?" he asked after a few silent minutes.

"I should be heading on home," Marcus said, sounding tired. Colby suspected that his encounter with Anna had exhausted him.

"Next time how about I visit you?"

"That would be fine with me. I mean I'd like that," Marcus said with obvious relief.

~~~

Bookwork had never been something Elliot enjoyed but, every Monday morning like clockwork he forced himself to fill out his ledger, using the sales receipts from the previous week. When he finally got to the stack from Saturday, he shook his head and chuckled. Marcus McClelland was, without a doubt, a curious man.

Even now he wasn't certain what made him decide to sit at that particular table, not when there were a good half dozen other vacant ones to choose from. Not to mention the partially filled tables where he might have enjoyed some good conversation.

Instead he felt compelled to sit with Marcus. Perhaps because he looked lonely. More likely,
~~~

though, because the man amused him.

In the nearly fifteen years since he and Margaret had moved to Charlotte, that young man had been painfully shy. Even as a young schoolboy, he couldn't recall seeing him around town with friends. And given the solitary life he seemed to lead, Elliot suspected he didn't have any. Then or now.

The bell over the door rang, interrupting his thoughts. When he looked up, his lips curved in a delighted smile and he walked quickly to meet his wife and youngest son.

"What brings you out this morning?" he asked, leaning down to kiss her quickly.

"I – need to talk to you," she murmured, not quite meeting his eyes. "Do you have a few moments?"

"Yes, of course. What is it, Meg?"

"Charles, why don't you go get the pail of blocks under the counter and play while I talk to your papa." Charles wasted no time in doing exactly that, and then Meg took his hand and said, "Can we step into the storeroom?"

Elliot felt his stomach knot up and wasn't sure he wanted to hear whatever it was she had to say. The faces of everyone back home, parents, brothers and sisters, nieces, nephews and cousins played in his mind like a picture show at the Nickelodeon, and he prayed that nothing had happened to any of them.

"We should have waited to have the family portrait taken until spring," were the first words Meg spoke when they were alone though. Having expected the worst news anyone could ever hope to hear, he was momentarily confused at what he was hearing.

"What?"

"We should have waited," she repeated, the beginnings of a smile on her face.

"And why is that?"

"Because it would be nice if the baby were old enough so he or she could actually look at the photographer when we have the next one taken."

"Baby?" Elliot mouthed, his breath catching in his throat? "We're having another *baby?*" Meg beamed at him as she nodded her head yes. Elliot let out a whoop and gathered her close, whirling her around the storeroom. When he stopped, he cupped her face and kissed her slowly before asking, "When?"

"Dr. Garland said he thinks it will be around Thanksgiving."

"A baby in time for Christmas? You couldn't give me a gift I'll cherish more."

Chapter 8

Colby cast his line out about mid – stream and sat contentedly on the bank of the Battle Creek River. Well, 'river' might have been a grander description than the narrow body of water deserved, but he was still fully prepared to spend the afternoon engaged in one of his favorite pastimes.

Even though Anna wouldn't allow so much as one fish in the house, he reveled in the thrill of the catch. And he never had a problem finding someone to take it, large or small, off his hands. If he managed to catch anything. The 'river' was running fast today due, he was sure, to the recent heavy rains.

Nevertheless it was a beautiful day and he intended to enjoy it. Life didn't get much better than this, sitting in the park with his fishing pole, listening to the laughter of children as they ran and played, a soft breeze caressing his face, and weather that was fully agreeable. Not too hot, and not a hint of chill in the early June air.

Sitting back against the trunk of a tree, he mulled over his lack of inspiration for tomorrow's sermon. Perhaps it was the fact that summer had descended upon them so abruptly, or maybe it was just an off week, as happened every now and again, but he was having little success in coming up with an appropriate subject. Or any subject at all, for that matter. So Colby Thornton decided he simply wasn't going to think about anything at all for a while.

He raised a knee and rested his pole against it. So far not so much as a nibble, but that really wasn't the point of fishing anyway. No, it was nothing more than the best way to relax, and he did just that, closing his eyes. Not to sleep, for he wasn't tired in the least. Just to listen. He sighed contentedly as he listened to the children, the birds chirping, the weeds along the creek bank rustling gently in the breeze.

The hooves of horses clopping by, a wagon wheel in dire need of some axle – grease squealing as it rolled along, and the occasional automobile speeding along Main Street. Not nearly as many on the road today as usual but then, in the name of patriotism, Charlotte's citizens were conscientious of conserving fuel for the war effort. In the distance the Methodist church bell chimed eleven times.

Another sigh escaped him. Yes, indeed, this was the life. A pleasant morning doing one of the things he loved above all else, in relative peace and solitude. Nothing to do but think, or not think, whichever he chose to do.

"Hey, Reverend Thornton!" So much for peace and quiet, Colby thought wryly, opening an eye as Jonathon Owens plopped down beside him on the bank. "Catch anything yet?"

"Not yet, but I'm hopeful," Colby said kindly, fixing his attention on the boy. Jonathon was one of his favorite people, always full of exciting tales and exploits, real or imagined. And this boy had more imagination than ten average young men.

"Me, too," Jonathon said, nodding at his pole and can of worms. "Told Mother I'd catch us a mess of fish for supper tonight."

"That's good of you. I'm sure she appreciates it."

"Well, she said she wasn't going to hold her breath, but I was welcome to try. I don't know why she'd want to hold her breath though. She'd faint dead away before I brought them home. Unless she meant after I bring them home. Cause some fish smell, you know." Colby smothered a chuckle with a cough.

"Well, let's see if I can help you out here. Mrs. Thornton can't abide fish at all so I was planning to give away anything I catch anyway. You're more than welcome to them."

"Say, that'd be swell, Reverend! I'd be happy to take them home. I don't know that I'd have been able to sit here long enough to catch enough to feed everyone. Thanks!"

"You're welcome, Jonathon," Colby said with a grin. If Jonathon Owens could sit still long enough to catch even one fish, he'd be surprised. "But shall we wait and see if I catch anything before you thank me?"

"Yeah. I guess that'd be a good idea." He swung his arm back unnecessarily far to cast his line, which, like its owner, landed with a soft plop quite near Colby's. They sat in companionable silence for a while. While he'd been sitting there alone, the silence had been welcome but was now too quiet to suit him.

"So tell me, Jonathon, what have you been up to lately?"

"Hmm. Well. I did beat Tommy Peters in trench warfare after school yesterday. Whipped him good! And let's see." Perhaps if Colby concentrated as hard as his young fishing companion appeared to be doing, he just might come up with his sermon. "Oh! Reverend Thornton, you're never gonna believe this!" His eyes shone with excitement.

"Then tell me quick," Colby encouraged, his smile stretching from ear to ear.

"It's Mr. Mertz. Pop says I still gotta get more evidence on him and all but this really should be enough."

"Enough?"

"Mmm-hmm." He was nodding his head vigorously. "It sure should. He got another package delivered today. A big one. A *real* big one! I think it's *a cannon*."

"A cannon!" Colby choked in surprise. "Just how big was this package, young man?"

"'bout this big." Jonathon rested his pole on his knee and placed his hands about three feet from the ground. "Really big. I'm not joshing, Reverend Thornton."

"I don't believe you are. But- A *cannon?* My

goodness. How many postal employees had to deliver it?"

"Oh, just Mr. Cavendish. But he's pretty strong, you know."

"I guess he is." Not able to resist, Colby reached out to squeeze the would – be hero's shoulder. "You know, with a young man such as yourself looking out for our safety, Charlotte is in good hands."

"Yeah," Jonathon grumbled, picking up his rod, a look of disgust on his face. "If Pop would let me write the president again about I all the things I seen Mr. Mertz do, why I bet they'd send General Pershing himself to arrest him!"

"But Elliot wants you to wait."

"Mmm-hmm. Hey! Revered Thornton, you got one!"

Sure enough, Colby caught his first fish of the day. If only the boy could catch his first spy so easily.

~~~

Daniel was about as nervous as he'd ever been as he walked slowly up the steps of the boarding house where Nina lived. It was ridiculous, given the outcome of yesterday's ride, but he couldn't seem to help it.

He smoothed the front of his suit jacket and removed the derby hat from his head, holding it with the same hand which held the huge bouquet of roses he'd just purchased as he rang the bell. The widow Thomas was quick to come to the screen door, the inside one already open in hopes of
~~~

attracting even the softest of breezes. Likely a vain hope because, as always seemed to be the case, the warmest of days arrived with the least amount of wind.

"Mr. Pullman," she greeted with a smile. "I suppose you're here to see our Miss Hakes?"

"Yes, Ma'am. If she's not otherwise occupied, I would please."

"I'm sure that even if she were, she'd want to see you. Would you like to wait in the parlor while I get her?"

"No thank you. I'll just wait for her out here."

"Make yourself comfortable and I'll send her right out," she told him, nodding toward the porch swing.

"I appreciate that, thanks." As she turned toward the stairway off the parlor, he paced the length of the porch instead. Fortunately it wasn't long before Nina was there, her smile of welcome easing some of his nervousness.

"Daniel. I wasn't expecting you until later."

"Do you want me to come back?" He hadn't considered that she might really be busy.

"No! Goodness, you know I'm always glad to see you," she assured him without hesitation. He watched as she glanced at the flowers. "Are those for me?" Daniel grinned, his nerves finally settling.

"They are. And you'll get them in just a moment," he teased, holding them out of the way when she made to reach for them. He took her hand and pulled her to the porch swing, where he commanded her to sit.

"Aren't you going to sit with me?" she wanted to

know when he remained standing, hoping she couldn't see how nervous he was.

"In a minute. But I have something to say and I want you to hush until I get it said." Her expression was puzzled until, with the aid of his cane, he lowered himself to one knee before her. Then she smiled, chin quivering, and her eyes filling with the tears he never wanted to see again. But he supposed if they were happy tears, that was all right.

"Yes!" she exclaimed before he could so much as open his mouth. Daniel threw his head back and laughed.

"I guess you misunderstood what I said. Hush means to – *hush*. I told you I wanted to do this right. Give me your hand." She held out her right hand and he shook his head, laying the flowers on the porch beside him, then fishing in his jacket pocket. "Your other one."

He took it tenderly in his, folded her fingers with his thumb and kissed them softly, smiling when her other hand went to her throat.

"Nina, I love you. I wish I could express how much but I don't think there are enough words in the world to tell you. From the day I first heard your voice I thought you were special. When I finally got my eyes to open-" she laughed quietly at that, "I knew you were. I knew that God had just allowed me to meet the most precious woman He'd ever created.

"I knew before I ever walked out of that hospital that you were the one I wanted to spend the rest of my life with." He smiled at her, her face swimming through his own tears. "Even though I jumped the gun yesterday, and even though you did today when you answered before I even got the question out, I'm asking you now if you'll be my wife."

"Yes," she whispered, reaching out to caress his face.

His hand trembled as he opened it to reveal a ring. The diamond wasn't large but it sparkled in the sunlight as he slipped it onto her finger.

Using his cane again, he rose to his feet and pulled Nina into his arms, kissing her tenderly.

"I love you, Daniel," she whispered, her arms wrapped tightly around his neck. From inside, Mrs. Thomas could be heard shouting to the other women in the house that he'd just proposed to Nina.

"I love you. And now, Miss Hakes," he said, kissing her temple, "if you have nothing else planned this afternoon, I would really like to show you my house. *Our* home."

~~~

Marcus was only vaguely aware that he was actually *humming* as he poured a cup of coffee and headed back to his office, and the desk where he could hardly wait to start penning a letter to Derek. Because, for the first time in his memory, the first time *ever* in fact, Marcus had something interesting to write about.

Sure he would make all the appropriate comments about the family, try to pretend he was tickled about the latest adventures of all those *kids*, and politely decline the most recent offer to join his
~~~

friend in the funeral home business in Philadelphia.

But *this* time, Marcus had some *real* news to share about himself. Nothing made up or embellished, but honest to goodness news. Derek might just faint dead away when he read it.

While he had resisted with all his might, and still wasn't entirely happy about it, allowing himself to be badgered into joining the baseball team wasn't a complete mistake. At least it made it appear as though he didn't lead the dullest life in town.

He carefully set the cup on the desktop, and then lowered himself into his chair, staring off into space with a hint of a smile on his face.

Even though being on the team meant he had to endure the other guys trying to engage him in the occasional conversation, it was worth it. Much to everyone's astonishment, Marcus was one of the best players in the league. A skilled third baseman, and one of the best batters in town.

Just Saturday afternoon his home run, with two men on base, had won the game. His smile grew into a self – satisfied grin and he snatched his pen out of the inkwell with enthusiasm.

~~~

It was another one of those sweltering summer days. The sort that made one wish for the swift arrival of autumn. Perhaps even for snow. Which would then, after a few weeks, make one wish for the warmth of a sweltering summer day. Elliot grinned when he realized where his thoughts had taken him. There wasn't a blessed thing he – or
~~~

anyone else – could do to change the weather so he might as well enjoy whatever there was to enjoy about it.

"I'm glad that's finished," Richard announced a little breathlessly, coming inside the store with a bucket of water and fistful of cloths.

Saturday's were reserved for cleaning and weather didn't allow for exceptions. Owens Shoe Store was immaculate, as was every other store in town. This morning, given the fact that it hadn't cooled down much during the night, Richard had decided to wash the outside of the huge windows first. A wise choice, learned from years of experience. This time of day, there was plenty of shade and it made the work easier than it would be if he'd waited until the sun was overhead.

"Thank you, son. I'll help move the chairs." A chore that had to be done so that the inside of the glass could be washed.

"I've got it, Pop. You keep dusting."

Dusting was done on a daily basis. Not because it was necessary on a daily basis but because there really wasn't much else to do while waiting for customers. Though business was always good, they rarely found themselves overrun. And so they dusted, rearranged displays, and washed windows. Not exactly exciting but Elliot always figured it was better than slaving away in a field or factory. Besides, selling shoes provided very nicely for his family.

"When you're finished with that, how do you feel about walking down to get us some lemonade from Mr. Spires?"

"I think that's the best idea you've had all morning," Richard said without hesitation, scrubbing a rag over the glass. "Never thought I'd say this but I'll sure be glad to see the last of summer this year."

"Because it's been so hot or because you're excited about the football team?" Elliot teased. He saw a flush creep up Richard's neck.

"Both," he admitted with an embarrassed laugh. "But I don't know if I'll try out or not. I don't think I'm good enough to make the team. I just like going to the games."

"And Mary Jane Whitcomb is homelier than a bent shovel."

"Pop!" The flush deepened at the mention of the young lady who had been the object of his son's affections for the past few weeks. Not that Mary Jane Whitcomb was aware of those affections. Elliot wouldn't have known had he not noticed the discreet glances Richard sent her way in church.

"You'll be the star of the football team and Mary Jane will fall in helplessly in love with you before you know it."

"Pop, stop it," Richard said weakly, putting more effort into the window washing. "Mary Jane is never going to notice someone like me."

"Someone like *you?*" Elliot questioned, dropping his dust rag and walking over to Richard. "And what, may I ask, do you mean by that?"

"Well, I think she kind of likes guys like Ted Porter."

"What does Ted Porter have that you don't?"

"A mustache." Elliot choked back a laugh.

"You're fifteen, son. Give it time. Anyway, Ted

Porter was never on the football team. As I recall, girls seem to like the boys who play sports."

"Do you really think so?" Richard asked, his expression hopeful.

"I know so. And I'll tell you something else-"

"Good afternoon, Elliot," Hank Andrews greeted, walking into the store. Richard looked away to hide his grimace and Elliot had to force a smile.

"Good afternoon, Hank. What can I do for you today?" God willing, it would be nothing.

"I'm in need of a new pair of boots."

"Well, then, have a seat and I'll show you what we have."

"Hey, Pop, I'm about finished here. I think I'll go in the back room and take the inventory," Richard said quickly, shoving chairs back into place as quickly as he could. Elliot leaned over and whispered in his ear,

"Coward. And Richard? The reason Ted Porter sports a moustache is because he *is* homelier than a bent shovel. You won't ever have to worry about having to hide your face." Richard's smile even made the prospect of fitting Hank better.

"Thanks, Pop."

"Hey. Open the backdoor while you're out there please."

"Yes, sir."

As Richard hightailed it to the storeroom, Elliot turned to face the customer his competition refused to serve. Because Hank Andrews had the foulest, sourest smelling feet in three counties. But he had never turned a customer away, much as he'd like to in this case. As Hank began removing his shoes,

Elliot steeled himself to not wrinkle his nose and hurried around collecting a few pairs of boots.

"Miserable weather we've been having," Hank boomed jovially, as the heavy, humid air began to reek.

"Sure is." He'd learned long ago to breathe shallowly, hold his breath as long as long as humanly possible, and keep his replies short and to the point. And to never, ever offer so much as a tidbit of conversation that might prolong the misery. At least until the sale was made and he could walk Hank outside and breathe freely again.

He quickly helped Hank into the first pair of boots which, of course, weren't quite right. He knew they wouldn't be. In the past, Hank would have to try on every pair in stock – before deciding the first choice was the right one after all. And so Elliot had taken to only bringing out three pair. Fortunately the man never asked if there were more. That meant only two would have to sit outside the backdoor to air for the rest of the day.

Finally, as he'd known he would, Hank chose and paid for the first and, for the first time in too many long minutes, Elliot walked him out and sucked in a deep, albeit discreet breath of sweet, fresh air. They never chatted long afterwards, Hank soon going on his way, but Elliot found, even in the dead of winter, that he needed a few moments before going back in.

"I don't suppose you've ever considered selling hats instead?" Richard, who was lighting match after match, asked when he came back inside. Elliot took a handful from him and joined in trying to, if not eliminate the odor, then to reduce it greatly.

"On days like today, selling horse manure would be an improvement," Elliot said good naturedly.

"Yeah, I'll just bet it would be. I already set the boots out back, Pop. I'll get started on the windows again in a-"

"*Oh my!*" came a gasp from the doorway. Mrs. Harrison's hand was at her throat, a pained look on her face as she asked, "Mr. Andrews?"

"Yes, Ma'am."

"Perhaps I should come back later."

"Might I suggest after lunch?" By that time the matches and open doors would have done much to dissipate the foul odor.

"I think I'll just do that," she murmured, turning quickly and beating a hasty retreat.

Elliot and Richard just stood there and laughed.

Chapter 9

Even though the sun was barely over the horizon the air felt heavy, promising more of the stifling heat that had made the day before seem unbearably long. It had been so bad, in fact, that several ladies fainted in the oppressive heat while tending to errands around town.

Instead of cooling down when the sun had finally set, there had been precious little relief. Without so much as a hint of a breeze, the night passed with excruciating slowness.

Elliot had listened to various members of his family pad down to the kitchen for glasses of water from the pitcher Meg never failed to fill and set in the ice box. He'd gone down several times himself for a refreshing drink, and refilled it twice during the long, miserable hours. As much as it had been in demand, he suspected he hadn't been the only one to replenish the supply.

By the time the bell at the Lawrence Avenue Church tolled six, he'd given up all pretense of trying to sleep. Rolling onto his side to rouse his wife, he discovered that Margaret had finally fallen into a restful slumber, so he decided not to disturb her. Stroking her cheek tenderly drew no more than a quiet grumble before soft snores resumed and he grinned, recalling the one time he'd mentioned the discovery to her. Horrified, she'd insisted that ladies simply did not snore, a declaration that amused him to no end. But he never did bring the subject up again.

He knew he really ought to get himself dressed and head down to start breakfast but the fact of the matter was, he enjoyed watching his wife. Usually she was up long before he was and busy doing some chore or another. Now she slept on her side, one hand beneath her pillow, the other tucked under her cheek. Her nightgown clung damply to her back and tiny beads of sweat peppered her face. She wouldn't sleep long because it was simply too hot to find relief for any length of time and, while he envied her the brief escape, he was glad that she was getting some rest. This pregnancy seemed to be sapping her energy more so than the others had.

Easing carefully from their bed, he slipped into his dressing gown and crept silently downstairs where he wasted no time in starting a pot of coffee. He would need all he could hold to get through this day.

Sundays and holidays meant a huge breakfast.

The sort that left one with a vague feeling of wanting to lie down for a nap – even though he or she hadn't been up long in the first place, and he decided there was no time like the present to get things started.

As was custom each Sunday morning, Elliot took the largest iron frying pan from the cupboard and set it atop the stove. Once he had it filled to the brim with thick slices of bacon, he lit the burner and turned the flame down low. The best bacon was that which was cooked very slowly, until it was *almost* crisp.

Once satisfied that the temperature was just right, he took a loaf of bread and sliced it. Usually Margaret made biscuits, but this morning he wanted her to sleep as long as possible. By the time he had a stack ready to be toasted, the coffee was done and he filled a cup on his way to the table.

He couldn't recall the last time he'd been the only one up so early in the day. He wasn't entirely sure he liked it either. Not much in life gave him as much pleasure as the noise and activity that could always be found in the Owens household.

He gazed out the door, overlooking the backyard, his thoughts on the day ahead. His favorite kind of day. One spent with his entire family. It promised to be enjoyable for everyone except Elizabeth, who chose not to enjoy any activity involving her family. Please, God, let this phase pass quickly, he prayed silently. He missed the sweet tempered girl she'd been before her involvement in the suffrage movement.

The smell of bacon began to fill the room and he knew it wouldn't be long before the aroma woke the rest of his family.

He took a sip of his coffee, the scalding liquid burning a trail down his throat, before getting up to turn the meat. Perhaps another thirty minutes or so before it would be ready. He took a dish of butter and a basket of eggs from the ice chest and set them on the counter. A bowl of potatoes, boiled the previous evening, was quickly sliced and sizzling in some of the bacon grease. They, too, would fry slowly to a crisp, golden brown.

"Good mo'ning', Papa."

Elliot turned to find Charles standing behind him, his little white nightshirt as rumpled as his sun bleached curls. He bent to lift him into his arms, kissing his cheek.

"Good morning, young man. How did you sleep last night?" There was nothing quite like the smell of a child and Elliot buried his face against his soft neck.

"Not vewy well, Papa. It was too hot!" the boy said vehemently.

"I know. It was very hot, wasn't it?"

"Did you have twouble sleeping, too, Papa?"

"That I did, son. That I did. Why do you suppose I'm up so early?"

"Because you is making bweakfast?"

"Yes I am. How about some water while I finish up here?" Charles nodded and he poured a tall glass from the nearly empty pitcher. Whoever had come down last should have refilled it he thought, as he did the job himself. It wouldn't have much time to chill before the others joined them.

"Papa? Today we can have the woaman

candles?"

"That's right."

"When?"

"When what?"

"When can we have the woamoan candles?"

"Oh. I'm sorry. Tonight. After dark."

"That's a long time," Charles complained, frowning his impatience.

"Not really. We have to get ready for our picnic at Bennett Park. That will take a while. And we can't do that until we've all eaten our breakfast." He turned the potatoes and bacon with long practiced skill. "After that we'll spend the day eating Mama's fried chicken and playing. You'll have so much fun you'll be surprised at how fast it gets dark," he promised.

"I like picnics. Jonafon told me that woaman candles are vewy pwetty."

"Jonathon was right. They're beautiful." If he didn't remember those from last year, he probably didn't recall the main display either. "So are fireworks. Next year the war should be over and if you think roman candles are pretty, just you wait."

"Jonafon told me they ow pwetty, too. He's mad because thewe won't be any today. B' he said all the money has to go fo' the owmy."

"It's true that it does. In fact, they need the money more than we need fireworks. But don't worry, Charles my boy. You'll have many years to enjoy them so this one time won't matter too much."

Their private time came to an end as, one by one, the rest of the family made their way to the kitchen. Margaret admonished him, insisting that

Elliot should have woken her but he simply gave her a kiss and told her to have a seat. He was in charge of the meal this morning.

Heat or no heat, this was going to be a wonderful day! Even taking into consideration the unbearable humidity, if things went as smoothly as they'd begun, it promised to be the best day ever. Even Elizabeth, though she didn't so much as smile, wasn't quite as dour as usual.

~~~

Most of the residents from in and around Charlotte – and a good many visitors from some distance away, if the size of the crowd was any indication – were gathered around the grandstand, erected the day before in preparation for today's events.

The mayor, members of the town council, a few of the more pompous businessmen, along with the preacher from the Methodist church (because he had the largest congregation, the mayor and his entourage being the most prominent members) waited patiently for the band to finish playing before starting the ceremony that would kick off the day's festivities.

The band consisted of five gentlemen who must also have taken their music lessons from Miss Abernathy, Elliot thought, grinning broadly. Like Jonathon, the horn, flute and tuba players managed to play just enough of the right notes so that one was able to tell what they were *trying* to play. Unlike Jonathon, however, the rest of the notes were not
~~~

consistently played wrong at all. No, they were all over the scale in random – oftentimes *painful* – order.

The two drummers merely banged their instruments enthusiastically, grinning broadly and obviously having a great deal of fun.

All – in – all it was an ear offending offering, if one had hoped to be entertained with musical ability. Fortunately everyone was present to simply have a nice day, visiting with friends and family, partaking of good food and fun games so no one minded the utter lack of talent from the band.

Which was a good thing since, before the evening concluded with Roman candles and sparklers, they would have played through every song they 'knew' several times. And their repertoire was quite extensive.

Elliot happened to glance down for a moment and caught the discreet tapping of a foot. A foot that happened to be peeking out from beneath the white and blue striped skirt belonging to his wife. He grinned down at her and his heart felt lighter when she smiled back.

Margaret appeared to most as a serious, sometimes grim woman with little sense of fun or lightheartedness, but he knew better. His Meg was tenderhearted and liked to laugh and enjoy herself as much as the next person.

~~~

"Are you sure we should?" Nina gasped, her eyes alight with excitement. Daniel chuckled and
~~~

almost dragged her to the starting line.

"If we don't hurry they'll run out of gunny sacks and we'll have to wait for the next race," he told her, unable to hide the enthusiasm in his voice. Nina had missed out on so much in her life that he wanted her to experience everything there was to experience.

"But your leg-"

"I'm already used to using the cane, and you know it hasn't stopped me from playing baseball. If you stand on my right, we'll be fine. I'll lean on you instead of it."

"If you're *sure*."

"I'm positive," he declared as they reached the line just in the nick of time.

It was in moments like this that he felt a sense of sadness because, though she hadn't talk much about her childhood since the day he'd proposed, he suspected that life in an orphanage had lacked much in the way of fun. He also suspected she hadn't had a whole lot of it since leaving that place either. Not that he knew anything for a fact. It was just a feeling he had based on her reaction to other things they'd done together. Like the first time he'd taken her fishing off the dam. Such simple pleasures, things he'd always taken for granted, seemed new and exciting to her.

Knowing that broke his heart. If orphanages denied the children who had nowhere else to go all of these things, what sort of life must it be? Even after his father had died, Daniel's mother still managed to find ways to make life special.

He would spend his life doing the same for Nina, he vowed.

She was giggling as they each worked a leg into the burlap bag someone handed them, her face flushed with excitement, and Daniel could hardly tear his eyes away from her.

She'd surprised him this morning, appearing at the door in a jaunty shirtwaist dress, its top a brilliant yellow, the skirt yellow and white stripes. When he complimented her, she told him she'd made it herself, then produced a straw hat, which she'd trimmed with the striped fabric and finished with off with a big white silk flower.

Stunning was the only word that came to mind then. As well as now.

"On your mark! Get set!" shouted the mayor. "*Go!*"

Though Nina's arm was wrapped tightly around his waist, with his around her shoulders, it still took several long moments to find their stride. A quick glance around him confirmed that most everyone else was having the same trouble. Not that it mattered because they, like he and Nina, were laughing themselves silly.

"Oh my goodness!" Nina squealed when another couple tumbled into them, nearly knocking them off their feet.

Daniel quickly maneuvered to his left and out of harm's way. Or so he thought. Another couple fell directly in front of them. There was no way to avoid them and they, too, tumbled to the ground. He had folded Nina in his arms and twisted so that he bore the brunt of the fall – and had the wind knocked clear out of him.

"Daniel! Are you all right?" Nina gasped,

pushing herself up off his chest. He couldn't catch his breath and she cupped his face, hers mere inches from his. "Are you hurt?" He tried to shake his head no but she was holding it so that he couldn't. "Daniel, please be all right!"

"Nina-" he finally managed to say. It sure felt good to breathe again. "I'm fine. It's okay. Don't- Oh no!"

Once again his arms went around her and he quickly rolled out of the way of another couple destined to join the casualties scattered all over the grass.

"Are you okay?" This time the question was from him.

"Yes. But maybe we should get out of here before we get crushed," she wisely suggested. He vaulted to his feet, pulling her up with him and they hurried to the sidelines to cheer the remaining few on. "That was such fun," she said a few moments later, after the last of the participants crossed the finish line.

"It was," he agreed, slinging an arm around her shoulders and steering her away from the crowd once first, second and third place winners were announced. "Maybe we can do something safer next time – like walking a tightrope."

"Thank you, but no," she giggled as he led her to their blanket.

"Why don't we eat instead?" he suggested, helping her down before seating himself. "My mouth has been watering since you told me you made fried chicken and potato salad for us. I'm starving."

"You're always starving," Nina teased, reaching

over to brush his hair away from his forehead, explaining, "There was a piece of grass -"

"Thank you for removing it for me, Miss Hakes. Now about that food," he said with a grin.

~~~

"Say, that was a great game on Saturday," Neil Andrews said, his aged voice as shaky as the hand that patted his shoulder in passing.

"Thanks, Mr. Andrews," Marcus said, trying to smile but knowing he failed miserably.

Mr. Andrews was the fifth to make his annual list so far today, which was a shame, too, because he was a really nice man. But there was no doubt that, before the year's end, the poor old gent would be gone from this earth.

He hated that he continued with the morbid game he and Derek had played in college. Except Marcus had shown an exceptional talent for predicting which faculty, students and alumni would die within a certain amount of time. He couldn't possibly guess who might die from injuries or accidents, of course. But for the ill and elderly, there was a certain...*something*...that he'd always been able to sense.

He'd asked his friend, a couple of years ago, if he ever thought about the game, and Derek admitted to still playing it. It just wasn't as easy to do in a city as large as Philadelphia. There were too many people, but in his neighborhood he figured he made twelve such predictions every July fourth and maybe two or three were ever right.
~~~

Unlike Marcus, who had a near ninety percent record for accuracy. Consistently, year after year after year.

He continued to stroll around the noisy fairground, figuring he could head for home in another hour or so. There weren't even going to be fireworks this year so there really was no point in staying much longer.

Looking at the crowd around him, engaged in games, splashing in the river and eating mountains of fried chicken, he realized how alone in the world he truly was. The only problem was, so did Colby. And if he didn't head out soon, he'd find himself roped into sharing a blanket and food with Anna Thornton. Just the thought of having to endure as little as thirty minutes in that woman's company made him shudder.

Maybe he didn't need to stay another hour after all.

~~~

Jonathon loved Fourth of July celebrations. He loved the food, the music, the crowds, the games. This year he particularly loved the fact that soldiers were there. Soldiers who would be leaving soon for France. Soldiers who had recently returned. Those were the ones he was particularly interested in. If a boy ever had heroes, it would be these brave, fighting men.

His attention was torn between getting close enough to be within hearing distance of them, and keeping an eye out on Mr. Mertz who was, at the
~~~

moment, chatting amicably with the preacher from the Methodist church. Given the fact that they were in a very public place, with hundreds of witnesses, Jonathon wasn't especially concerned. Surely Mr. Mertz wouldn't do anything suspicious here. Not with all the soldiers in attendance.

His desire to be near his heroes won out and he slipped through the crowd to where he saw Arnold Bodell holding court amid a small crowd of men. They appeared to be hanging on his every word. When he got close he spotted a safe place where he could listen and not draw attention to himself. Some grownups didn't like children hanging around and listening in, and he didn't want to risk being told to go play.

Seeing that no one was watching, he hunkered down behind a bush and sat back to hear the most amazing stories a boy could hear.

"...couldn't get rid of 'em. No matter how hard we tried," Arnold was telling everyone.

"You don't say," someone responded, sounding shocked. "I hadn't heard that lice were a problem from anyone else. But then I don't have any family in the war so I don't get letters."

"I think a lot of the guys try to pretty it up so their families don't worry," Arnold explained kindly. "But lice, bad as it was, wasn't the worst of it. Some of us had trench foot because it was so wet and cold. My feet swelled up so bad I couldn't even tie my boots. And the itching was just awful. But I can't complain too much because a lot of the fellows got gangrene from it."

Gangrene? Jonathon's eyes got wide and his

stomach felt a little funny. People had parts of their bodies cut off because of gangrene. Some people even died from it. *And soldiers got it from fighting the war from the trenches?*

"I had no idea," another voice gasped, clearly shocked. Jonathon knew how he felt.

"Yeah, I'm glad I was able to serve my country but it wasn't glamorous like the songs make it out to be. We were overrun with frogs and slugs and beetles. Oh and the smell? I think we all got kind of used to it after a while but when the new people came, well they would get so sick you just had to feel bad for them."

"What was it from?"

"The latrines. The dead soldiers. Couldn't bury them deep, you know. We had to do everything at night 'cause those snipers were good. Couldn't make a lot of noise so we dug 'em quick and shallow. That way we didn't draw a lot of attention. Heck, you couldn't even look out of a trench during the day without gettin' your head blown off. You wouldn't believe how many new soldiers died the same day we got 'em because they had to have a look at what was out there."

"Well, I'll be," Mr. Spiros murmured. Jonathon knew it was him because he'd been in the shop so many times for candy and ice cream he'd recognize his voice anywhere. Not that any treats sounded very good right now. He was starting to feel very sick.

"It was definitely the worst experience of my life," Arnold said softly, sadly. "I'll never forget what I saw. I still have nightmares. Made a real good friend over there. His name was Thomas Larson. Real nice guy. Married, had three boys. He was on the burial detail one night and a sniper got him. I wrote his wife. Hardest letter I ever had to write. Hope no one tells her the stuff I've been telling you, though. Nobody really wants to know that you could go a couple of months without a bath, or that the trenches were infested with rats."

"Rats!"

"Yeah. You're not gonna believe this but some of them were as big as cats."

"Now you're pulling my leg."

"No, sir, I'm not. It was all the bodies, you see. They had an endless supply of food. Makes me want to throw up remembering it. We tried to scare them off at first but there were too many. Didn't matter what we did, we couldn't get rid of 'em."

Jonathon had heard enough. More than enough, and he quietly got up and walked away. How could he have been so wrong about what war was? How could he have thought that trench warfare was a fun game to play?

Well, one thing was sure. He wouldn't be playing it anymore. He didn't think he could and not remember the things Arnold had been talking about. Jonathon shivered just thinking about rats as big as cats. He didn't even really like mice, though he'd never admit such a thing to another living soul. Men weren't supposed to be afraid of anything. Especially not stupid little mice.

~~~
~~~

"Hey, Reverend Thornton!" little Billy McGuire called out, waving on his way to only the Lord knew where.

"Good afternoon, Billy."

Colby couldn't help but smile at the joyful chaos around him. He'd watched an enthusiastic Nina Hakes enter the sack race with her beau, Daniel Pullman and worried, for a moment, that they would be crushed as one couple after another fell in a heap after one young man tripped and tumbled to the ground with his wife. They did, however, emerge laughing and Colby was relieved. He thought it was long past time someone noticed what a sweet girl Nina was. Obviously Daniel had because it was as plain as the nose on his face that he adored her. The engagement ring she wore so proudly bore testament to that.

In the open area of the park, boys and young men played a hearty game of baseball. Little girls jumped rope, older girls played hopscotch and young women batted eyelashes at potential beaux. Near the bandstand, where a small brass band played George M. Cohen tunes with more enthusiasm than ability, members of the Suffrage movement milled around with banners and sashes, telling anyone who would listen of the importance of women's rights. Elizabeth Owens was one of their most fervent supporters, much to the dismay of her mother.

As he settled back against the trunk of a big, old oak tree, on blanket spread over the grass, he thought that life couldn't get a whole lot better than this. He loved being out among people on happy occasions like this. Actually, he just liked being around people period. Especially on days like today. Not even the war could cast a pall over the festivities which, in his opinion, was good. People needed a chance, every now and then, to relax and forget about the cares of the world.

He, for one, intended to do exactly that. With Anna off gossiping with her cronies –always seeking out new subjects to blather about – he could do it in peace. When suppertime came, she would return to eat with him and then be off again because, of course, she knew better than to try and interest him in her tales.

From the corner of his eye he saw that Jonathon Owens was walking his way, shoulders slumped and clearly not happy. An unusual occurrence, as Colby had never seen the boy when he wasn't nearly bubbling over enthusiastically about one thing or another.

"Why the sad face?" Colby asked when Jonathon reached him.

"I'll tell you," he said, sighing mightily as he flopped down beside Colby. And he did, relating what he'd learned about the war just moments ago. Despondently he finished his story by saying that he was never going to play Trench Warfare again. "It sounded so awful, Reverend Thornton. Nobody ever told me it was like that over there."

"I imagine it's like Arnold said. I also think that a lot of people do suspect what's going on, but it's easier to pretend it isn't. It's hard to support any cause when you have to face the less than pleasant aspects of it."

"I guess. I just wish it wasn't like that."

"So do I, Jonathon. So do I." Colby squeezed his shoulder in commiseration.

Chapter 10

Daniel rubbed his leg absently, waiting for the next batter to step up to the plate. He was glad that he'd been a pitcher before the accident because he knew there was no way he'd have been able to play a fielder's position now. Just running the bases three times had caused an uncomfortable ache in his leg. It was good that this was the final inning and he wouldn't get up to bat again. Unless a miracle occurred and the opposing team was finally able to catch up. Mostly due to Mr. McClelland's surprising skill, they were ahead by three runs.

He walked the first player, but struck the second one out. The third batter hit a fly that Carl Bodell caught. Just one more out and the game would be over.

But it wasn't meant to be. Not only did Wilson's

Wildcats score the three runs needed to catch up, they brought in another for good measure, leaving Bodell's Bulldogs behind by one.

The game would continue. At least until they scored two more points. Mr. McClelland was third in line to bat. If just *one* of the men before him could get on base, there was a good chance the funeral director would hit a home run. He nearly always did, and this would be a good time to continue that trend.

If only he hadn't tripped on the steps when he'd stopped to pick Nina up, for she always insisted on attending the games. But he had, and now suffered the consequences.

~~~

Jonathon was hurrying down the street, intent on meeting a couple of his friends for a lively game of - Well he wasn't sure what they were going to play today now that he'd been put off by Trench Warfare. Knowing what life in the trenches was really like had taken all the fun out of the game. It made him feel things he didn't like feeling, which kind of made him mad, and when he spotted Kathleen standing in front of them, hands on her hips, he was even madder. Now what, he wondered irritably. Couldn't he ever be free of the babies?

Girls in fancy white dresses had no business playing games with boys. Sure as shooting if she got her clothes dirty, Mother would blame him. He quickened his pace until he reached them.

"Kathleen, go home now," he snapped, brushing
~~~

past her to stand by the other boys.

"They took Maggie!" she wailed, her eyes full of tears. Jonathon growled in frustration and looked to see that red headed, freckle – faced Steven Powers was the one who had the doll. Beside him stood Tommy Underwood, blond hair bleached almost white after spending most of the summer out in the sun. He was grinning wickedly.

"Give it back to her so we can go play."

"Give her back this *ugly* doll?" Steven taunted, holding it almost within Kathleen's reach and then dancing away with it.

"C'mon, Steven, give it back. We don't have all day you know."

"You mean this *stupid* doll?" Tommy asked, grabbing Maggie from Steven. The tallest one of their small group, he held the doll above his head. "Na. I don't think so."

"What? You wanna play with a *doll* instead?" Jonathon asked sarcastically.

"No. We just don't want an *ugly, stupid little girl* to play with her *ugly, stupid little dolly*."

"I'm not stupid!" Kathleen cried, stamping her foot. "And I want my baby back right this minute! You're scaring her!"

"Scaring her?" Tommy gasped, eyes wide. "If you think this is scaring her, I wonder how she'll feel about this?" He waltzed over to a nearby tree and hit the dolls head on the trunk.

"No!" Kathleen screamed, running at Tommy, who stepped aside just before she reached him. Kathleen stumbled and fell on the ground, crying out as her knees scraped along the hard packed dirt.

"Now look what you've done!" Jonathon yelled, rushing to her side to help her up. Kathleen was holding the hem of her dress up to reveal her white hose stained and torn – and there was very definitely blood. He shot a furious glance at his friends.

"Look!" Steven cackled. "She's crying like a baby! Poor ugly baby!"

"Leave her alone," Jonathon shouted angrily, wrapping an arm around his sister's shoulders. "And give her the doll back. *Now!*"

"Who's gonna *make* us?" Steven sneered, catching the doll as Tommy threw it. He, too, hit the dolls head against the tree nearest him, causing Kathleen to howl.

"If you don't give it back to my sister *now*, *I'm* gonna make you!"

"Oh, we're so scared!" Steven hit the doll so hard this time that the head rolled right off the body, landing within inches of Kathleen's foot. She snatched it up and began sobbing in earnest.

Jonathon took off at a run and tackled Steven. They both landed hard on the ground, which didn't bother him at all, considering that Steven broke his fall. They wrestled viciously over the now decapitated doll, landing hits anywhere they could.

Jonathon felt a fist against his nose, the pain so sharp it brought tears to his eyes. He punched Steven in the eye. Steven punched Jonathon in the eye and Jonathon bit his ear.

They were pretty evenly matched until Tommy got in on the act, throwing himself to his knees and pounding Jonathon on the back. All the while

Kathleen stood there sobbing and screaming at them to stop hurting her brother. But it wasn't until the commotion drew the attention of a neighbor that the fight finally ended, Tommy and Steven running off like the cowards they'd proven themselves to be.

"Are you okay, Jonathon?" Kathleen wept, kneeling gingerly down beside him. "Your nose is bleeding!"

"Are you all right, Jonathon?" Mrs. Connors asked anxiously, also kneeling beside him. She pulled a handkerchief from her apron pocked and pressed it carefully against his nose. "Can you hold that there?"

"Yes, Ma'am. Thank you," he mumbled with as much courtesy as he could manage. Someone had split his lip and he could feel it swelling.

"Here. Let me help you up."

Jonathon figured there wasn't much on his body that didn't hurt and he groaned mightily as he got to his feet.

"What happened?" Mrs. Connors asked gently, looking closely at what would probably turn into a black eye. He could feel that swelling, too.

"They stole my baby," Kathleen cried piteously, "and Jonathon tried to get it back for me. They broke her!"

Mrs. Connors, he noted, looked outraged as she checked his arms and lifted the back of his shirt, gasping.

"You're going to have some pretty bold bruises there, young man. Do you need me to help get you home?"

"No thank you," he declined politely, or as

politely as he was able given that he was now speaking around a lip the size of a football. Holding the handkerchief snugly on his nose didn't help a whole lot either.

"Are you sure?"

"Yes, Ma'am."

"All right then. You go on then so your mother can tend to you. I'm calling those boys' mothers *this minute*."

Jonathon was glad. They deserved spankings, not only for teasing Kathleen, but for ganging up on him like that. Some friends they turned out to be. It was days like today that he really missed his best friend, Luke. And he hoped his father would come home from the war really soon so his family could move back to Charlotte.

"I'm sorry for getting you in trouble, Jonathon," Kathleen whispered, still crying. "I didn't want those nasty boys to hurt you."

"You didn't do anything wrong, Kathleen," he told her fiercely. "They're just stupid."

"But now they're mad at you."

"I don't care. They're not my friends anymore." It was one thing to tease one of the babies, but Steven and Tommy had gone too far this time. They had been downright mean. Breaking her doll hadn't been funny either. Sure he thought that playing with dolls was a dumb pastime, but he wasn't a girl. And Kathleen loved her dolls like they were real people.

"I'm glad. They're mean!"

"Yes they are. Do your knees hurt bad, Kathleen?"

"A little. Mama's probably gonna be mad about

my hose."

"I'll tell her what happened. If she is mad, she'll be mad at them, not you."

And hopefully not at him either. Mama didn't take too kindly to fighting. Although, from the look on her face as she hurried around the corner toward them, he didn't think she was going to be mad at either one of them. Apparently Mrs. Connors had called her before the other boys' mothers.

"Oh dear Lord in heaven!" she gasped, coming to a breathless stop beside them. "Oh, Jonathon!"

Margaret hurried them toward home, trying to comfort Kathleen as best she could, but most of her attention was given to Jonathon's battered face.

~~~

Alerted by a telephone call from Edna Connors, Elliot hung the "Closed" sign in the window, locked the door and literally ran all the way home. Meg and the children were within two houses of theirs and he hurried to meet them, feeling a little nauseated when he saw Jonathon's bruised and bloodied face.

"Steven and Tommy did this to you?" he demanded, squatting down in front of him to examine him more closely.

"Yes, sir."

"Because you were trying to get Maggie back for Kathleen?"

"Well, not exactly."

"What exactly then?" he asked, looking at his left eye, swollen nearly shut and turning a brilliant shade of purple.
~~~

"Elliot, can we get him back to the house please?" Margaret nearly begged. "We need to get something on that eye. And I need to check to see if his nose has stopped bleeding yet."

"I- Yes, of course." He hoisted Kathleen onto his hip and helped hurry them along.

"Papa, they didn't start fighting until Steven broke Maggie's head off and Jonathon got mad. They were so mean!" she said, beginning to cry again.

"It's okay, Sweetheart," he soothed, holding the door open for his wife and son.

"First it was just Jonathon and Steven fighting. And then Tommy started hitting his back. Real hard, Papa. I couldn't make them stop hurting Jonathon. Only Mrs. Connors could when she came out."

Elliot felt like hitting someone. Or, specifically, two cruel young boys who needed a good thrashing!

He sat Kathleen in a kitchen chair then, at Meg's request, ran upstairs to make sure that Charles was still napping. In a panic, she hadn't thought to let Elizabeth, who was holed up in her room reading, know.

Seeing everything was as it should be, he hurried back down with a fistful of washcloths. Meg relieved him of them and told him to tend to Kathleen's knees while she saw to Jonathon, who was now sitting at the table, shirtless, his back a colorful assortment of bruises.

Elliot couldn't believe his ears when he heard his wife say,

"I hope you got in a few good licks of your own."

"I think I broke Steven's nose."

"Good boy."

~~~

"Daniel, *please?"* Nina implored him. "You might have fractured one of the breaks again. You need to let Dr. Garland look at it."

"I'm fine, Nina. It doesn't feel broken, it just aches."

"That's why you're so pale?"

"It's really hot today," he pointed out, wishing she'd let the subject of his leg go.

Maybe if she would distract him with news of the sanatorium, or something that happened at the boarding house, he could get his mind off just how much his leg really *did* hurt. So much so that he was afraid she might be right. But he couldn't bear the thought of wearing a splint for another six weeks. Not with the days as hot as they had been, and promising to get nothing but worse as August drew to a close. Septembers were often just as bad, if not worse.

"I'll worry all night if we don't go and see him."

"Nina-"

"Looks like you could use a lift," Colby Thornton called out, pulling his buggy to a stop just ahead of them.

"Thank you for the offer, Reverend, but we're fine."

"*I* would love a ride home, Reverend Thornton," Nina said defiantly. "It's so *hot* today, after all."

"Nina!" Daniel muttered. "Stop it."

"No. If you won't go see the doctor, then we at
~~~

least need to get you off your feet. If you would just stop being so stubborn about it."

"Talk about the pot calling the kettle black! You need to stop *nagging* about this."

"Daniel?" she asked, clearly hurt at the harshness in his tone. She stepped away from him.

"Nina. I'm sorry!" He reached out to pull her back to her side, but she continued to back away.

"No. No, you should let Reverend Thornton take you home," she whispered, then turned away and hurried down the road. But not before he saw the tears that filled her eyes.

~~~

"Mr. Owens!" One of the young clerks from the post office rushed into the store shortly after Elliot had returned from dealing with the fight. He was red in the face and breathless, waving an envelope in Elliot's face.

"Good afternoon, Milton. What's that you've got there?"

"It's from the White House, Mr. Owens! The postmaster thought you would want it right away!"

Stunned, he took the envelope and stared at it in awe. Sure enough, it was from the White House – and addressed to Master Jonathon Owens.

"Imagine that," Milton said enthusiastically, adding almost reverently, "Someone from Charlotte has mail from the *White House*"

"Imagine that," Elliot breathed, sitting hard in one of the red leather chairs usually reserved for his customers.
~~~

It hadn't been all that long since he'd mailed the letter to the president for Jonathon and here was, he assumed, a reply. Not that he ever figured his son would receive a one but he had, and very promptly, too.

"Mr. Nelson was so excited he was almost beside himself. In fact, if it weren't so hot out I think he'd have brought it to you himself."

"Well give him my thanks," Elliot said, getting to his feet and shaking the young man's hand. "And thank you for bringing it, Milton. I think I'm going to take it home to Jonathon right now."

With that decision, Elliot Owens locked the door to his store, earlier than he should have for the second time that day.

Despite the fact that he wore a suit, and that the day was another scorcher in a long string of exceptionally hot and humid summer days, he all but ran the three blocks home – again. He failed to notice the people he passed pointing and whispering because Milton and Mr. Nelson had told anyone who would listen that the Owens' household had received a letter from the White House.

"Jonathon!" he shouted, rushing into the house. "Jonathon!"

"Mother went for a walk. Jonathon went with her to make sure she was all right," Richard informed him as soon as he had come in the front door. Elliot watched his eldest son reading to his youngest and wondered what had happened this time. Meg often went for walks but it was usually in the evenings after supper, always with him, and often with one or more of their children tagging along. Given the fact that Richard wouldn't meet his eyes, Elliot had a pretty good idea why his wife had gone. "Did she and Elizabeth have another argument?"

"Yes, Sir," Richard admitted reluctantly.

"Did your sister take a walk, too?"

"No. She's in her room."

"Thanks," Elliot said, deciding that enough was enough. Tucking the letter in his jacket pocket, he turned on his heel and took the stairs, two at a time, rapping on her door in seconds.

"Go away!" came the terse order. Elliot turned the knob and strode into the room where he found Elizabeth at the window.

"We need to talk," he said firmly, walking to stand beside her.

"I'd rather not," she told him, still looking at the backyard.

"That's fine then. All you need to do is listen – *without* interruption."

"More orders, I suppose?"

"I believe I said *without* interruption, young lady." It wasn't often that Elliot lost his temper with one of the children but Elizabeth had brought this upon herself, what with her attitude and ugly disposition.

"Yes, sir." This was said through clenched teeth and Elliot felt his fingers clench into fists.

"I have tried to understand your position as far as the Woman's Suffrage Movement, Elizabeth, but if this is what it's turning you into, then I have to forbid any future involvement." Her eyes flew to his, but a raised brow forestalled comment. He continued, "If this is what the movement encourages

– insolence, rebellion, anger – then it's a movement I cannot support. And neither will any member of my family."

"That's not fair!" Elizabeth wailed, folding her arms across her stomach, her eyes filling with tears.

"And it's fair to treat your family this way? You are sixteen years old. You are not a woman, but a girl. As such, you are subject to the rules of this house. And one rule that you *will* obey is respecting your parents. Your mother in particular."

"She won't even try to understand, Papa."

"Understand *what*, Elizabeth? *I* don't understand. One day you are a sweet tempered young lady and the next you are impossible to get along with. You seem to go out of your way to make everyone around you as miserable as you appear to be." He took hold of her shoulders and shook her gently. "*Why*, Elizabeth?"

"Because none of you understand how important this is!" she cried out, jerking away from him and flopping down on her bed.

"Important enough to alienate your family?"

"It wasn't supposed to be this way."

"You made it this way," he said in exasperation, running a hand through his hair in frustration. "I know many women involved with the movement and they haven't turned into – into-" He couldn't think of a word he'd care to use in the presence of his daughter. Especially not in *reference* to his daughter. None had passed through his lips in all of his thirty – seven years, and he didn't intend to allow them to now. Or ever.

"Papa, you just don't understand." He sank

down beside her on the mattress and sighed.

"Then help me to understand, Elizabeth." He watched as tears began to slide down her cheeks.

"It's Mrs. Mitchell."

"Mrs. Mitchell?" He asked, and finally understanding dawned.

Mrs. Harold Mitchell, Elizabeth's favorite teacher. The teacher who, the previous autumn, found herself divorced after her husband had run off with his young clerk, selling the house and taking the couple's young children with him. Mrs. Mitchell, devastated at the loss of her family, had committed suicide, placing a pistol to her temple and pulling the trigger.

"She had no rights, Papa," Elizabeth wept into her hands. "The judge wouldn't give the children to her, he took away her home and – well, just everything. Because Mr. Mitchell was a man, he was given the right to take *everything* from her."

"Mr. Mitchell is *not* a man," Elliot muttered, wrapping an arm around her shoulders.

"I know I've been difficult to live with-" Elliot rolled his eyes and had to bite down hard on his lip to stop himself from heartily agreeing with that declaration. "Not all women are as fortunate as Mother. Even if you were to divorce her, you're still an honorable man. You wouldn't hurt her like Mr. Mitchell hurt Mrs. Mitchell. You wouldn't leave her with nothing. I don't even think you'd take us away from her."

Just the thought of being apart from his Meg made Elliot shudder, even as he found himself agreeing with his daughters logic. She was right.

Most husbands were decent, upstanding men who treated their wives well. It was the Harold Mitchell's of the world that had made the movement necessary.

"Please don't make me stop, Papa. You have no idea how important it is."

"You're wrong, Elizabeth. I understand completely. And you've just won my support, though I have always planned to vote for its passage. But I still can't condone the way you've been treating your mother and the rest of us. It has to stop. Immediately."

"Yes, sir. Does that mean I can continue attending the meetings?"

"I don't know. Your mother is very concerned about your relationship with Edgar Perkins. He's eight years older than you and she's afraid that he may try to take advantage of you."

"*Edgar?*" Elizabeth gave a strangled laugh and Elliot knew that his suspicions were correct, that she was infatuated with the man. He was just as sure that the man wasn't interested in her – as anything but one of the masses. "Edgar doesn't even notice me. Believe me, Papa, she has nothing to worry about."

"I do believe you. But we have one more issue to discuss before I can make my decision, Elizabeth. That would be your attitude concerning God."

"God- I thought faith was a choice that even *He* allowed us." Her sarcasm returned, full force.

"That is true. But why is God so repugnant to you now? You used to like to go to church, and to sit at the table with us when we read the bible. What's changed your mind about Him?"

"He's the one who made women with no value. He's the one who allowed men to have all the rights and women to have none." Elliot chuckled softly at her ignorance. Yet she wasn't alone in that. Many men believed that lie, too.

"God did neither one of those things, Elizabeth. He created woman as a *helpmate* for man. He commanded men to love their wives as Christ loved the church. To love them as they love themselves. Does that sound like He intended women to have no value or rights?"

"N-no. I guess not," she admitted, looking at him in surprise.

"You're not sure? It's right there in your bible." He reached past her for the bible lying on the small table at her bedside, thumbing through it until he found one of the passages he sought. "Here it is. 'Husbands, love your wives and be not bitter against them.' And here's another one. 'Likewise, ye husbands, dwell with them according to knowledge, giving honor unto the wife, as unto the weaker vessel, and as being heirs together of the grace of life, that your prayers be not hindered.' So you see, Elizabeth, God tells men their prayers may not be answered if they don't treat their wives well."

"I didn't realize, Papa."

"I know. That's why I thought you should hear what *He* had to say on the subject." He closed the bible and laid it back on her table. "Men are to love, respect and cherish their wives. And, like Christ, be willing to lay down his life for her." As he'd give his life for his own wife if the need ever arose.

"Thank you, Papa."

"You're welcome." He hugged her tightly. "And now that we've cleared that up, perhaps we could come to an agreement that will satisfy everyone?"

"What do you mean?" she asked, resting her head against his shoulder.

"What I mean is this," he said, trying to force some sternness into his voice, and failing miserably. "If you wish to continue attending the suffrage meetings there will have to be some changes around here. First, I insist you start treating your mother better. God is also very clear on that subject. Children are to honor and respect their parents."

"Yes, sir. I'll try." Elliot raised her chin so that she had to look at him and raised his brow again. "I *will*. I promise."

"That's better. The second thing is this. You will attend church with us and participate in bible readings without complaint."

"All right." He kissed her temple.

"Good girl. I'll talk with your mother as soon as she returns. As long as you continue to honor those two conditions, we have a deal."

"Thank you, Papa!" she said, with more enthusiasm than he'd heard her express in months.

"You're welcome, young lady. Now we're going to go and wait on the porch for your mother and Jonathon. I have something very important for your brother."

~~~
~~~

Colby glanced at Nina's retreating form and then back at her very pale, distraught fiancé. As hurt and shocked as Nina had been, he suspected that this was the first argument they'd ever had. From what little he'd heard, Daniel was hurt and, in the way many men tended to react, didn't want to have whatever it was checked out.

Climbing down from the buggy he thought, perhaps, he might convince him to change his mind.

"Daniel?" The young man started when Colby laid a hand on his shoulder. "Let's get you off your feet."

"But Nina-"

"Son, it's been my experience that there are occasions when a woman needs some time alone. This looks to be one of those times."

"But I need to apologize to her," he protested as Colby pulled him to the buggy. It was clear that there was something wrong with his leg, and that he was in a great deal of pain, and Colby decided he wasn't giving him a chance to change his mind. They were heading directly to Doctor Garland's office.

"Come on, let's go."

After a few minutes of silence, Daniel finally turned to Colby and asked,

"Do you think she will forgive me?"

"What happened?"

Slowly, with a great deal of reluctance, Daniel told him about falling on the steps at the boarding house, and how much trouble he'd been having with his leg since then.

"So Nina wanted you to have the doctor take a

look?"

"Yes. I just don't want to wear a splint again. It was bad enough when it was cold out. It's going to be worse with this heat," he muttered, sounding much like a petulant child.

"I can see where that would be uncomfortable," Colby commiserated, "but I'm not sure that, if it were me, I'd want to take a chance. If the bone *is* broken again, not having it tended to could cause it to heal badly, and then you could be in pain for the rest of your life."

In the end Colby didn't have to force the issue. Daniel just sighed and asked if he could take him to Doc Garland's house.

"I think that would be for the best. And look at it this way. You're making the board happy."

"*What?*"

"Well," Colby said with a chuckle, "I know for a fact that some of the members on the hospital board weren't too happy about getting a Crookes Tube. They didn't think it would get enough use to justify the expense."

"I guess I proved them wrong this year," Daniel sighed again.

"Indeed you have."

~~~

Before she noticed him sitting on the steps, Elliot noticed that his wife looked tired. Of course her pregnancy was nearing six months so that was to be expected. But the heat was making it worse and he vowed to make sure she got more rest.
~~~

"*Elliot?*" she asked when she finally noticed him. He wasn't due home for a few more hours and he could see that she was alarmed. "What's happened?"

"It's all right," he assured her, getting to his feet as she and Jonathon approached. In just the short time since he'd returned to the store the bruising on his son's face was even worse and Elliot felt a renewed sense of anger, and a desire to thrash those boys. Instead, he reached into his pocket and withdrew the envelope and showed it to his wife.

"Oh my!" He caught her as she swayed. Jonathon just stood there looking from him to Richard and Elizabeth, who had been watching from the window but now came out to join them.

"Pop?" Jonathon said hesitantly. Elliot handed him the envelope and grinned at the expression of stunned surprise on the boy's face. "It's from the White House."

"What!" Elizabeth exclaimed dubiously.

"The White House?" Richard asked, equally uncertain.

"Open it," Elliot urged, still holding his wife who now fanned her face with her hand.

Jonathon started to rip the envelope open then, thinking better of it, took out his pocket knife and carefully slit it open. With trembling hands he removed a single sheet of paper, unfolded it and read it slowly. It felt as though the whole family held their breath waiting to hear what it said and who had sent it. After a moment, Jonathon handed it to his father, his hand shaking, and Elliot read aloud,

'My Dear Jonathon, On behalf of a grateful

country I would like to thank you for your diligence in helping to keep the United States safe from the enemy. I would like to ask you to continue keeping an eye on Mr. Mertz and to send me a full report in two months' time. I look forward to hearing from you again. Thank you again. Best regards, President Woodrow Wilson.'

Even Elizabeth, who wasn't impressed by much these days, was awed into silence. Richard looked as though he couldn't believe that the president had written *his* brother. Meg was wiping her eyes with her apron, and Elliot was just so proud of his son that he thought his chest would burst with it.

~~~

The sun had almost set when Reverend Thornton pulled the buggy to a stop in front of the boarding house. Telling Daniel to stay put, he jumped down and hurried up to the door, returning with a reluctant Nina a few moments later. When she caught sight of the splint, and crutches leaning against the seat, she gasped and ran to him.

"Oh, Daniel! I'm so sorry," she whispered, clutching his hand to her cheek.

"No, I'm the one who needs to apologize," he told her softly, reaching out with his other hand to stroke her hair. "I should have listened to you, and I can't tell you how sorry I am that I snapped at you."

"It's all right. I understand."

"You shouldn't. I was such a chump, Nina. I love you *so* much."

"I love you, too."
~~~

Chapter 11

"Marcus? Marcus, are you still there?" Derek's voice came over the line, across several hundred miles as clearly as though he were standing in the next room.

"I- Uh - yeah. Yes, I'm still here," he finally managed, wishing he had a chair nearby so he could sit down.

"Did you hear what I just said?"

"I heard."

He wiped a hand across his eyes wishing with all of his heart that he hadn't. Thousands were dying from a particularly bad strain of the influenza that was sweeping relentlessly from the eastern coast of the United States westward. Nothing, no precautions no matter how determined, seemed able to slow it. He felt the blood leave his face when Derek went on to tell him of the vast number of people who had died in a single week in the state of New York, the city of the same name being particularly hard hit.

"If it keeps moving at the same pace, Marcus, it will be here soon. And in Michigan not long after." He heard his friend sigh deeply. "We're not prepared for anything like this. There aren't enough undertakers in the whole of Philadelphia to take care of the bodies if we get hit like New York did."

"What will you do?" Marcus asked, reluctantly, slumping back against the wall. If Derek and the others in Philadelphia weren't prepared, what would happen in Charlotte if it reached this far. It *couldn't* reach this far. Could it?

"We all met a few nights ago and we're trying to keep it as quiet as possible so we don't cause a panic, you know. But each and every one of us have ordered as many pine boxes built as we can afford. I've spent nearly all of my savings and it makes me ill just thinking about it. Seventy – five caskets, Marcus. And that's only what I ordered."

"Won't your builders be suspicious?" he asked after a moment's silence.

"We had to be honest with them. They know what's coming anyway. It's all over the newspapers. And they know what will happen if the general public discovers that we're preparing for the deaths of thousands. So they're keeping quiet. Not that it really matters because everyone knows it's coming. They just try to pretend that it won't come *here*."

"It doesn't seem possible," Marcus almost whispered.

"Oh it's possible," Derek laughed, but there was

no humor in it. "There have been returning soldiers heard to say that it's all but wiped out small villages overseas." After a lengthy pause he added, fear lacing his voice, "Some people are wondering if this might not be the plagues written about in Revelation. They're afraid this is the end, Marcus."

Marcus swallowed hard and closed his eyes tightly as he asked, "Do you think it's the end, Derek?"

"I don't know. I wish I did. All I can say, friend, is to make sure you're prepared. As best you can be anyway. If someone doesn't find a way to stop it, it's going to be on your doorstep before you can blink twice."

"How can this be happening?" Marcus asked, knowing that even as he did, there was no answer.

"Marcus. What if the worst were to happen to Amanda and me?"

"Don't say that!" Marcus exclaimed, stiffening his spine as he came away from the wall. "Nothing is going to happen to you or Amanda."

"I *have to* think about it, Marcus. Her parents are gone and my mother has all she can do to take care of my father. He's getting worse every day." No one knew what was wrong with Edgar McGovern, except that he appeared to be wasting away before their very eyes. No treatment or medicine had helped. "My brothers all have families of their own, as do Amanda's. There's no one else we can ask."

"Ask?" Ask who what? Marcus wondered, snapping out of his stupor and giving his full attention to his friend.

"You remember the promise we made in

college." It wasn't a question and he swallowed hard.

"Yes." It was the hardest word he'd ever had to utter.

"Will you keep it?"

"Nothing is going to happen," he assured Derek with all the force he could muster.

"But if it does, *will you honor your word?*"

"You know that I will," he swore. And prayed that the need to keep it would never come.

"Thank you," Derek said softly. "I need to go now. I'm late for supper. But I didn't want to call from home. I didn't want Amanda to overhear."

"I understand."

"Take care, Marcus. I'll keep you posted on what's happening out this way. Just whatever you do, be careful, okay?"

"You, too," Marcus said, and hung his telephone up when Derek ended the call.

Without conscious thought, he walked out to his porch, clutching the railing as he bent over and sucked in several deep breaths of the crisp autumn air. Try as he might, he couldn't get his mind to accept the devastating news he'd just received. Maybe this was just a bad dream. A nightmare that he'd wake up from shortly and laugh at his fears.

Yet he knew it wasn't a dream. A nightmare? Definitely. But it was real. He, too, had heard stories about the vicious influenza sweeping the earth, and had hoped they were nothing more than rumors. But they were real. And it was coming this way.

He took one last deep breath then straightened and looked around at the houses in his neighborhood. If it reached Charlotte, would he have any neighbors left? Would *he* survive?

Shaking his head as though to clear it, he strode back inside and into his office. Sitting at the desk, he pulled open the top drawer and took out his savings book, a sheet of paper and a pencil. After determining exactly what he had to spend he walked back over to the telephone, signaling the operator that he needed to make a call.

"Roland Lumber," came the greeting from Andrew Roland's assistant several seconds later.

"This is Marcus McClelland. May I speak to Andrew please?"

"Certainly. One moment please." It wasn't long before Andrew's voice came over the line.

"Marcus! Good to hear from you. What can I do for you today?"

"I need to order thirty-six pine caskets, Andrew. And I'd like them delivered as quickly as possible."

"You want *what?* Thirty-six caskets!" His booming laugh forced Marcus to move he earpiece slightly away. "I never realized you had a sense of humor, Marcus," Andrew chuckled. "Now how many do you *really* want?"

"Thirty-six," Marcus answered seriously. "And you should know, you may be getting more large orders, Andrew. You see, I just got a call..."

~~~

After listening to Arnold's tale of what it was really like, Jonathon hadn't been able to enjoy trench warfare anymore. After all, the game had
~~~

been exciting and fun, and war obviously was not. Why anyone had ever thought it was fun was a mystery. Some of the guys still liked playing because they hadn't heard all the awful stuff he had. Still, he'd started playing with some of the other kids, even though his heart wasn't in it. He wished Luke would come home.

It appeared, though, that he wasn't the only one lacking enthusiasm. Gordy Cartwright and Sam Collins were definitely distracted, whispering together far more often than playing. Jonathon wanted to know why, so he crept up behind them.

"My pop told my mother that thousands of people were dying out on the east coast," Sam whispered, looking at his dusty shoes.

"Big deal. That's on the east coast. Michigan is a long way from there."

"He said it's moving west. He sounded really scared."

"It'll never come here. That's *hundreds* of miles away from us."

"So is London and Berlin, and people are dying everywhere. It's all over the world, Gordy."

Jonathon felt chilled, and a little sick. Were they talking about the Spanish influenza? He'd heard a little talk of it, seen photographs in the newspaper with people wearing masks, but he hadn't paid much attention to it.

"Did he say anything else?" Gordy was running a hand that shook through his bright blond curls.

"Just that cities are closing everything. Schools, stores, even churches. But it's not stopping it. More and more people just keep getting sick and dying.

Oh yeah. He also said it's killing more younger people. I don't know what he meant."

"How young?"

"He didn't say."

"Do you think he meant young like us?" Jonathon blurted out, finally letting them know he'd been listening. Sam looked up at him, his brown eyes wide with fear.

"I don't know. I hope not."

~~~

With the extreme heat of summer behind them, Daniel wished that everyone could just enjoy the pleasant, early October weather. But no one was enjoying much of anything. Not with the threat of the influenza epidemic. It had swept through most of the eastern coast of the United States and was moving westward at an alarming rate, killing thousands in its wake. And now it had reached inside the borders of Michigan, new cases in cities as near as Battle Creek were being reported daily in the Charlotte Republican.

Even Nina's enthusiasm over their upcoming wedding, less than two weeks away now, had paled in light of the fear that it might come here. He reached over and squeezed her hand, and she looked up and smiled at him from where she sat on the seat of the buggy beside him. Even that wasn't as bright as it had been even a week ago.

"It's going to be all right, Nina," he promised gently. She didn't have to ask what he meant.

"I hope so. It's getting closer all the time."
~~~

"Well, I've heard talk around town that if it comes much closer, they're going to close the roads and stop everyone from coming in. If they quarantine Charlotte, I don't think trains can stop here either. The mayor is even recommending that people avoid traveling unless it's an emergency. We won't get it here. I'm sure of it."

"What about the buses that takes the workers to the automobile factory in Lansing? They come through here every day."

"They'll deal with it if it becomes a problem. No one wants the epidemic here and they'll do whatever they have to do to prevent it. Even if they have to make those men stay in Lansing until the threat has passed."

She laid her head against his shoulder and they rode in companionable silence for a while. As hard as he'd tried to convince her that everything would be fine, he had to work harder to convince himself. Since the word had first come that the epidemic had reached Michigan, he'd felt a sick fear in the pit of his stomach.

Life had been hard when each of his parents had died, but he couldn't remember ever being terribly unhappy outside of those events. On the other hand, he couldn't ever recall being this happy either. Nina was everything he'd ever dreamed of and he desired, more than anything, to spend the rest of their lives together. Their *long* lives. The epidemic might be a threat to those dreams.

The newspapers were saying that this influenza was different. It was killing people of all ages, but far more people their age than any other. People in the prime of their life. The young and not the old this time.

He wished that there was a safe place to take her. Somewhere that the influenza couldn't ever hurt her. But, from what he'd read, there wasn't a place on the face of the earth that wasn't being affected by it. All they could do was hope and pray.

"I was thinking," Nina said after several long minutes. She was staring at her lap, wringing her hands nervously. "Maybe we shouldn't wait to get married."

"Not wait? What do you mean?"

"Maybe we should get married now. Just in case."

Daniel stared at her in surprise. He knew she'd been looking forward to having a fussy wedding, though it had taken much encouragement from both him and Reverend Thornton before she'd agreed to one. In fact, the reverend had been the one to bring the subject up and had, of his own accord, taken it upon himself to enlist the ladies of the church to help make it happen.

"Nina, don't do this because you're afraid. As much as I'd love to marry you this very minute, I know that you've been having the time of your life planning the wedding. Don't give it up because you're afraid. I promise, I won't let anything happen to you."

"It's not me I'm worried about," she murmured. Daniel covered both of her hands with one of his.

"Nothing is going to happen to me either."

"You can't know that, Daniel. No one can know

how this will all turn out. And you can't control something like the influenza."

"No, we can't control it, but we can take precautions against getting it."

"Like the surgical masks? They didn't do a lot to help in New York or all of those other places in the world."

"Well how about we do this then?" He kissed her softly.

"Kiss? That's what we're supposed to do to prevent it?" she gasped. Daniel laughed and shook his head.

"I just couldn't resist. But no, if it gets closer to Charlotte before the wedding, we'll get married, buy enough food to last us a month and lock the house up tight as a drum. We won't go out and we won't let anyone in. That should keep us safe."

"What about work?" Nina asked, pointing out a serious flaw in his plans. "If it comes to Charlotte, they'll need every nurse to help."

"No!" Daniel exclaimed, jerking the horse to a halt. He turned and grasped her shoulders, fear making him nauseous. "You absolutely *will not* be working around anyone with the influenza! I forbid it!"

"But-"

"No. You were going to quit after the wedding anyway. You can just quit now. In fact, you're right. Let's go back to town and have the reverend marry us *now*." He wanted the right to forbid her to work. There was no way he was going to risk losing her if the worst were to happen.

"But, Daniel-"

"No. We're getting married today."
"But you just said we should wait."
"I've changed my mind."

~~~

"I don't want you going downtown anymore," Elliot said softly, holding Meg close, his hand resting on her rounded stomach. From time to time he could feel the baby moving around and kicking.

"The paper said there haven't been that many cases in Michigan yet," she reminded him, but he could feel her trembling. "At least not compared to how bad it's hit other states."

"I don't care. It's not worth the risk. You know what they're saying." They both did and it terrified them. Expectant mothers were more susceptible than most of the population. "From now on, I'll do all the shopping."

"All right."

"I'm scared, Meg. I want to take us all somewhere far, far away, but there doesn't seem to be a place on earth that's safe."

"We'll be fine, Elliot. We already know what we're going to do when it gets close. The influenza would have to learn to open locked doors and windows to get to us," she whispered, trying to ease his fears.

"I hope you're right. I couldn't bear the thought of losing any of you."

"And I couldn't bear the thought of losing you. We'll be okay, Elliot. I promise you."

He could tell she was having trouble staying
~~~

awake. This far along in her pregnancy found her tiring out quite easily these days. He didn't remember her being quite so exhausted with the other children, but she was nearly four years older than she'd been when Charles was born.

A smile curved his lips when her soft snores filled the air a few moments later and he held her just a bit closer. Not enough to wake her, but he felt like he needed her as near as possible.

An especially strong gust of wind blew in through the open window, parting the sheer curtains and caressing his bare back. But he couldn't enjoy it. Couldn't be grateful for it. Because he knew it carried with it a risk.

Elliot couldn't remember ever being so afraid in his life. Like everyone else, his mind hadn't been able accept that something as horrible as the Spanish influenza could affect their lives. Sure the stories in the newspaper saddened him, but those things were happening in faraway places.

Battle Creek was only about thirty miles from their front door. It wasn't far away at all anymore. That thought hadn't been far from his thoughts for most of the week and had, in fact, left him feeling sick to his stomach more often than not. Even knowing that more people were surviving than dying didn't comfort him.

Because too many people were dying. Hundreds of thousands of them. Some estimates were said it numbered closer to the tens of *millions*.

If it reached Charlotte, if it got too bad, he didn't know what he would do. His thoughts had jumped from one outrageous idea to another, including confining everyone to the basement. He could haul enough food and water down, along with mattresses and clothes to last them awhile – and nail the door shut until the danger had passed.

Of course they would have no way of knowing when the danger had passed, not being cut off from everything like that.

And, deep down, he knew it wouldn't stop it anyway. The sickness, if it came – *when* it came – would be carried in with the very air they needed to live.

Chapter 12

Elliot closed himself in the storeroom, leaned against the wall and closed his eyes. Even so, a few tears managed to squeeze through and slide down his cheeks.

He couldn't recall ever having been as afraid in his life as when Charles started throwing up that morning. Meg had put in a frantic call to Dr. Garland, who hadn't wasted much time in making a house call. Only to assure them that, although there were a few cases of Spanish influenza in the southernmost areas of the county, there weren't any nearby. Or at least none that he was aware of. Charles simply had a case of stomach flu, which a number of residents in the city limits had come down with during the past week or so.

He'd thought for sure that the ruthless killer that was already causing some people to hole up like hermits had afflicted his youngest son and he'd been almost paralyzed with terror. No one knew where he'd been exposed, and he wasn't even in school yet, so it could have been anywhere.

What if someone brought the influenza home that way? It could be here already and they wouldn't know.

But he was going to make sure they stayed safe from it. When he locked the doors at six, he was hanging a notice saying that the shop would be closed until further notice. Then he was going to the mercantile and having a large order of food and canned goods delivered to the house.

After that he would go to the meeting the mayor had called, but then everyone was staying at home. No to school, church or trips downtown. They should be safe enough in the house and yard, at least until word came that it was here – and then no one was leaving the house at all.

~~~

The turnout for the meeting had grown so large that everyone had to be moved to the lawn of the courthouse, where the mayor and public health officer were having little success in trying to call everyone to order from where they stood at the top of the stairs on the southern side of the building. Colby, who had left with what he thought was more than enough time to get there early, had been forced to stand near the road and he wondered if he'd be able to hear anything at all. He *knew* he wouldn't if the rightfully panicked crowd didn't calm down.

"Quiet!" the mayor said loudly. He had to repeat
~~~

it several times, his voice rising in volume with each command, but slowly everyone quieted, giving him their undivided attention. Colby noticed that the mayor's face and bald head were red from the exertion of shouting. "If you haven't already heard, there were two cases of Spanish influenza diagnosed in Potterville yesterday. As a precautionary measure, Mr. Densteadt, our Public Health Officer, the town council and I have decided to close all roads leading into Charlotte, effective at dusk today.

"At this time we urge you to spend as much of your time as possible in your homes and avoid gathering in groups. We feel it's necessary to close our schools, churches, nickelodeons and other business establishments, and we would like to remind you that the more that you're out and among others, the greater the risk of spreading the disease, should it reach our town.

"As for the issue of food, our fine grocers have decided that they will deliver orders to your doorsteps, but you have to telephone them before eleven each Monday, Wednesday and Friday. Those who don't have telephone service should wear their masks and *quickly* drop them in boxes that will be left outside their doors. But no one will be allowed inside. When it has been determined that the threat has passed, you will be notified that it's back to business as usual."

At this point Mayor Taylor announced that Mr. Densteadt would now step forward with his suggestions.

"Many medical practitioners feel that the

wearing of surgical masks will help prevent the spread of the influenza epidemic. Fortunately the mayor, in anticipation of the need for them, has enough masks available for the citizens of Charlotte. We ask that you pick them up after the meeting and encourage those who weren't able to come, to stop by to get their own as soon as possible. They will be available in the courthouse lobby until the supply is exhausted.

"While the masks may, indeed, help prevent the spread of the influenza, I must reiterate what the mayor has already said and encourage you to stay in your homes as much as you are able. Avoid crowds and eat a healthy diet. Plenty of fruits and vegetables. And make sure that your masks are washed, and sterilized in boiling water after each wearing.

"One final word. While it is true that the entire city will be closing down, there are a few notable exceptions. The sanatorium will remain open, as will the police and fire stations. All doctors will remain accessible to those requiring medical care. And, although we are *not* anticipating a problem with the Spanish influenza, we thought it best to be prepared in the unlikely event that we are wrong. Mayor Taylor, I think I'll let you share this last bit of news."

Colby bit his lip to keep from laughing out loud at the expression on Fred Taylor's face. Hearing the snickers spread through the crowd, it was clear that most everyone else hadn't even tried. Obviously the good mayor didn't want to say whatever was left to be said.

"Yes. Well- Uh-" He sent a withering glare at

George Densteadt before continuing. "Please keep in mind that, again, while we do *not* expect the influenza to affect anyone in town, we have tried to plan for every contingency. In order to ensure that our citizens receive the best care available, should the need arise, we've had to make some decisions that-" He scowled at PHO Densteadt again. "Well, you know that most of our doctors are over in France caring for our wounded soldiers. That leaves us a little shorthanded in case of an emergency. So if worse comes to worse, and you can't get hold of a physician, we're advising you to contact one of the local veterinarians."

Colby had to cover the lower half of his face with his hands as an outraged, offended protest went up all around him. There might have been others chuckling, too, but he would bet that they were in the minority. He laughed harder when the mayor and public health officer beat a hasty retreat, closing themselves inside the courthouse in short order. Apparently they'd bolted the door behind them because when the council members tried to follow, they couldn't get in.

As the small group men huddled together at the top of the steps, eyes wary as they watched the angry masses, he had to wipe tears from his eyes. He knew he should get hold of himself but seeing the city leaders turn into a pack of cowards before his very eyes was just plain funny.

Finally, as the crowd began to calm down, and he managed to rein in his mirth, Colby took his place in the line that was growing so long that it would probably circle twice around the courthouse.

He wanted to pick up masks for himself and Anna, but he also wanted to ask if he could have a few more. Some of the elderly members of his congregation would find it a hardship to come and get their own. While he waited for his turn, he began to pray that all of these measures would be enough.

It wasn't that he feared dying or anything like that. He knew his eternity would be spent in heaven. In fact, he looked forward to it. It was just that he wasn't in any hurry to get there. There was still too much he wanted to do and experience here on earth.

He loved being a minister. He loved his congregation. They were his life, if truth be told, and he wasn't sure what he was going to do with the churches being closed, too. The prospect of spending endless days trapped inside his house was almost unbearable. He loved every moment spent away from home. Away from Anna.

She was already making his life miserable because of the influenza. In her opinion, as soon as it had reached Michigan, he should have closed the doors to the church and holed up in the house until she felt sure the danger had passed. That was before it had even reached Battle Creek. Just the thought made him shudder.

He hadn't told her yet, but if the influenza did become a problem, he still had no intention of hiding out. Chances were good that at least some members of the church would need him and he intended to do his job. God willing, that wouldn't include having to perform any funerals.

"Hello, Reverend Thornton." Colby saw that

Elliot Owens was standing next to him as they neared the courthouse steps.

"Elliot." He wasn't sure what to say, how to reassure someone as afraid as this man obviously was.

"I can't believe they're telling us to call on veterinarians," Elliot murmured tonelessly.

"I know. It's hard to think about, but if it came down to a choice between no care at all and a veterinarian, they're better than nothing."

"How do you figure that?"

"They *do* have some medical knowledge."

"I'm scared," he whispered. Colby clasped his shoulder and nodded. "It's in *Potterville.* That's only six miles away. Maybe it's already here and we just don't know it yet."

"I hope not, Elliot. I truly hope not."

~~~

"If it gets too bad," Gerald McKimmon said quietly, "I'm not going to take a chance on catching it. I have a family."

"But if we don't deal with the bodies," Paul Brighton argued, "who will?"

"I don't really care. Those bodies are going to be in homes with other people who may be sick."

"I have a friend in Philadelphia," Marcus said reluctantly. "He said some of them are insisting that the families wrap the bodies in a sheet and lay them outside. They have to hang a flag to alert the funeral directors."

"Alert them how?" Paul asked.
~~~

"I guess they're just going around with wagons and picking them up from porches and lawns."

"Does anyone know that we won't catch anything just from touching them?" Gerald demanded? "Or from touching the sheets they're wrapped in?" Marcus shook his head slowly. He hadn't thought of that.

"I guess we just need to make sure we're wearing our masks and a heavy pair of gloves. And then make sure we boil all of them every night."

"I don't know," Gerald muttered, glancing around at the quickly dispersing crowd. Everyone who had gotten their masks seemed in a hurry to get home instead of milling around talking as they usually did after other town meetings. "If it comes here, I think I'm done. People can just go out to the shed and get a casket if they need one, but they can stay far away from me and my family."

"I think I might do that, too," Sam decided. He, too, had a wife and a couple of children and Marcus really didn't blame either one of them for being scared.

He couldn't remember ever having been this scared in his life.

~~~

It was in Potterville.

Six miles northeast of Charlotte. Battle Creek was to the southwest so how was it possible, he wondered, that it had it passed them by? He didn't think it *was* possible. In fact, Daniel was sure it was already here, they just didn't know it yet.
~~~

He felt himself break out in a cold sweat and, lightheaded, he had to stop and lean against a tree until it passed.

It hadn't been easy losing both of his parents, but he hadn't been terrified when he knew their deaths were imminent. Just unbearably sad. Now, for a woman he'd known less than a year, fear was choking him, making it hurt to breathe. What would he do if his *wife* was struck down by the Spanish influenza? Would she die like so many others had?

No.

He pushed off the tree and started walking as fast as his leg would allow, grateful that the splint had come off the week before so he didn't have to deal with the crutches.

Nina must have been watching out the window because she met him at the door, wringing her hands. Daniel pulled her close and held her tightly for several long moments before raising her face to his.

"What is it?" she whispered, her eyes wide with fear. "What's wrong?"

"It's in Potterville. Nina, you're not going to the sanitorium until the threat is over."

"But-"

"No. No arguments. I've waited my whole life for you," he said, gently cupping her face in both of his hands. She was so beautiful! "You're going to stay here where it's safe. Tomorrow I'll stop after work and pick up enough food to last us awhile and, if it gets really bad here, I won't go to work until it's over. I'm not going to take a chance on losing you. I won't."

"All right, Daniel," she murmured, turning her head slightly so she could kiss his palm. "I'll stay home."

"Thank you," he whispered, pulling her close again.

"Do you want some coffee and pie now?" she asked, when it must have seemed to her like he intended to hold her in the hall for the rest of the night. "I'd like to know what the mayor said."

"That sounds good. But you're not going to like what he had to say." He hadn't liked a single word he'd heard. Because the danger was right in their backyard now. It wouldn't be long before it was knocking at the door.

~~~

"Well that's it then," Anna huffed, pacing the kitchen like a caged animal. Colby was sorry he'd told her about the meeting now. Wished he'd stopped by the church and stayed until long after she'd fallen asleep. But he hadn't, and she'd nagged like a fishwife, demanding to know what happened, and he'd finally given in. "You're not leaving the house until it's passed us by."

"I have a duty to my congregation, Anna. It's my job to be there for them when they need me. I can't just lock myself in our house while they're sick and possibly dying."

"You certainly *can* because you're not going to go out *there* if the influenza is here. Do you really think I'll allow you to be out there around people who have it and then come back *here?* Because I
~~~

won't have you bringing it home to *me,* Colby Thornton!"

"You won't *allow* me, Anna?" he asked so softly he wasn't sure she even heard him.

"I'll make your life hell on earth if you take so much as one step out that door." He almost laughed aloud at that. Her threat didn't mean a whole lot given that she'd been making his life hell on earth for nineteen years. What else could she do to him that she hadn't already done?

"I'll wear my mask," he sighed. He was so weary of her incessant selfishness he just wanted to shake her sometimes. He'd never known another soul who cared so little for others.

"What if it doesn't help? People are wearing them everywhere else and they're *still* getting sick and dying." She did have a valid point, he admitted reluctantly. No matter how many precautions were taken, nothing seemed to stop the spread of this awful plague.

"I'll stay at the church until it's over then."

"You will not! You know I'm afraid to stay here alone at night."

"Anna-"

"What if *you* get sick, Colby?" She seemed to realize she was getting nowhere with her viscous demands and apparently decided to change her tactics. She curved her lips in what she probably hoped would pass as a smile, walked slowly to him and began rubbing his shoulders. When she spoke again, her voice sounded much like he remembered it from their courting days. Soft and sweet. "What would I do if something happened to you, my darling husband? You could stay here with me. And – and come to my room every night until the influenza is gone."

"That might be weeks, Anna." He sighed, closing his eyes during the long pause that followed.

"I- I know. That's all right. I – don't mind."

But he could tell from the tone of her voice that she minded very much. Even if she didn't, he would still fulfill his duties as minister to his flock. He hadn't chosen to enter the ministry lightly, ready to hide out in fear when the going got rough.

"I'm sorry, Anna. I know what the offer to share your bed cost you." And he knew it had cost her dearly as she couldn't bear his touch. "But I made a commitment to God and these people, and I'm going to keep my word."

Something between a scream and a growl sounded behind him as she began to pummel his back with her fists. He shot up out of the chair, catching her hands in his, but she continued to try and hit him.

"You made a commitment to me, too, Colby! What if you *die,* you fool? Who will take care of me then?"

~~~

"Elliot!" Meg breathed, hurrying from the kitchen when she heard him enter the house. Elliot pulled her close and didn't want to let go. Especially when he felt the baby kick against his stomach.

"We need to get everyone in the parlor, Meg. Now."
~~~

"What did they say?" she asked, her voice trembling. He could see the fear in her eyes and reached up to stroke her cheek.

"It's in Potterville. Go sit down, I'll get the children."

"Charles is sleeping."

"That's all right. He's too young to understand this anyway." He walked to the foot of the stairs and called the other four down, then went to sit by his wife on the settee.

One by one they made their way down the stairs, looking at him curiously when he held out his hand to indicate that they, too, needed to sit.

"What's up, Pop?" Jonathon asked, flopping on the floor. He tried to give the impression that this was a normal family discussion but Elliot could see the fear in his eyes, too. Something he'd seen in too many faces over the past few days.

"The mayor told us that there are people in Potterville with the Spanish influenza." Richard leaned forward, his hands on the arms of the chair, his face pale. Elizabeth gasped, her face the same shade as her brother's. Jonathon glared at the floor, his hands curled into fists, and poor Kathleen just looked confused.

"It's coming here," Richard said tonelessly. "It's coming to Charlotte."

"It appears that way," Elliot said quietly, clasping Meg's hand tightly. "That means there are going to be some changes around here. Everything is going to close, effective tomorrow, so you will all be staying home until this is over. You can still play in the backyard if you want, but as soon as I hear that it's reached Charlotte, we're all staying in the house."

"But, Pop! That's not fair!" Jonathon cried out, looking at his father in indignation.

"That's too bad," Elliot sighed, wishing he didn't have to impose such strict rules, but desperate times called for desperate measures.

"But-"

"No exceptions, Jonathon. No one is to leave this house, except in an emergency, until it's safe."

"But that could be weeks."

"Yes it very well could be. Again, that's too bad." He looked at his middle son hard. "And if I so much as suspect that you're disobeying me, young man, I *will* spank you. I may, in fact, *beat* you. Is that understood?"

"Yes, sir," Jonathon muttered, scowling at him.

"Now you may all go play or read. I want to talk to your mother alone."

He held out a hand and Margaret took it, rising to her feet, and they walked quickly up to their bedroom where he closed the door, just in case someone took it into his curious little head to eavesdrop. Meg had wrapped her arms around her middle, her eyes filled with terror. Elliot truly wished he could reassure her as he took her in his arms, but he couldn't. If he tried, it would be nothing but lies because no one knew what would happen, how they might be affected by this deadly killer.

"Do you think it will be enough?" she asked. "Locking ourselves in the house?"

"I don't know. Nothing seems able to stop it, but this seems to be the most reasonable course. I don't know what else to do, Meg."

"Do you think we're at greater risk living across street from the sanatorium?"

"I've wondered about that, too. Maybe not. The mayor acted very fast when he heard about the cases in Potterville. He issued the order to close everything immediately. Even the roads coming into town at dusk. Hopefully it hadn't had much of a chance to spread before that. Everyone has been staying home more so it might not be as bad here as it has been in other places."

But there was no way to know if an infected person had already been in town. From everything he'd learned about this influenza, and that was only what he read about in the newspaper, symptoms might show up show up within hours of being infected – or it could be longer, only no one knew for sure how much longer. In fact, no one knew much about it at all. Why some people could be sick with it for days and recover, while others could contract it and be dead in a matter of hours.

"I don't know what else to do," he repeated helplessly.

He'd made two stops on his way home. The first at the druggists for aspirin and any other medicine he thought they might need, and then at one of the other grocers where he placed an order for a delivery in the morning for foods in cans and boxes. There was only so much he could carry, and his was a large family. The butcher had decided days ago that should the need arise, he would close up shop, though he would make deliveries early each morning and so Elliot had arranged to have meat brought to the porch twice each week until the danger had passed.

"I suppose there isn't much else that we can do," Meg said, taking a deep breath and forcing herself to calm down. Elliot had to smile. His wife had the ability to rise to any occasion, good, bad or otherwise. She would be a tremendous help over the next days or, God forbid, weeks – should it come to that.

"No. I hope our biggest problem is five bored children."

"And two bored parents?" she suggested, smiling up at him.

"Will we be bored, Meg? I foresee arguments, bad tempers, and a whole lot of complaining. Boredom may come as a pleasant change of pace, I think," he said with a chuckle.

"Jonathon will be the worst," she guessed, stepping away and going to look out the window. "At least he can see Mr. Mertz's house from our room. I expect he'll be spending most of his days in here."

"Whatever it takes to get through this." Because they would get through this, he vowed, unwilling to accept any other outcome. He'd always taken care of his family and that's what he planned to do for many years to come.

"Do you think we've given them enough time to feel sorry for themselves?" Meg wanted to know. "It might be a good night to pop some corn and play charades, or read Charles Dickens. Start it off the way we mean to continue?"

"You're a good wife," Elliot told her, kissing her tenderly. "Have I told you how much I love you?"

“Not since you got home, but you’re welcome to tell me as often as you like.”

“I love you very, very much,” he whispered as he kissed her again.

Chapter 13

Derek had begun to sob and Marcus felt his stomach begin to churn. It was happening, just as his friend had predicted.

"There are so many," Derek wept. "More every day. It's getting worse."

"I-" He couldn't think of anything to say, could hardly breathe. Fear was pressing down upon his chest like a boulder.

"They're putting the bodies on the porch. The families can't come out because the men picking them up won't stop if they do. They just stack them in the wagons, Marcus."

Marcus could feel himself begin to panic. He'd never known his friend to be this upset over anything. Not even his father's illness and that had shaken him pretty badly.

"We're running out of caskets. People are stealing them. Stealing *caskets,* Marcus. We have to hire guards to protect what's left and- Oh God I still can't believe this. One man was shot and killed trying to take one for his son. He'd already paid for two when his daughters died and he couldn't afford another. His wife is alone now. How can this be happening?"

"I don't know." Marcus felt faint. Dying because you needed a *casket* for your son? He'd taken a loss for destitute families in the past. But to be so desperate that someone would try to steal one? What sickened him even more was the fact that someone actually took a man's life over a *casket.*

"They're talking about mass graves, Marcus." He could almost hear Derek shudder as he said the words. "They don't know if the bodies can still be contagious or not. And they're worried about new diseases if they pile up." By 'they're' Marcus assumed he meant city and health officials. Of course they would worry about those things. How could they not?

"What about you? Your family? Are you all well?"

"We're not sick, if that's what you mean. Scared? Terrified? Yes. People are dying all around us, Marcus. They can be healthy in the morning and dead by nightfall. It's so quick with some of them."

"Everyone who gets it dies?" It was a question he hadn't wanted to ask but supposed he needed to know.

"No. Not everyone. At least not yet. I hear that east of us, a lot of people who got it are recovering, but that's a slow process. Many who get the influenza wind up with pneumonia. It's just that *so many* are getting it. I don't even want to open my eyes in the morning, Marcus. I've never seen anything like it."

"God, please don't let it come to Charlotte," Marcus prayed. He hadn't realized he'd said it aloud until Derek snorted.

"Keep praying, my friend. It's the only thing that might save you. But I'm not sure even God is powerful enough to stop this from spreading."

~~~

Jonathon knew he was beating the rug with more force than was necessary, but he had woken up that morning angrier than he could ever remember being. Three days now the whole family had been trapped in the house for nearly every waking hour. When someone had called to say that there were cases being reported in Charlotte the morning after everything had been closed down, Pop had decided that everyone could go out for half an hour very early every morning. But only in the backyard, and only if everyone stayed close to the house.

And so Jonathon was pretending that the rug he hit over and over with the wicker paddle was the Spanish flu.

"Son, I think you've beat the dust from next week out of that thing. Maybe you should do the other one now," Pop suggested from where he sat on the porch reading to Kathleen and Charles.
~~~

Jonathon grinned sheepishly, pulled the rug off the line, folded it in half and laid it on the steps. Before he hung the second one up he glanced around the yard.

Mother was on her knees snapping the heads off the shriveling Marigolds and tossing them into a small basket. Later she would remove all of the seeds in preparation for planting next spring then store them on a shelf in the cellar. Elizabeth sat in the grass, leaning back against a tree trunk looking frightened as she stared off into space. And Richard just stood there, hands on hips, like he was on guard against anything that might try to sneak in and harm them.

Jonathon knew how he feeling. It was the same way all of them felt. Except the little ones. They were too young to understand what was going on. Kathleen seemed to know that something was up because she had been pretty quiet, like she was trying to figure it out. But the rest of them knew.

Only Jonathon knew even more than his brothers and sisters.

They didn't realize it, but he'd overheard his parents talking quietly in the kitchen before they knew he was awake. Pop said that Mr. Grundy, from the hardware store, had passed away from the influenza during the night. Mr. Grundy wasn't old like Pop either. And Phyllis Landry. She was in Elizabeth's grade. And they were both dead. Jonathon wanted to throw up.

He hadn't known too many people who had died. And most of those were just old ones from around town. That always made him feel a little bad, but it was hard to be really upset. It was different with Mr. Grundy and Phyllis. He and Pop went to the hardware a lot, and he saw Phyllis all the time at school. It made him feel sick to his stomach to know that she wouldn't be there anymore.

As he beat the second rug, just as hard as he had the first, he wondered where the influenza came from. He'd heard people talk about it and they thought maybe God was making everyone sick. That they were so bad that He was tired of giving them chances and wanted everyone to die.

Jonathon didn't think that was true. Except for Mr. Mertz, and Steven and Tommy, he didn't know any bad people. But if it wasn't God, he didn't know what it was. For the first time he could ever remember, he wished he could go to church and talk to Reverend Thornton. If anyone would know if God was going to kill all the people in the world, it would be him.

~~~

"I don't know why you have to go out *every* day," Anna complained as she flounced across the kitchen. "The more you're out there, the more you risk catching that awful influenza and bringing it home to me!"

"I offered to stay at the church to minimize your risk," Colby reminded her. "And I have an *obligation* to be out there, Anna. This is what ministers do. These people depend on me."

"*I* depend on you, Colby."

It took every ounce of self – control he
~~~

possessed to not roll his eyes heavenward. Of course she depended on him. To provide the money to buy her everything her heart desired, to put food on the table, and to give her the prestige she craved from his position as a respected minister. Except for those things, though, she had little use for him.

"You knew what I was when you married me," he finally said with a heavy sigh. "Do you honestly believe I would abandon these people in their time of need?"

"What about *my* need, Colby? What about what *I* want?" she shrieked, flinging a bowl off the counter in her fury. It shattered all over the floor, some of the pieces coming to rest on Colby's shoes. He shook them off absently and walked to get the broom from the pantry.

"All you want and need is my money and the things you can buy with it," he muttered, his voice too low for her to hear as he swept the shards of glass into a neat pile. More loudly he said, "Robert Grundy died last night, Anna. Do you even care?"

"No. No, Colby I do *not*. I'm sorry but I won't lie to make you happy. I barely knew the man."

"That was your choice. He attended our church for eight years and I'm not going to turn my back on his wife and children now."

He went back to the pantry for the dust pan, thrusting it into Anna's hand before picking up his mask from the counter.

"When will you be home?" she demanded.

"Expect me when you see me," he told her, turning his back on her and walking out the back door without a second glance.

After all this time it shouldn't have surprised him that Anna didn't care for anyone but herself. But her callous attitude about Robert- He'd had to get out of the house, away from *her*, immediately.

As he walked down the sidewalk, not a soul in sight for as far as the eye could see, he thought about his marriage. He had been happy the day of their wedding. Happier than he could ever remember, and his life to that point had been a good one. But the morning after, every dream he'd ever imagined for them had been shattered when she moved out of their bedroom – and never shared it with him again.

She had denied him love, companionship, and intimacy for nearly two decades, and she wondered why he was more devoted to the members of his church than to his wife. It might have made him laugh if it weren't so tragic. They *could* have been so happy- They might have had children, too.

Oh how he longed for children, even now. Sons to fish and hunt with, daughters to cuddle and protect. But she'd crushed that dream, too.

He thought he'd come to terms with everything. Accepted his lot in life and thrived, as much as one could in a situation like this. But the threat from the epidemic had brought out a side of Anna that Colby hated passionately. Sometimes, these past few days, he was afraid he hated her.

~~~

For the first time ever Jonathon realized he knew what real fear felt like. Everything in him felt
~~~

funny, a painful sort of tingling. He could hear his heart beating in his ears. It was hard to breathe. Like the dreams he had sometimes. The ones that scared him about as bad as a body could be scared, but he never really remembered what it was he'd dreamed about. Just that he'd awaken shaking and feeling like this.

He knew exactly what was causing it now though.

It was here. The Spanish influenza was in their house. Despite all the precautions Pop had made them take. Even though they'd hardly gone outside, and hadn't seen another person in days, it had gotten in anyway.

Mother and Pop were up there now, in Elizabeth's room. She'd begun coughing long before dawn, and it had gotten nothing but worse since then. Really bad. He knew it had to be hurting her because you couldn't cough like that and not have it hurt.

Charles was playing with his blocks on the floor while Kathleen had all of her dolls on the dining room table. He and Richard had just been sitting in the parlor, casting frightened looks at one another – and at the stairway – since they'd been banished from being upstairs a few hours ago.

Every now and again they'd hear quiet arguments from the hallway outside Elizabeth's door. Pop wanted Mother to come downstairs with the rest of them but she wouldn't do it. He kept saying she needed to take care of herself and the baby, and she kept telling him that Elizabeth was one of her babies.

And through it all, she kept coughing.

Pop had called the doctor a while ago and Jonathon hoped he would come soon. Probably there were a lot of people who were sick and he needed to see them first. But he didn't want anything to happen to his sister.

And so he prayed that it was just a cold. He knew it wasn't though. They all got colds sometimes. They were never like this. Not this bad.

~~~

"Do you have any idea how many people are actually *sick,* Daniel?" Edward Hinkle hissed into the phone. "We need you here. Ted is at the end of his rope."

His boss was generally an easy going fellow to work for but, when under stress, everyone tried their best to give him a wide berth. And this was, without question, a stressful time for everyone.

"I'm not coming in until it's over, Edward. I can't. I'm sorry."

"You may not have a job to come back to then."

Daniel ran a shaky hand through his hair. He and Nina hadn't even been married a month and now he could lose his job? That was just a chance he was going to have to take. He could always find work somewhere else. His wife was irreplaceable.

"Tell Ted to do whatever he needs to do. She's all I have."

From the kitchen doorway Nina watched him, wiping tears from her eyes with the edge of her crisp white apron. He replaced the receiver and walked to
~~~

stand in front of her, a wry smile on his face.

"Are you in trouble?" she asked softly, reaching out to lay a hand on his chest. He covered it with one of his own.

"Probably."

"Daniel-"

"Hush. We've already had this discussion and I'm not changing my mind. I meant it when I said that it isn't worth it, Nina. This isn't like anything we've ever seen before. This is *dangerous.* In the few days since the mayor said it was in Potterville, *four people* that *I* know have died here. It's just barely here. What's it going to be like in another week?"

"Worse."

"Yes," he murmured, pulling her to him. "A lot worse based on what's happened in other places. And the more I'm out and about, the more likely I am to catch it. And I can't take that chance, Nina. I will do everything in my power to make sure that *you* don't get it."

"Even if it means you lose your job?"

"Even if it means I lose my job."

"Good. Because you're all I have, too, Daniel," she whispered.

"You'll probably be so tired of my company in a day or so that you'll be praying harder than anyone else in town for the influenza to go away," he teased, kissing her forehead.

"That will never happen," she said fiercely.

"Ah, but you don't know what I have in store for you yet, Mrs. Pullman." He grabbed her hand and pulled her along with him to the back porch.

"What's that?" she asked, noting the presence of two large crates, one filled with rolls of paper, the other with a couple of very full burlap bags.

"That, my darling, is what we're going to apply to the walls in our parlor and dining room. As long as we're confining ourselves for who knows how long, I thought we could do some work on the house."

He laughed as she knelt down to inspect his surprise. If her gasps of delight were anything to judge by, she was quite pleased with the things he'd chosen. It was a delicate pattern with tiny roses and vines that she'd fallen in love with when they looked through the samples at the hardware a couple of weeks ago. One of the more expensive patterns, she'd decided against it, and was still undecided over three she hadn't liked nearly as well.

"Can we afford this?" She looked up at him, torn between worry and joy.

"I had some savings and thought this would be a good way to spend some of it."

"Can we start today?"

"Well, we'll have to get the furniture moved and wipe down the walls down, but we could probably start putting the paper up tomorrow. Is that soon enough for you?"

"I guess it will have to be," she said with a smile.

~~~

Three days. Three days since the meeting and this was the eighth call he'd gotten to pick up a body. Fred Latimer. He was younger than Marcus.
~~~

Why were so many young people dying? Usually it was the very old or the very young. But the newspapers had been reporting all along that it was school children, college students and younger adults who were succumbing to this horrible strain of influenza. Certainly some of the others were being lost, too, but most of the victims were in the prime of their lives.

He didn't know how many calls the other three funeral directors in town were getting but, if it was anywhere near what he was receiving, that meant more than thirty people gone in seventy-two hours.

They had all grudgingly agreed to keep working at the urging of the mayor and public health officer. But they had done it on one condition. The same condition that they had set forth in Philadelphia. The bodies had to be wrapped in sheets and left outside. If a living soul was anywhere to be seen, they would leave.

Marcus walked wearily to the kitchen, sitting at the table where an almost untouched cup of coffee waited. His first sip reminded him that it had been there awhile. It was cold.

He hadn't realized he'd been pacing quite that long, walking from one window to another, peering out the drapes. Watching. Waiting to see if someone walked past his house. But no one had. Not one person all morning. Once, though, as he was looking out of the window on the north side of the house, Henry Franklin was looking out his window, eyes filled with fear – staring straight at Marcus. He wondered if Henry had seen that same fear reflected in his face.

Sighing, he carried his cup to the sink and emptied it before filling it from the pot warming on the stove.

Colby wasn't due until early afternoon, still a few hours away. He'd volunteered to ride around town with him because everyone felt that it was safer for two people to lift and carry the bodies than it was for one person to try and sling someone over his shoulder. Since no one knew for sure, he didn't want to take a chance that a sheet would come unwrapped, possibly exposing himself to the influenza.

Three days.

What was going to happen in a week, or two or three, as the Spanish flu continued to wreak its havoc? If he didn't get any more calls today, his stock of pine boxes would be depleted to twenty-seven. And this nightmare had barely even begun.

He prayed that the telephone wouldn't ring again but less than a minute later it did. Marcus closed his eyes.

Chapter 14

"Maybe she doesn't have it," Jonathon whispered hopefully as he and Richard sat close together on the settee. Charles and Kathleen were still playing, blissfully unaware of what was going on upstairs. At least the doctor had finally arrived. "I mean, maybe it *is* just a cold. Or a sore throat." But he knew he just *wanted* it to be something that wasn't scary. He also knew that it was exactly what they feared it would be. He'd known it from the moment he'd opened his eyes that morning.

"Maybe," Richard agreed, though Jonathon knew he was expecting the worst, same as him. "That's how the influenza starts. Just a cough."

"You don't think she'll die?" While it was true that he hadn't much liked Elizabeth as of late, she was still his sister and he didn't like to think of her not being in their family anymore.

"No! Don't even say things like that," Richard snapped, angry enough that Jonathon figured he'd been worrying about it, too. "She's going to be *fine.*"

"I heard Mother and Pop talking yesterday morning. Mr. Grundy died. So did Phyllis Landry."

"How do they know that? We haven't talked to anyone in days."

"Someone called on the telephone. Mother was really upset. I don't think Pop was very happy about it either."

"Well who would be happy to find out someone they knew had died? Mr. Grundy was a really nice man."

"I know he was," Jonathon muttered. Sometimes Richard made him feel stupid and he didn't appreciate it at all.

From upstairs they heard Elizabeth coughing something awful and they looked at each other fearfully. That didn't sound like a cough from a regular cold.

"I wonder how long the doctor is going to be up there?" Richard worried, turning to peer out of the draperies. They had been drawn tightly closed since their father had announced that no one was to leave the house. Apparently he didn't see anyone because he turned back around and stared at the wall.

"Do you think she snuck out of the house during the night?" Jonathon asked. "If she didn't, how do you suppose she got it? *If* she has it, I mean?"

"I don't think she went out. She knows how dangerous it is."

"Then how did she get it?"

"She doesn't have it, Jonathon! Stop talking about it."

Maybe Richard didn't want him to talk about it but it didn't keep him from wondering. How could something like that get in a house that had been closed up tightly for three days? When they were outside in the mornings? When Pop hurried out to the porch to bring the meat or newspaper in? Was it in the meat? Would the rest of them get sick, too? There were so many things to think about. So many things that scared him.

Mr. Grundy hadn't been the first person to die from the influenza. The paper was full of news every day. Dozens of people sick and forty-three dead so far. One article told about cities that had thought it was over, only to be struck down again as soon as public places like schools and churches reopened. It didn't look even close to being over for the first time in Charlotte. Would it come again, like it had in those other places?

If it did, would others in his family get sick, too? Even if Richard didn't want to admit it, he was pretty sure that Elizabeth *did* have the influenza. Maybe they would all get sick from it this time. Would they all die? He didn't like to think of there being no more Owens' living here. What would happen to the shoe store? To their house and their things?

The sound of a door opening upstairs had them both sitting at attention, their eyes on the stairs, but even though they'd heard footsteps in the hall, no one came down.

"No!" Margaret Owens groaned. "No, no, no,

no!"

Jonathon jumped up and ran for the kitchen because now he knew he was going to throw up.

~~~

Colby had been a minister long enough that he knew how influenza worked. Every winter, without fail, too many people got sick and some, inevitably, died. It was just the way it was.

But winter wasn't upon them. It wouldn't arrive for weeks. Autumn had barely begun, which meant that daytime hours were still very comfortable. In fact, the only time he'd needed a sweater was in the early mornings or after sunset.

Influenza *shouldn't* be sweeping through the city right now. Yet it was. A viscous, virulent sickness, it had already stolen the lives of more people in a few short days than the virus last year had taken over the entire season.

The number of residents getting sick was simply staggering. Some were estimating that at least one person in more than half of the households in the city limits had come down with it. No one knew for sure what was happening in the countryside. The roads were still closed, but now it was more to keep residents in than others out. Word tended to spread fast so afflicted areas were to be avoided at all cost.

So there was no way to know how those living in the country were faring. Telephone service was pretty limited outside cities and towns, unless one happened to live on the main roads. Colby really hoped they were safer. It was possible since there
~~~

tended to be several miles between houses. The virus couldn't be spread from person to person as easily as it could in town.

Except people *in* town had been avoiding one another for days. Shutting themselves up inside their homes in an attempt to avoid catching it. So *how* was it spreading? Because it was spreading with the tenacity of a wildfire, even with streets so deserted that it made Charlotte feel like a ghost town.

For the past two days he knew he could count on one hand the number of people he'd seen while out and about on his rounds. Obviously one of them was Marcus because he was helping to collect bodies. But the three or four others had been slinking around town looking like bandits in their masks, running away from him like he had the plague.

He snorted when he realized what he'd just thought. 'Like the plague.' Very appropriate considering the circumstances.

Sitting in the pew in the front row of the dark and chilly church, he stared at the stained glass window behind the pulpit. Even though the light coming through was faint, the cross, a centuries old symbol of hope, was clearly visible. But for the first time in so long that he couldn't remember the last time, Colby didn't feel that hope anywhere inside him. Just fear and uncertainty.

He'd been praying about this for weeks. Mostly for everyone in the countries the newspaper wrote about. And then for Americans on the east coast. Like most other people he supposed he never believed the influenza would make it this far. Or didn't *want* to believe it. He still didn't want to.

With a sigh, he got to his feet. It was time to head over to Marcus.' He knew it wouldn't do much good, but he sincerely hoped they wouldn't find more than the two bodies he'd seen laid out on the porches he'd passed earlier.

It had been one of the hardest things he'd ever done yesterday, helping Marcus pick them up. Seeing the family members standing at the windows, clutching at draperies and one another, sobbing helplessly because, if they wanted their loved ones to have a proper burial, they were forced to remain inside. He couldn't imagine how difficult it would be to see your loved one carted off like so much garbage and then tossed in the back of a wagon.

Not that that's what they did, of course. They treated the bodies with the utmost respect but still, that's what it must have seemed like to everyone watching them.

As he closed the door behind him, Colby looked up to the heavens and prayed that this awful *plague* would soon leave Charlotte. That no more lives would be lost because of it. But he was afraid, even as the words passed through his lips, that countless more would die as the Spanish influenza ran its course.

~~~

Elliot wanted to hit something as he stood at the stove stirring a pot of soup. His daughter was sick,
~~~

and getting sicker. His wife refused to leave her bedside, even though she stood a greater risk of contracting the influenza than anyone else in the house. Arguing had gotten him nowhere, so there she stayed.

And it wasn't that he blamed her. He didn't like being away from Elizabeth for even a minute. It had taken all the courage he could muster to leave her long enough to open a few cans and pour them into a pan to heat. It had been all they could do to get sips of water into her, though they had encouraged her to drink throughout the day. And so they hoped that the broth might sound better to her, its warmth soothing her raw throat.

The other children needed to eat, too, in order to keep their strength up. He knew Richard had given them sandwiches and milk at some point during the afternoon, but he didn't know enough about cooking to do anything for supper. Not that warming canned soup could be called cooking, but it would have to do for the moment.

Oh he hated this. Since the moment he'd married Meg she, and then their children, had become his reason for living. All he wanted was to provide for them, take care of them, and protect them from anything that might ever hurt them.

He didn't know how to protect them from this though. Everything he'd tried had failed. And he'd done everything the public health officials recommended and more. In spite of it all, his daughter lay upstairs fighting for her life.

He reached up to take some bowls from the cupboard when he thought he heard muffled coughing coming from somewhere near the kitchen. He could hardly breathe as he lowered his arms slowly to his side, listening carefully and praying that it was something else.

But there it was again. Pain seemed to race from the top of his head to the soles of his feet before he took that first reluctant step toward where it seemed to be coming from. Behind the door to the cellar. His hand shook as he turned the doorknob because he already knew what – *who* – he was going to find down there.

Jonathon sat on the floor in a shadowed corner, leaning against the wall and barely able to stay upright. Even in the dim light Elliot could see that his cheeks were flushed and he wanted to cry out, to scream at how unfair this was. *Two* of his children?

"Jonathon?" he whispered, squatting down and laying his palm against his son's cheek. He was burning up.

"Hiya, Pop," he said weakly, trying to smile but failing miserably.

"Why didn't you tell someone, son?"

"I'm not sick," he denied without much conviction. "Just tired."

"Come here," Elliot groaned, pulling him into his arms and holding him close for several long moments. He kissed the top of his head as tears rolled down his face. He loved this boy so much. Loved every one of his children more than he could ever say, and he prayed with everything in him for God to spare them all.

And then, as gently as he could, he lifted Jonathon and carried him up to the main floor. As he walked past the parlor he heard Richard inhale sharply and glanced up to see his eldest son ghostly white. Elliot wished he could assure him that everything would be just fine. But he couldn't.

"Keep Charles and Kathleen down here," he murmured, looking away before his oldest son could see the tears in his eyes. "There's a pot of soup on the stove. And, Richard, please call Dr. Garland. Hurry."

~~~

Marcus stood in the doorway of his store room shaking his head in denial. Nineteen caskets left from the thirty-five he'd ordered such a short time ago. In five days sixteen people had lost their lives to this cursed virus. And those were just the ones he had been called about. The others were reporting fewer, but the death toll was more than fifty now.

The fact that scared him the most is that they weren't even a week into this. It didn't just scare him, he realized, it terrified him. Would they have to resort to using mass graves like so many other areas had done? It went against everything he'd learned throughout his life, first from his father, and then in the years since he'd taken over.

He wished he hadn't thought about his parents. They were so far away and he worried about them constantly. He prayed they took his warnings seriously. Most of the operators weren't working, either because they were sick, taking care of sick family members, or just plain afraid and refused to leave their homes, but a couple of women were still
~~~

manning the board. Marcus had finally gotten through to his mother late the night before.

He told them to stock up on food enough to last a few weeks and stay inside with their windows and doors closed. To not go outside no matter what. But he knew they wouldn't. It was too hot out there to close their house up like a tomb. That's exactly what it would become if they followed his advice.

With a determined effort he looked at the stacks of ugly pine boxes again. There weren't enough. There just weren't. He supposed it was time to put in a telephone call to the mayor, and hope it didn't take all day to do it. They needed to implement a plan for when the caskets were gone. They should have done that before, but who could ever have known it would be this bad?

Locking the door he walked wearily to the back porch and sank down on the steps, burying his face in his hands. Was it just a month ago that he'd thought this was the best year of his life? He still wasn't entirely comfortable around other people, but everywhere he'd gone, after their team won the season, men would clap him on the back and encourage him to try out for the Detroit Tigers.

And ladies had actually looked at him like he was something special. Not that it made much difference. He still hadn't been able to do more than stammer and stutter when they tried to talk to him. But he'd begun to hope that he might get better at it and maybe, finally, work up the courage to court one of them.

The best year of his life had quickly turned into the worst. Former glories, fleeting as they might have been, didn't mean a whole lot today. Not when he thought about the list lying on his desk. Four more names had been added to it this morning. Who knew how many more he would have to write down before Colby came?

Marcus had never wanted to run away from home when he was growing up. No, his parents had been wonderful and he loved his life, as much as a painfully shy young man could love anything. So running away had never even crossed his mind. Until this week. Only there was nowhere to run to. The influenza was everywhere. There was no escaping its reach.

~~~

The air was stagnant, the smell of sickness thick and heavy as Elliot dipped a cloth into the cool basin of water. He wasn't sure how many times he'd repeated the action, or how many more times he would continue to do so. She was too sick, he thought as he squeezed the excess water from the rag.

It struck him that other than the sound of Elizabeth's labored breaths, and Jonathon's painful coughing and cries from across the hall, the tinkle of that water as it dribbled back into the bowl was the only thing that broke the silence in the dimly lit room. In the entire house it seemed.

He couldn't recall a time when his home had been so quiet, except when the family was slumbering at night. It was broad daylight now. There should be laughter, the sound of awful piano
~~~

music offending every ear in hearing distance. Charles or Jonathon running from one end of the house to the other. *Something* other than this cursed silence.

Fear threatened to choke him as he gently wiped the damp cloth across his daughter's brow, down her neck and then her arms. And then he started over again.

The vicious monster influenza that inflicted his babies with the high fever and painful cough was a terrifying thing. Daily the papers told of the thousands of deaths it had already caused. Tens of thousands, in fact. Just in America. But death would not strike in this place, he vowed, willing his children the strength to fight against its powerful grip. If love alone could heal them, they would have bounded out of their beds in that moment.

But Elizabeth only lay there, looking fragile and small against the pillow. And pale. So pale, much as her brother had looked when he and Meg traded places a short while ago. He drew in a long breath, letting it out slowly, and dipped the cloth into the basin again.

She was hot, her skin flushed as though she'd stayed too long near a roaring fire. Heat radiated from her and Elliot hurt at her suffering.

Even though the past year had been difficult with the change in her attitude and her enthusiasm for the Suffrage Movement, his love for her had never waned. Now it welled up within him as he sat there, on the edge of her bed, trying in vain to make the fever leave her.

"Please, God," he prayed fervently, leaning

down to place a light kiss against her hair. “Let her live. Let Jonathon be all right. God, *please*.”

She’d had the influenza once before, he remembered. When she’d been not much older than Kathleen was now. Just a few days of a relatively mild illness. Back then he’d been concerned, as any parent would be. But he hadn’t felt this crushing fear. That sickness hadn’t been a real threat to the life of his sweet girl.

This threat was all too real.

He pushed those thoughts away and plunged the cloth back into the water with more force than he’d intended. A small wave washed over the side and onto the bedside tabletop. He didn’t care, or even much notice, his attention fully on Elizabeth as another fit of coughing seized her.

A sob escaped him as he pulled her into his arms, hoping to ease the severity of it. She’d coughed so hard and so often since sometime the previous morning that it was torture to watch her suffering – and to be so utterly helpless to stop it. All he could do to help was to hold her as she fought to expel the fluid from her lungs. And watch her trying to breathe. That was the worst. Listening to her struggle to draw each breath.

By the time the spasm ended, she’d collapsed against him and he held her close, feeling the dampness of her skin from the exertion. Feeling the rage well up again, he wanted to hurt something. To *kill* something. Instead he just held his daughter.

“Papa?” she whispered, lacking the strength to speak aloud.

“Yes, Darling?” Reluctantly he laid her back

against the pillow and resumed wiping her face with the cool cloth.

"Where's Mama?"

"Tending Jonathon."

"Jonathon?" she gasped, her eyes wide with alarm. "Please tell me he's not ill!"

"Just a bit," Elliot said evasively. She needed to concentrate on getting well herself, not on her brother laying in much the same condition down the hall.

"*Oh no.* Oh God, please no!" Fear had lit her eyes before but terror replaced it now that she realized that her brother, too, was at the mercy of this ruthless virus.

"Shh," he soothed, gently smoothing her hair. "Jonathon is going to be fine. I was with him just a while ago. And he's going to be all right. You're *both* going to be just fine."

"But he's so little-" Tears spilled down her cheeks. "I'm so scared, Papa."

"Elizabeth-"

"I don't want to die." Elliot was taken by surprise at the fury that exploded in his chest when he heard the words he couldn't even bear to consider.

"*No one is going to die*," he said harshly. "Do you hear me? *No one* is going to die!"

"But-"

"No. I won't let anything hurt you," he promised softly. "Haven't I always taken care of you?"

"Yes, Papa," she murmured, a slight smile curving her dry, cracked lips. As though weighted, her eyelids began to close. "I'm so tired-"

"Then rest, my darling. Rest and get well."

He cupped her face with his hands and wiped the traces of the tears that had dried swiftly from the heat of her skin, and placed another kiss against her brow.

"I love you, Papa," she murmured just before sleep overtook her again.

"I love you, Elizabeth."

As the words left his mouth he had to resist the urge to wake her long enough to repeat them. Because she hadn't heard him and he needed her to hear it. So she knew, beyond a shadow of a doubt, how much he loved her. Just in case-

He began to pray harder than he'd ever prayed in his life.

Chapter 15

Colby dressed warmly, buttoning his coat clear to his neck. If yesterday was anything to judge by, there would be a chill in the air again today. The same chill that had seeped into his bones and stayed firmly put no matter how hard he tried to get warm. Less than a week ago the days had been very pleasant, but the temperatures had dropped steadily until it seemed that winter might make an early appearance. Had it been as cold this time last year, or was he just getting old? Feeling it more than he had in his younger years?

Maybe he was too tired, even though he knew he was sleeping more than usual. By the time he crawled under the covers since the influenza had come to town, he was so exhausted that he was falling asleep faster than ever before. Oh how he longed to return to the bed he'd so reluctantly left behind a short while ago – and not come out again until this nightmare was over.

Instead he walked purposefully to the kitchen for a sip of coffee before he had to leave. And he knew he had to go. So many people needed him that there was no choice.

Anna sat at the table, a scowl of disapproval aimed his way but, as had become customary, he didn't quite meet her eyes. He didn't want to see the hatred and anger there. Didn't want to see the fear that he might, today, bring the dreaded killer home with him. She seemed to feel that his duties as a minister of the gospel should begin and end with his Sunday morning sermons.

She was wrong.

Trying to keep a normal tone in his voice he informed her that he would try to be home for the mid – day meal. If not then, possibly for supper. Though he couldn't make any promises for he didn't know what he might find waiting for him. He chose his words carefully, neglecting to mention the death he would greet him in too many homes. This sort of news terrified her, and only served to feed her anger.

This past week or so she'd been more hateful to him than at any time during their marriage – and she'd been very hateful for most of it, so he found her silence this morning a refreshing change of pace.

Mumbling a vague goodbye, he let himself out the back door, closing it quietly behind him. The crisp October wind hit him full force and he reached up to hold his collar close, wishing he'd opted for his heavier winter coat.

Pausing at the bottom step, Colby donned the white mask he would never grow used to wearing. The way it covered his nose and mouth reminded him of stories from the Wild West, a time when outlaws wore kerchiefs tied over their faces to conceal their identity.

He would have made a poor bandit, he decided, his steps taking him along the walk that ran in front of the house. The mask made him feel claustrophobic. A complaint he'd heard mumbled from others he talked to the day after the town meeting, before everyone had closed themselves up in their houses.

This mask wasn't meant to hide identities, though. And no matter how uncomfortable it might be, it was a necessary evil.

Not that it made a whole lot of difference. The influenza struck down those it would, regardless of even the most meticulous measures taken to prevent its spread. The dozens of bedsides he'd knelt at to pray was proof enough of that.

Wearily he wiped a gloved hand over his brow and made his way down the deserted street. Except for an occasional flutter of curtains as vigilant inhabitants kept guard against unwelcome intruders, nothing stirred for as far as he could see.

An eerie feeling came over him. The wind howling through the trees, bits and pieces of paper and other debris blowing here and there – and not a soul in sight. Almost as though he were the lone survivor of some horrific disaster that had wiped mankind from the face of the earth. His stomach rebelled at the thought and he fought a wave of nausea as his steps quickened.

His first destination would be the church. He felt the need for some time alone to pray before facing the frightened faces of his parishioners. Like Anna they, too, feared he might bring the sickness with him, though he never went near the homes that didn't have a black flag on the porch. No flag meant no influenza. Yet. Those were the houses he preferred. The ones where he wasn't needed.

Not like the others, where family members were ill. Dying. Wanting assurances that they would spend eternity in heaven. Most would, he was sure. And where there was doubt, he reminded them of the way to get there. Some, he knew, were there now who a week ago would have missed out.

The worst, though, were the situations where it was obvious, to his eyes anyway, that the victim wouldn't be granted entrance at the pearly gates. And even in such tragic circumstances, he couldn't lie to the surviving family and say things would be all right. Instead he would suggest that, at the end of life, people tended to see beyond this world and make things right between themselves and God. And like the families he tried to comfort, he hoped it was true.

His path took him past Marcus' house and an involuntary shudder passed through him. He'd helped him collect far too many bodies, and performed more funerals in the past week than he normally did in two years' time.

"Why?" a young mother had wept the day

before, clutching the still form of her two year old to her bosom. How, when she'd prayed and believed for a miracle?

How many other mothers, other fathers, husbands, wives and children had asked the same question? How many more times would he have to say that God had a good reason, even if they didn't understand it now?

He wished he could understand how God could allow the deaths of thousands, no, hundreds of thousands of people. Was this it? The end of the world? One of the plagues foretold of in Revelation? The beginning of the end?

Somehow, though he'd been paying little attention, Colby found himself standing at the door of his church. Feeling older than Methuselah, he turned the knob and let himself in.

The stained glass allowed very little of the gray light inside and, even though the sanctuary was filled with eerie shadows, Colby made his way to the altar. He knew this place as he knew no other, and could find his way around blindfolded if need be.

"What!" he exclaimed. As he neared the pulpit, one of the shadows moved and he started violently. "Who is it?" he demanded, a tremor in his voice. The figure rose slowly.

"It's me, Reverend Thornton," a soft voice spoke. "Nina Pullman."

"Goodness, Nina, you gave me a fright!" He laughed shakily and pressed a hand to his chest.

"I'm sorry," she apologized, sounding tired. "I needed a place to pray."

"Me, too." As he neared he saw that her face

was flushed and he knew. "Would you like me to pray with you?" he asked softly, taking one of her too warm hands in both of his. She looked at him tearfully and nodded.

"Please." Her face crumpled and she almost choked on a sob. "Reverend Thornton?"

"Nina?"

"I'm so scared," she whispered. "I don't want to die."

~~~

"When you and Elizabeth are feeling better," Mother was saying as she wrapped an arm around his shoulders, helping him to sit up for a sip of water, "I'll have your father go out to the lake and get some ice, and then we'll make ice cream."

"It's not summer anymore," Jonathon croaked, his voice nearly gone from all of the coughing he'd done since he'd realized he was sick this morning.

"Who said it had to be summer to have ice cream?" she asked, easing him back against the pillows. She quickly wrung the cloth out in the bowl that sat on the table beside his bed and resumed the gentle wipes across his face, neck, arms and bare chest.

"Ice cream sounds good," he whispered.

It would feel good right now, too. His throat felt raw and he didn't want to cough anymore. But hard as he tried not to, it wouldn't stop. Sometimes, like now, it was better, then it would get so it was hard to breathe and it would start all over. He remembered the day that Steven and Tommy beat him up when
~~~

he tried to get Kathleen's doll back, how he felt afterward. He hurt worse now. A lot worse. Like a hundred boys had been beating him for a week.

"In a few days, when the influenza is gone, we'll have a party to celebrate," she continued, trying to make her voice cheerful. Jonathon could tell she wasn't though. She was scared, same as him. "It will just be us, but we'll have cake and ice cream. Then, before you know it, Thanksgiving will be here and we'll have forgotten all about this. You'll be out sledding and skating."

"Not in November. Ice will be too thin," he said, beginning to gasp. It was going to happen again. Mother knew it, too, because her voice began to shake a little.

"We sure don't want you on thin ice, do we? I think one time in freezing water is enough for anyone."

And then it started. The horrible coughing, so hard he could hardly catch his breath. He curled into a ball and wrapped his arms around his ribs, hoping that would help. It had for the first few hours, but now nothing helped at all. Except that Pop or Mother would hold him until it passed.

"Shh, shh," Mother wept, wrapping her arms around him tightly. "It's going to be all right. Shh."

She had been crying a lot and he wondered, vaguely, where the tears kept coming from. It seemed like she would have to run out by now, but they kept coming. When she changed rooms to spend time with Elizabeth, he could tell that Pop wanted to cry, too. But even though he could see tears in his eyes sometimes, they didn't fall very much. He guessed that men didn't make as many as women did.

When the coughing finally ended she raised him up for another drink. He'd just taken one swallow when the door to his room opened and Pop came in – carrying Charles. Mother looked up and Jonathon was afraid she might be sick, right there on the floor beside his bed. But he knew how she felt because he wanted to be sick, too.

"No, Elliot. *No!*" she moaned, crying even more as she hurried to take Charles from him. Pop was crying, too. Maybe men did make as many tears after all.

~~~

"Nina, we're going to have to get you home. It's cold this morning and you shouldn't be out," Colby said, helping her to sit in the front pew.

He knelt before her and prayed more fervently than he had in his life – and this week he'd sent up some pretty fervent prayers. When he finished he stood and told her to stay put while he went home and hitched up the buggy.

"Thank you," she whispered, beginning to weep. He reached in his coat and pulled out a handkerchief.

"I'll be right back."

As exhausted as he was, Colby ran fast as he could for the small barn behind the house. Much as Anna coveted an automobile, she'd been unwilling to curb her demands for other costly things and his salary only went so far. But he was very grateful for
~~~

their horse. Never more so than this moment.

"Please, Lord, not her," he prayed, jumping out of the buggy to close the barn door. "Not her! She and Daniel have just found each other and they're so happy. I know that heaven is a wonderful place, but let them have a little heaven here on earth first."

In short order he'd settled her on the seat and was tucking three quilts around her snugly. For a change he was glad that Anna hated the cold and insisted on keeping a pile folded under the seat.

"Does Daniel know you came to the church?" he asked, snapping the reins. Elijah took off at a slow trot.

"No. He was sleeping. I- I was afraid to tell him," she admitted, dropping her chin to look at her lap.

"Do you want me to go in with you when we get to your house?"

"Would you? He's going to be upset."

"Of course he will be. He loves you, Nina." He reached over to pat her hand. "I'll telephone the doctor while he gets you settled, and then I'll be back later with some soup."

"I was going to make soup," Nina whispered, beginning to cry again.

"For the sick?"

"Yes."

The mayor had called on those who hadn't been afflicted with the influenza to help where they could, and many stepped up to do just that. Countless women were, at this very moment, making huge pots of soup to fill Mason jars. This afternoon he and other volunteers would pick them up and deliver them to the porches of homes where families were sick. George Densteadt had asked residents to hang a white sheet on the porch if even one person in the home had been stricken with the flu.

The grocers and butchers were supplying all of the ingredients and jars. Some were donating what fresh fruit remained in their stockrooms. Even the pharmacists were doing all they could to help, offering cases of aspirin and cough remedies to be given to anyone who needed them.

Never had Colby been so proud of his fellow citizens. But he wished more than anything that they didn't need to be so unutterably generous.

~~~

"Papa?"

If Elliot hadn't been sitting on the bed he doubted he'd have heard her weak voice. He leaned close and felt the heat radiating from her. Reaching out, he brushed his fingers against her cheek. It didn't seem possible but the fever seemed to have risen even more.

"What, Sweetheart?"

"Where's Mama?"

"She's- I'm not sure," he hedged, not wanting to admit that she was tending the boys.

"I need to talk to you both," she told him, the effort to speak visibly tiring her.

"You should be resting," he said gently.

"Please, Poppy?"

Poppy.

His heart constricted painfully as he remembered. It seemed only yesterday when a
~~~

golden – haired baby girl had toddled up to him, a smile guaranteed to melt the coldest of hearts lighting her face, calling for her Poppy.

"I'll get her," Elliot whispered. The bed springs creaked as he rose and strode quickly to the doorway so she couldn't see his tears. "Margaret," he called out, "could you come here for a moment?"

He watched his wife scurry out of the boys' room, her face so white it scared him. Elliot realized she was thinking the worst and wasted no time in saying,

"Elizabeth wants to talk with us."

He caught her as her knees buckled and held her tightly. Did he look as haggard as she did? Neither had been able to sleep more than a snatch here and another there for the past two days. It seemed like so much longer ago that.

"She's waiting, Meg," he said quietly, taking her hand and feeling a small measure of comfort.

Margaret eased onto the bed and leaned down to place a kiss on her daughter's cheek. Watching, Elliot felt utterly useless. He couldn't ease his children's pain nor his wife's fear. He wished he could ease his own as he sat carefully behind his wife and took Elizabeth's frail hand in his own.

"Mama?"

"What is it, Darling?"

"I'm so sorry," Elizabeth said, her voice faint.

"For what?" Elliot asked.

"For being so horrible to everyone." A fit of coughing seized her and Margaret drew her into her arms until it passed. Elliot wrapped his around both of them, wishing he could do something as feeble sobs mingled with the violent coughs that racked her body until, finally, she lay limply against her mother's breast. It was several long moments before she was able to speak again, only to repeat,

"I'm so sorry."

"It's all right," Elliot assured her. The last thing he wanted was for her to be worried about silly adolescent moodiness.

"I hurt you both."

"We've forgotten all about it. I won't give it another thought. Neither will your father," was Meg's tender reply.

"It's forgotten," Elliot echoed, stroking her hair. She seemed to relax a bit.

For a while they sat there together and Elliot wished he could freeze this moment in time. To let it never end and, perhaps, rid himself of the awful fear that had taken root in the pit of his stomach.

"Will I go to hell?" came the fearfully voiced question.

"*Elizabeth!*" Margaret gasped, holding her closer.

"*No!*" Elliot exclaimed forcefully, the hand against her hair trembling. "You're not going to die. Not for a long, long time. And when you do, you'll be going straight to heaven."

"But what if I do? Die, I mean," she persisted. "I wouldn't pray. I didn't want to go to church-"

"You listen to me," Margaret said firmly. "You *listen.* You were going through a very confusing time, Sweetheart. God understands that."

"But what if He's mad at me?" Margaret began to rock her back and forth gently.

"Remember the story of the prodigal son? His father forgave him and God will forgive you if you ask Him to. As long as you believe that Jesus is your Savior, Elizabeth, you're going to heaven. But not for a long, long time – like your father said. Do you understand me? Not for a long time."

~~~

Marcus wandered around the now empty storeroom, his steps slow and labored. Thirty-six pine boxes. Plus seven nice ones. Mahogany, walnut, and another made of very costly metal.

Forty-three people. *Forty-three.* And he didn't know how many more would be waiting for him when he went out today. Too many. There had already too many but it didn't stop them from dying. They just kept *dying*.

He leaned his forehead against the wall, pressing a fist against his mouth as he began to sob.

He didn't know what to do anymore. He'd tried calling Derek, had been trying for two days but he never got an answer. If things were this bad in Philadelphia, with so very many more people, he imagined that his friend was being run ragged. He knew he and his fellow funeral directors could barely keep up with Charlotte's population, diminutive by comparison.

But it wasn't going to be as laborious now. When Colby finished delivering food to the sick this afternoon, their jobs would be a little easier. With no more caskets to be had anywhere in town, and the
~~~

mayor loathe to consider mass graves, all bodies were being delivered to the ice house behind Zourdos and Spires. He was determined that there they would stay until the threat had passed and construction could begin on dozens of crates. Not even pine boxes, just crates, the easiest and quickest way to give the victims proper burials.

Before *this*, Marcus would never have considered that a ‘proper’ burial. But given the alternative, it was the better choice.

Chapter 16

Margaret Owens rarely allowed her voice to rise above the gentle tone befitting a lady. Even raising five children made little difference. An expression of disappointment on her sweet face accomplished far more than the volume with which the reprimand was spoken.

That wasn't to say she didn't have her moments. Like the time Jonathon fell out of a tree at the home of the family they had been visiting out at Pine Lake. She not only shouted for help, but shouted so loudly that everyone within a quarter mile had heard, much to her distress.

No, Margaret Owens didn't often raise her voice. But she did this late, overcast morning. One single word.

"*Elizabeth!*"

The anguish in the cry was heard by each member of the household and, for a brief moment, all activity ceased.

Elliot, fixing a tray with bowls of broth for Elizabeth and the boys, held a ladle in midair. Richard froze in his tracks, an armful of wood momentarily forgotten. Kathleen, reading softly to herself, stilled and looked toward the stairway.

Even Jonathon, dozing fitfully as the influenza induced fever ravaged his weakened body, woke and was lucid enough to realize that something was wrong. Terribly wrong. Charles managed to look at him, barely able to turn his head where it lay on the pillow, fear in his eyes.

Because Margaret Owens only shouted when something was truly wrong.

When her sobs filled every corner of the house, terror filled five pairs of eyes and Elliot finally moved, dropping the ladle with a clatter. Murmuring a numb, "stay here" to no one in particular, his reluctant feet led him to, and quickly up the stairs.

He didn't hear the soft footsteps padding behind him. Only the wild sobs of his wife.

Nausea gripped him as he neared the bedroom and he had an insane desire to turn right around and run. Run until he could run no more. Until he could return home to find this had all been a dream. A nightmare.

He reached out a hand that shook, grasped the door jam and literally pulled himself into the room.

Margaret sat on the bed, Elizabeth's still body clutched in her arms. She rocked their daughter frantically, stroking her hair as she wept.

Elliot knew he should cross the room. Try to do something to comfort her. But he couldn't move. Could only stand there and stare in horror while the reality of the scene before him sank in.

And when it did, pain such as he'd never known hit him like a physical blow. He wrapped his arms around his stomach as the agony spread to his heart, his head, his face, even his fingernails.

Tears stung his eyes, spilling over and rolling down his cheeks. In the far recesses of his mind, in the place where all good memories were kept safe, the past sixteen years rolled by like a moving picture.

A red – faced, squalling infant, moments after birth, howling her way into the world, and the pride he'd felt as he nervously held his baby girl for the first time.

A beautiful, toothless grin directed at him that had him grinning from ear to ear, filling him with pure delight. Her first, wobbly steps toddling toward Poppy's outstretched arms. How she'd cried the first day of school, gripping his hand like a vice.

So many sweet memories crowding in, one after another, reminding him of happier times, even as his eyes took in the horror before him. His heartbroken wife clutching the forever still form of his precious darling.

Elliot had always felt a tremendous sense of pride in his ability to take care of his family. Now everything was spinning wildly out of his control and an awful feeling of helplessness warred with his pain.

As his knees gave way, an awful sound filled his

ears. Something between a scream and a deep, gut wrenching groan, followed by out of control sobs. It was only when he hit the floor that he realized the sounds were coming from him.

Richard and Kathleen stood silently behind him, tears coursing down their cheeks, landing silently on the carpet on which they stood. Even Jonathon had managed to drag himself out of bed and stagger down the hall, now supported by Richard who immediately wrapped his arms protectively around his brother.

Their eyes met, each with an unspoken question reflected in their depths. Would Jonathon be next? Charles?

~~~

Every muscle in Colby's body ached and he groaned as he lifted yet another wooden crate filled with canning jars of soup. The ladies from all the churches in town who hadn't yet succumbed to the influenza were generously supplying the food to the families who had. And there were so many families. Forty-two on his list alone. He didn't even want to know how many his fellow ministers had on theirs.

They would, as he had already done, pick up boxes of oranges from the grocers to deliver with the soup. It seemed like pitifully little to do for the families, but the doctors and nurses kept them supplied with aspirin powders and other medicines. Not that it seemed to be doing a lot of good. People just continued getting sick. And dying. So many had died.
~~~

He climbed into his wagon and wearily rubbed a hand across his jaw. He, himself, had officiated twenty-three funerals this week alone. Many from his own congregation.

His eyes burned with tears when he thought about Elizabeth Owens. Of her father standing alone at her grave because he feared exposing Richard and Kathleen. Of her mother, Margaret, who dared not risk leaving Jonathon and Charles alone. Not even to bury her beloved daughter. He prayed often that the good Lord would spare that family, but most especially Jonathon. He couldn't begin to contemplate a world without that young man and his vivid, wonderful imagination.

"Enough of that," he admonished himself. There was work to be done. People depended on him to do his job and so he couldn't give in to his grief. Not yet.

Two houses down he stopped for another crate, then delivered food to the next four. Another pick up, followed by several more drop offs.

In the three blocks he'd gone so far, he had seen seven covered bodies lying on porches, waiting for the wagons. There were only four being sent around Charlotte, and so many to take care of that it could be hours before they might be picked up. Marcus, he knew, had begun working from sunup until sundown the past few days. Several volunteer firemen had finally offered to help, for which everyone was grateful. Nevertheless, there were too many people working too many hours, doctors, nurses and every veterinarian in the county. A few men were working at the lumber yard, but many more were too sick to help out. There just weren't enough healthy, able bodied adults to keep up with the need.

Even though he'd had some warning, and ordered all he could afford, Marcus had run out of caskets less than a week after the first case of influenza had been discovered. Now it was simply a race between death and the woodworkers. They weren't even bothering to shape them anymore. Just oblong boxes built as quickly as possible. Even so, the ice house downtown was being used to store a staggering number of bodies.

Earlier in the year someone had asked him if this was what had been foretold of in Revelation. Colby had even preached a sermon on it, assuring everyone that the war wasn't the beginning of the end of the world. But that was before they'd known about the epidemic.

Could he have been wrong?

~~~

Daniel sat at his bride's bedside praying for the countless time that God might spare her life, even as the influenza waged a mighty war against her. A war it seemed to be winning, stealing her strength in a matter of hours. Weakening her so completely that she had been unable to fight off the pneumonia that had settled deep in her lungs.

He squeezed the excess water from the cloth, as he'd done hundreds of times. Or was it thousands? He'd lost track.

It had begun to feel as though a lifetime had
~~~

been lived in this room, listening to the shallow, labored breaths from the small form beneath the sheets. As though all eternity would be spent here, fear overwhelming him in wave after excruciating wave.

Gently, he wiped it across her brow. Down her temple, her cheek, her jaw. Starting over on the other side of her beautiful, flushed face.

So beautiful.

It never ceased to amaze him that Nina loved him. A gift that surpassed any he'd ever received, or could ever receive. One he'd hoped to cherish for decades to come.

God knew this. Surely He wouldn't take her away. Not now. Not this soon. Of course He wouldn't! Daniel forced the thought from his mind, unable to entertain even the remotest possibility that it could happen.

He plunged the cloth back into the bowl.

"It's going to be all right," he promised, his voice barely above a whisper.

Tears filled his eyes as he reached out his other hand to brush the hair from her face. Her skin was so hot he could feel the heat from it before his fingers actually touched her. And that's all he wanted to do. Just touch her. To somehow lend her some of his strength so she could fight her way back to health. Back to him.

~~~

"I can't do this anymore, Colby."

Marcus had pulled the wagon over near a
~~~

vacant field and began to sob. It seemed like that's all he'd done for days now. He prayed all the time that it would stop. That the influenza would go away but it just kept getting worse. He was afraid that Derek had been right when he said that God might not even be powerful enough to stop it.

"I know," Colby sighed, rubbing his back as his friend bent over his knees. "It's getting harder every day."

"They're all dying. I'm afraid everyone is going to die. And I don't want to see it anymore."

"I don't believe everyone is going to die. I *won't* believe that."

"The ice house is almost full. It's not right, Colby. Bodies stacked like that? Like bricks or boxes, almost to the ceiling. Where will we put them when we can't get any more in there?"

"I don't know, my friend. Maybe in some of the private ice houses outside of town. I don't know."

"Mass graves is what's going to happen. Instead of a decent burial, they're going to be thrown in big holes and – I can't do it. It's wrong. It's just so wrong!"

Marcus knew that his friend didn't know what to say to that, but he continued to rub his back, trying to comfort him. But there was no comfort to be had now. No one in the world could have been prepared for a disaster of this magnitude and everything was spiraling out of control.

The mayor wasn't even answering his telephone now. No one knew if he was actually sick, or if he just couldn't handle the pressure anymore. Not that Marcus would blame him if that were the case. He didn't know what he might do if everyone in the city expected him to figure out solutions to problems that there were no solutions for.

Except the one that no one wanted to accept. Even if he didn't make his living in the funeral business, Marcus would have a hard time handling the thought of people being buried in mass graves. He couldn't even begin to imagine how the families of the victims might react to *that*.

A few men in town, when their wives or children had died, were so appalled at the thought of their bodies being stacked in the ice house that they asked Marcus to return the next day. They had torn down shelves and broken apart chests of drawers and tables to build crude boxes in which to bury their loved ones.

Elliot Owens had done the same thing, with the help of his oldest son, when his daughter died two days ago.

It wasn't right. A father and brother shouldn't have to do that. But he understood that the alternative wasn't acceptable.

"It's hard for everyone," Colby was saying gently. "We're needed, Marcus. Desperately. What will they do if we stop helping? They're suffering so much already. We can't do anything that will make it harder for them. Can we?"

Marcus took a deep breath. And then another. Colby was right, as he usually was. It didn't make it any easier, but he supposed he'd needed to hear that. The last thing he wanted to do was hurt these people more. Somehow he would have to find the courage to do the right thing.

He just wished it wasn't so hard.

~~~

The sun, barely over the horizon, cast eerie shadows in even the deepest corners of the house. The little light that managed to peek through the closed draperies promised a bright autumn day.

A day to walk around town, wading through the crisp brown leaves that hadn't been blown away by the strong night's wind. A day to listen to children's laughter, to sit by the fire with a steaming cup of cocoa.

But it wasn't going to be that kind of a day. In fact, it was going to be the second worst day of Elliot's life.

Something about his slow steps descending the stairs must have alerted them because Richard and Kathleen were waiting in the hall before he'd gone even halfway. Kathleen had come only because her brother had, not fully understanding the impact the influenza had already had in their lives.

Richard, on the other hand, knew full well what the threat to their family meant and was looking at him, his expression a mixture of hope and fear. An expression that changed instantaneously when he saw the tears streaming down his father's face. So suddenly, in fact, that it was almost comical to watch. Elliot had an insane desire to laugh. But no sound came. Not even a whimper. He doubted he could utter the words. Not even if someone held a gun to his head and demanded he speak. If his lips parted even a little, he feared he might start
~~~

screaming. And never stop.

"Jonathon?" Richard finally asked hoarsely, though he clearly didn't want to know. Obvious in the way he'd wrapped his arms around his stomach, bracing himself against the blow he knew was coming.

Elliot could only shake his head and watch his son's face contort as the agony of realization washed over him.

"*Charles?*" he whispered in a disbelieving squeak.

Elliot nodded, just once, as another wave of pain cut at the gaping wound in his heart. Somehow, knowing that someone else knew made it more real. More horrible. Unbearable.

"*No!*"

The deep, anguished shout was unexpected, but the way Richard turned and bolted down the hall even more so. His footsteps echoed to the kitchen, paused, then resumed, following the resounding bang of the door against the jamb. He hesitated but a moment before hurrying the rest of the way down the stairs, stopping momentarily to rest his hands against Kathleen's hair.

"Stay here," he said tonelessly, before hurrying after Richard.

His head start only a brief one, Elliot was surprised to see that he had already crossed Krebs Court and was quite a distance into the field that ran behind the houses on Main Street. Running as though the devil himself were after him. As if he could escape the nightmare. But it wouldn't help. He couldn't run fast enough, or far enough because if he could, Elliot would follow him every step of the way.

As he was now, though he was gaining precious little ground. Vaguely he wondered if he would ever catch up. Wondered why he was even trying.

All he wanted to do was crawl into a safe, warm place and hide, maybe never to come out. Because here, in this cruel world, two children had been viciously stolen from him, a third lay waiting, his fate not yet decided. And Elliot didn't want to know because he couldn't bear anymore. He just couldn't.

Finally, as he approached Warren Street, Richard came to an abrupt stop, reaching down to rest his hands against his thighs. Even from the distance still separating them, Elliot could see his chest heaving as he gulped in great breaths of air, huffing out billowing clouds of steam.

It took another minute or so to reach him and he promptly collapsed against the trunk of the nearest tree, his lungs on fire, ready to burst as he gasped for air, doubting he would ever regain the ability to breathe normally. And not particularly caring if he did.

Quite a sight they made, neither able to stand fully erect, alone in a field in a city that appeared deserted, its inhabitants locked behind closed doors, hoping in vain to escape the ravages of the influenza. But it was a futile hope. Elliot knew that nothing would stop it. *Nothing*.

"Is Jonathon going to die, too?" Richard asked raggedly, glancing over at his father. His face was wet with tears.

Elliot looked at him for a long while, his silence

speaking the answer more clearly than any words ever could. Still he said,

"I don't know, son. I just don't know."

Slowly, as though time had nearly stopped, Richard dropped to his hands and knees, oblivious to the leaves and twigs snapping beneath his bare hands. The sobs that began deep in his belly and filled the air could probably heard a block away.

Elliot went to kneel beside him. He could offer little in the way of comfort because he hurt too deeply himself, so he just wrapped his arms around his son and held him.

He knew that they should go home. Knew that Meg needed him. That Kathleen probably needed comfort, too. He knew men couldn't just run away. And yet, knowing all of this, he didn't want to go back.

Home was no longer the haven it had been. Now it was a place filled with unimaginable horrors. Rooms echoing with silenced voices, filled with memories of his babies. It was a place where another sweet boy lay fighting for his life. A place where Elliot had become helpless to protect his family from danger.

Icy claws of fear closed around his heart and wouldn't let go. Rooted him to Richard's side. Not so much to comfort him but rather more because he couldn't bear what he might find when he returned home.

And so he knelt there, the sounds of his son's grief filling his ears, the cold numbing his flesh. Maybe if he waited long enough, it might numb him so completely that he would feel nothing at all.

Chapter 17

Colby wanted nothing more than to close his eyes and sleep for a week. He'd never been so utterly exhausted in his life. Ten days it had been now. Ten excruciatingly long days that he'd given everything he had to help as many people as he could. And now that he was confined to the house, whatever it was that had kept him going had deserted him so completely that he didn't know how he could go on. It fled the second Anna had come to him during the night and slapped him awake because she was sick.

"Come, Anna," Colby coaxed, holding a glass of cool water to her parched lips. "You're burning up. You need to drink this." He could feel the extreme heat from the fever through the thick tangle of hair as he tried to raise her head so she could take a sip.

"No, I don't want it!" she hissed, hitting it away

from her with enough force to knock it right out of his hand. It shattered against the floral paper on her bedroom wall, water and shards of glass raining down on the floor. "I don't want anything from *you*."

"Anna. How can you get better if you won't help me try to bring your fever down?"

"*Help me?* You *brought this to me!* I *begged* you not to go and visit all those sick people but *you*- You did it anyway! And then you brought it home to me!"

"If I did, I'm sorry," he soothed, leaning down to pick up the fragments, wiping the water up with one of the rags that lay on the bedside table. That done, he squeezed the water from the cloth in the bowl of water and gently wiped her face and neck. He didn't bother trying to explain to her that the influenza was making people sick who hadn't been in contact with anyone in more than a week. She wouldn't have believed him anyway.

Because he'd been in such close contact with so many other victims, he knew the fever would get bad but, because his visits had been brief, he hadn't realized the endless challenge involved in trying to keep the fever under control. It was getting to the point where he couldn't remember the last time the palms of his hands hadn't been wrinkled from constantly holding the wet cloth. Since Anna had taken ill the previous night it seemed that he'd been sitting at her side for an eternity. A long, miserable eternity. Not just because the tending to her needs was never ending, but mostly because in her waking, lucid moments, Anna complained endlessly, accusing him of making her sick. And her waking, lucid moments were many.

If he had inadvertently brought this illness home to her, he truly was sorry. He would never intentionally harm another human being. Not even the wife who, it seemed, despised him. And had almost from the moment the marriage ceremony had concluded, if her ramblings were anything to go by at any rate.

"I'm going to get you some broth," he said softly, replacing the cloth in the bowl. "You need nourishment, Anna."

"Why can't you just leave me alone?" she shrieked, her eyes filled with hatred. "I don't know why I thought you would make my life better. All you've done is make me *miserable*, and now you're *killing me!*"

"I'm only trying to help you, Anna. I'll be right back," was all he said, leaving the room as quickly as he could. On the way to the kitchen he prayed, "God, give me strength."

He also prayed for compassion but didn't feel it well up within him as he hoped it might. In all the homes he'd been in these past days, no 'patient' had been as bitter and hateful as his wife. Most seemed to spend the majority of their time resting or sleeping. Anna would have to be the exception. The one who seemed to gain some kind of energy from weakness.

Colby carefully took a china bowl from the cupboard, one of the ones with the rose pattern Anna so loved. Personally, he thought it was a little gaudy but it might cheer her.

After filling it with one ladleful of the chicken broth that had been simmering on the stove all day, he sat it on the counter and sank into a chair. Just a few moments peace and quiet wouldn't hurt. It might even do Anna a world of good. Without him in the room to complain about, she might get some much needed rest. Maybe the good Lord would have mercy on him and actually let her fall asleep for an hour or so.

"Please, Lord," he whispered, folding his arms on the tabletop and resting his head. He was so tired he wished he could sleep for a little while. Just a short nap. And maybe when he awoke, this nightmare would be over.

"Colby Thornton!" Like fingernails being dragged across a chalkboard, her voice cut through the silence, broken only by the harsh coughing he'd heard too often. "Help me, you good for nothing fool!"

He shot to his feet and dashed back into the bedroom, sitting on the edge of the bed she'd so seldom allowed him to share. As carefully as he could, he helped her to sit up, supporting her until the spasm ended.

Anna finally collapsed against his chest in a heap, her thin cotton gown soaked with perspiration. He laid her back against the pillow and, quickly as he could, retrieved a clean gown from her armoire in hopes she'd be more comfortable. He wished he could change the damp sheets but, even had he not been exhausted, he would need the help of at least one other person to move her enough to do so. Instead, he hurried back to the kitchen to get the broth.

"Open up, Anna. It's warm. "It'll help sooth your

throat," he encouraged, holding the spoon to her mouth. She stubbornly refused, turning her head away like a petulant child. "Anna, please."

"Go away," she snapped. "Let me die in peace."

"You're not going to die."

"Everyone else dies, why shouldn't I?"

"Not *everyone* else," he assured her. "Most people survive."

"I won't. Because you *want* me to die!"

"That's not true. You're just feeling bad because you're so ill."

"You want me to die because you hate me!"

"I do not hate you, Anna." Colby sighed deeply, sitting the bowl on the bedside table, and then reached to wring the cloth out again.

"Tell me you love me then. Tell me you want me to get well."

"Of course I want you to get well," he said, wiping her brow, reaching deep within himself to find even the smallest measure of love for her because it wasn't in him to lie. But lie he would have to do because it was no longer there. She'd killed it long ago. "And I do love you."

"You're a liar! You don't love me. You haven't for a long time."

"Anna, you need to rest now. Rest and get better." He wanted to reassure her that he did, in fact, love her, but the first lie was one too many. The first one tasted bitter enough without adding to it.

When it appeared that she finally slept, Colby sank into the arm chair he'd placed near the bed, wishing he could rest. Wishing he could turn the clock back to find the sweet tempered, lovely woman he'd married. Where had she gone, he wondered, tears filling his eyes.

~~~

Jonathon thought his eyes felt funny. They were sure seeing funny because everything looked very odd. Like things were moving back and forth, maybe like they were swaying in the wind. He wondered if it was because it was so hot. Which was odd because summer was over. Wasn't it? He tried to push the covers away but felt them being tucked snugly around him almost instantly.

"You don't want to catch a chill," he heard his father saying gently. "Maybe this will help."

Jonathon felt a damp, cool cloth being wiped across his face and thought it was one of the nicest things he'd ever felt. It made him wish he were sitting on the dam because the water there was always nice and cold.

"Elliot, lift him up a bit so I can give him a drink," his mother said from somewhere to his right. Ah, cool water. In a glass, not at the dam, but that was fine with him. He hadn't realized it until he swallowed but his mouth felt funny, too.

"More," he whispered, wondering why his voice didn't want to work.

"Not too fast," Pop cautioned as he drank greedily. "You don't want to choke."

Choke? And then Jonathon remembered. The influenza. Elizabeth had died. He and Charles were sick with it, too. They'd both coughed so much and so hard. No wonder his voice didn't work. His throat,
~~~

now that he thought about it, hurt really bad.

"Am I going to die?" he croaked painfully. Boy he sure didn't want to!

"No!" his parents gasped in unison.

"You're not going to die," Elliot assured him firmly.

"But -"

"You're not going to die," his mother told him, sounding just like she did when she meant business. "We won't let you."

"But if – I do, you have to watch Mr. Mertz."

"If you do, we'll watch him," his father said roughly. "But you're going to get well and can do it yourself."

"Okay. Can I have another drink? My throat is sore."

"I'm sure it is."

Oh but that felt good. He thought he might drink every drop of water there was in the world and never get enough.

"Is Charles better? I don't hear him crying anymore."

~~~

It felt as though someone had twisted a knife in his heart, Elliot thought as he fought against the tears his wife had lost the battle with. She could only shake her head when Jonathon asked about his brother before rushing out of the room. He didn't know if she meant for him to ignore the question, or to lie and tell him that his brother was fine. It wouldn't actually be a lie to tell him the latter
~~~

because Charles was in heaven now, no longer sick.

"Pop- Is Charles okay?" Jonathon asked again in a whisper that sounded as painful as it must feel.

"Charles is just fine," he said. "Don't you worry about him. Just worry about getting better. Do you hear me?"

"Yes, sir. Everything looks – funny."

"That's because you have a fever." A very high fever. They hadn't been able to bring it down more than a degree or so, even with the aspirin powder and wet cloths.

But, after three days, Jonathon was still here. Both Elizabeth and Charles had died within twenty – four hours of coming down with it. Surely that had to be a good sign. Please, God, let it be a good sign, he prayed, wringing the rag out again.

It seemed like that's all he'd been doing for four days now. Four days that felt like forty. He didn't think his hands would ever be the same again, but that was okay. As long as Jonathon got well. That's all he wanted now. That and to have Richard and Kathleen stay healthy. He didn't know what they'd do if those two got sick. He doubted that he'd gotten a full eight hours of sleep since Thursday night, and he knew Meg hadn't slept much more than that.

He worried about her, too. Constantly. With the baby due in less than seven weeks, this wasn't good for either of them. Not the fear, the grief, or the never – ending care she'd been giving to their children. He kept reminding her that expectant mothers were especially susceptible to the influenza, and fought against the fear that came with it nearly every second of every day.

So he kept praying, fervently, that Jonathon would get well and the rest of them would stay that way. Surely God would allow him that much.

~~~

Whump!

Marcus didn't need to look at the clock atop his dresser to know the time. Six a.m. And this paper would join the growing pile on the porch. The papers that had been delivered yesterday, the day before, and the day before that.

He couldn't read it anymore. Couldn't bear to see in print the names of the newest victims. Or those who would soon become victims.

Charles Owens and his homemade casket had been the final straw. He couldn't make arrangements for anyone else. There had been too many already.

Even now he could see Elliot Owens again standing there alone, staring at the graves of two of his children. Pain, disbelief, and shock distorting his face. And the fear. That awful fear.

A father who should be holding his babies, not burying them. Fear that the three that were left might be snatched from him as cruelly and quickly as these ones had been. Fear for the wife who should have been at his side but was at home caring for a third child, and carrying another.

Something in Marcus died as he stood there watching. He'd always known death was horrible. He just hadn't known how bad until the influenza
~~~

had come to town.

Walking home that day – could it have only been three days ago? – his steps had been slow, labored. And it was then that all feeling within him had ceased to exist. He'd walked into the house, locked the door and drawn all the drapes before walking up to his bedroom.

And there he'd stayed, but for trips to the outhouse, or to the kitchen for a simple meal. Persistent knocking at the door had been ignored. The telephone, which seemed to ring incessantly, had gone unanswered. No light, other than the few rays that managed to sneak in from behind the curtains lit the darkened rooms.

Marcus now lived in his nightshirt and dressing gown, spending nearly every waking minute in the leather arm chair beside his bed staring off into space. Trying to clear his mind of every thought that entered. Because when they did, it hurt too much.

~~~

"Today would have been our wedding day," Daniel murmured, sitting beside the bed, the wet rag in his hand too warm once again. He dipped it into the basin of water that would need to be changed very soon. "I'm sorry you didn't get to wear your pretty dress, or have your cake and flowers.

"It doesn't matter," Nina said weakly, struggling to keep her eyes focused on him. He smiled down at her, tears stinging his eyes.

"No, I don't suppose it does."

"I got the husband and that's the most important
~~~

part." Daniel tried to smile again but his lips started to tremble. He bit the bottom one until he knew he could control it.

"Well, when you're better, I'll buy you all the flowers you want. Anything you want."

"I only want you," she whispered. He could see she was losing the battle to keep her eyes open.

"Rest, Darling. I'll be right here."

She smiled again as her eyes closed. And he sat there. For hours. Cooling her often with the cloth. Praying for mercy. Listening to her struggle for each breath. Willing the sickness from her. If love could work a miracle, she would be well in that instant.

"So beautiful." Her voice was so low he barely heard it. Her eyes were open and she was staring at something beside the bed. "So white, so clean. I've never seen anything like it."

"Like what?" Daniel asked, his eyes going to where she looked – and seeing nothing.

"The light. Don't you see it?" she asked earnestly. "Such peace and beauty. And love, Daniel. It feels so good."

"Nina?" A chill ran up his spine and Daniel shivered.

"Shh." She smiled at him. "Would you hold me for a while?"

After the merest hesitation, Daniel carefully laid down beside her, drawing her against him, so that she rested in the circle of his arms, her head safe against his shoulder. Gently he stroked her hair.

"I've always believed," she whispered, "but I never realized-"

"Realized what?" She sounded more lucid than she had since the fever had gotten bad.

"That there was a heaven. And angels. Do you see them?"

The chill squeezed his heart and the pain of it radiated throughout his body, throbbing in its intensity.

"Don't say things like that," he pleaded, pressing his lips against her hair. "I need you, Nina. I love you!"

"I love you so much, Daniel. You'll never know how much. Being with you has been the most wonderful thing that's ever happened to me. I've never been happier." Her voice was growing faint.

"Neither have I," he said thickly. "And we're going to have the rest of our lives to be happy. Do you hear me?"

"I do love you." She sighed deeply.

"I love you. So much-"

"Hold me, Daniel."

"I've got you." He held her closer, as close as he dared, as she sighed again. He waited for the next raspy breath to come. When it didn't he whispered, "Nina-"

A soft sob sounded deep in his throat as the tears that had been threatening to spill over, trickled down his face. "I've got you."

~~~

"Too hot," Anna moaned, rolling her head back and forth.

Colby continued to wipe her down with cool
~~~

cloths, giving her aspirin as often as the nurse recommended, but nothing seemed to help. The fever continued to rise, and the coughing had gotten to the point where she actually sobbed during an attack. He wasn't sure if it was because she'd always had a low threshold for pain or because it was actually bad enough to make her weep.

He wished he could muster more sympathy for her plight. Truly he did. But it was hard as she'd been a complaining, vicious patient from the first hour. He'd been around dozens of people, in far worse condition that hadn't been nearly as contrary.

It hadn't helped when he'd received the telephone call about Charles Owens. Anna hadn't been sick when Elizabeth had died. That, alone, had almost broken his heart. But precious little Charles. And Jonathon was still sick. He'd never felt as useless as he had when he had to tell Elliot that his wife was sick and he would have to postpone the service for his son.

He truly wanted to be able to comfort him. And Margaret and the three remaining children. But even if he had been free to go to them, he didn't know what he could have said or done that might help. Actually he knew there was nothing he could say or do. Nothing would help. The loss was so great he wasn't sure if even time would.

"I hate you," Anna growled as another fit of coughing gripped her. Rather than allowing him to help her sit, which sometimes made it easier, she curled into as tight a ball as her large belly would allow, her back to him.

He didn't bother to respond. She'd been saying

that particular phrase often over the course of the past few hours. That and she hoped he would come down with the influenza, suffer and die. All he could do now was rub her back during the attacks, offer her sips of water and try to keep her as comfortable as possible. She refused to forgive him for making her sick, refused to listen to reason, that she could have caught it when she visited the grocers on several occasions. In her opinion, it was his fault and no other explanation was acceptable.

When she lay back against the pillow, Colby saw something that made his blood run cold. As discreetly as he could, he ran the cloth over her lips and chin. There it was. The telltale pink froth. He didn't know anyone at this stage of the illness who had survived. Still he prayed for God to heal her. He couldn't do anything less. Even though if He did, Colby's future would be nothing but miserable. Anna would never forgive him. And yet he wanted her to get well.

But she didn't. Throughout the evening, not twenty-four hours since her symptoms first appeared, she continued to get worse. The coughing spasms came more frequently. The fever inched up ever higher. The froth grew darker. And the hateful words spewed from her mouth without ceasing.

"I should have married a real man," she mumbled. "Someone who loved me and took care of me."

"I tried, Anna," Colby whispered, but she didn't hear him.

"But I married *you*. You have *never* made me

happy. I just want you to know that."

The coughing started yet again. Worse than before. So bad she could hardly catch her breath. This time, however, instead of curling up, she leaned up, grasped the front of Colby's shirt and hissed,

"This is your fault! *You* did this to me!" And then she fell back and simply died, a snarl frozen on her face. Colby knew that his wife hadn't found any peace at all in death. Just as surely as she wouldn't find any in the afterlife.

Numb, he slowly pulled the sheet over her face and waited for grief to wash over him. A measure of loss, or even a hint of sadness.

But the only thing Colby felt was an overwhelming sense of relief. As though a millstone had been removed from his neck. Like he'd been given a second chance. A gift.

Next he waited for the guilt he would surely feel. After nineteen years of marriage, a husband should feel bad that his wife had died. Especially if the husband in question happened to be a minister.

But, as he slowly rose from the bed and headed downstairs to alert the public health officer that he had a body to be picked up, Colby murmured a quiet and heartfelt, "Thank You, Lord."

Chapter 18

"I've got you," Daniel whispered again, holding the still form of his wife close, as tears slid down his temples.

At least she wasn't suffering anymore, he tried to tell himself. But it brought no comfort. Two weeks hadn't been enough time to be with her. Not nearly enough. They were supposed to have a lifetime, which meant *years*. It shouldn't have been able to be measured in days. How was he supposed to go on without her?

"Nina, please," he said, and began to weep. And then he stilled as he felt her take a great, deep breath.

It couldn't be! Could it?

He hauled himself up on one elbow and cupped her cheek with his other hand. The fever was gone, and she'd begun to sweat profusely.

She wasn't dead? Please, God, he prayed, sobbing now as he brought his face near hers. She *was* breathing! But how long had it been since she taken that last breath? Twenty seconds? Surely no more than thirty.

"Nina? Nina, wake up!" he begged, patting her face. All she did was moan softly. But it was enough. She was still with him.

~~~

Elliot's first thought, before he even opened his eyes, was that he must have dozed off at some point during the night. But whatever rest he'd gotten hadn't helped. He was so tired he could have slept for a month and it wouldn't have made a difference. He wished he could sleep forever rather than face a new day, and the pain that never left him. Wondering if Jonathon, too-

Jonathon!

His eyes snapped open and he sat bolt upright. Why hadn't Margaret woken him? Where *was* Margaret? She'd been sitting on the bed wiping a cool cloth across Jonathon's face the last time he recalled seeing her.

Where was Jonathon, for that matter?

The room was empty, but for him. A faint ray of hope swelled and he shot out of the chair, searching the rooms on the upper floor. He only found Kathleen asleep in her bed, her face tear stained. She must have brought every doll she possessed under the covers with her.
~~~

Elliot reached out a reluctant hand and gently laid it against her forehead, breathing a sigh of relief at the still cool skin.

A smile lighting his face, Elliot hurried down the stairs, noting that Richard was sprawled out, sleeping in a chair in the parlor. He'd check on him in a moment. After seeing for himself that Jonathon was all right.

But the kitchen was empty.

More than a little perplexed, he scoured the main floor but found no trace of his wife or son. They weren't out back either. His brows furrowed, he headed out to check the front porch. When he opened the door and saw them, he felt as though he'd been hit with a sledgehammer.

Margaret sat on the swing, slowly pushing it back and forth, humming softly. She held the stiff, lifeless body in her arms.

Jonathon was gone, too.

It had to be a nightmare. Three children in a matter of days? How could he bear this?

A curious numbness washed over him. He wanted to cry or scream at the unfairness. At the cruelty. But he could only stand, rooted to the spot, staring in anguish at this wonderful boy whose brilliant mind would be ever at rest. At his wife who tenderly stroked his hair and placed light kisses on his face.

"Did you sleep well, Dear?"

It took a moment before Elliot realized she'd spoken. To him. Why was she smiling?

"Margaret?"

"I know how exhausted you were," she

continued softly, "so when Jonathon's fever broke I thought it best to just let you rest."

She smiled down at her son and kissed him again before looking back at her husband.

"Sweet boy. He's tired, too. But I thought he should have some fresh air after being cooped up inside for so long. And it's helped. He's resting comfortably."

"Meg-"

"I'm going to make him an apple pie tomorrow. I know it's Wednesday, but you know how much he loves apple pie. I'd like to make it today, but the baby is coming. I don't think he'll mind though, do you? Not that I care!" She laughed softly then continued to talk. Rapidly. Much like Kathleen often did, barely stopping for a breath. "You will run to the market for me, won't you?"

"I- Yes. Of course," he murmured. She had to know. *Didn't she?* And *what* had she just said? The baby is coming? *Now?*

"I knew you would. Thank you." She began humming again and Elliot walked slowly to stand before her.

"I think you should come inside now," he said gently. He pressed his hands against her stomach and felt how hard it was. Yes, it was time. "There's a chill in the air and it's not good for- Jonathon. And you don't want to have the baby out here for all the neighbors to see, do you?"

"Jonathon is warm enough," she said quickly, looking pointedly at the quilt wrapped snuggly around him. "And there's plenty of time before the baby gets here. We've been cooped up in the house for so long, we just want to enjoy some time out here."

"*You're* not warm enough." She wore only a skirt and thin blouse. He reached out and touched her cheek. She *felt* warm, but it was from the fever. For a moment he closed his eyes then, swallowing hard, looked at her again. Please, God, not his wife, he prayed fervently. He couldn't bear any of this without her.

"I'm fine, Dear."

"I insist you come in and get into bed. I'll call the doctor and then you can concentrate on bringing our new son or daughter into the world. Let me take Jonathon, and then I'll help you upstairs."

"No!" she cried out, clutching the still form even closer. Her eyes were wild when she looked up at him.

In that moment he knew that she knew.

"Margaret, please let me take him."

"I've got him. Elliot, he just needs me right now. And you can't blame him. The poor child has been so ill."

"I want you to come inside *now*," he repeated firmly.

"I-" For a moment she looked desperate, then smiled suddenly and said, "All right. But I think it would be best if Jonathon laid down with me."

"If he's well, he can sleep in his own bed."

"No. Elliot, *please*-"

"Come. Let's go *now*." He reached out to take Jonathon but she slapped his hands away.

"No! I'll take him inside!"

Elliot was too weary to argue and merely helped

her to her feet. She struggled valiantly to carry the son who was nearly as tall as she across the porch. He wondered how she'd gotten him from the bedroom upstairs all the way out here without waking anyone.

As they neared the door Elliot noticed Richard there, tears coursing down his cheeks. How much of this had he witnessed, this tenderhearted young man who had lost two brothers and a sister?

"*No!*" Margaret screamed as Jonathon slipped from her arms.

Elliot whirled around as his body landed on the wooden planks. He nearly collapsed at the awful thud. Instead he grabbed Margaret, who made to lunge for her son.

"Let me help you inside. I'll come back for him."

"No! I can't let him lay there. Elliot, he'll get cold!"

"I'll bring him inside, Mama," Richard said quietly.

Margaret calmed immediately, patting his face as she allowed Elliot to lead her through the door.

"You're a good boy, Richard. All of you boys are, aren't they, Elliot?"

"Indeed," he murmured, glancing at Richard with gratitude.

"Be careful not to wake Charles and the girls, won't you?"

"I'll be careful, Mama."

~~~

Elliot stood at the window staring at the dark
~~~

blankets covering the neighbor's windows, scoffing at the futility of it. Did they really think that would protect them from the sickness? That they were above the invisible killer? That their pitiful attempts to keep it out would work? That it would pass by their family when it had destroyed his own in such a cruel fashion?

"Elliot?"

He turned quickly when her weak voice, barely audible, reached his ears. Her eyes were actually clear and focused now, and he felt the barest glimmer of hope as he hurried to sit on the edge of the bed.

"Meg," he said softly, smiling gently at her.

"Elliot-" She ran the tip of her tongue across dry, parched lips.

"Yes, my darling. I'm here."

"How is the baby?"

"She's fine. A little smaller than the doctor liked, but he said if we keep her warm and fed, she'll be just fine. She's sleeping in Kathleen's room. Doc Garland said you can see her when your fever is gone. She's so beautiful, Meg. So tiny. I'd forgotten how small babies are," he told her, stroking her cheek. He didn't think her fever had gone down at all.

"I was sure she'd be a boy. I don't know what we should name her."

"We'll come up with the perfect name when you're well again."

"Elliot? Will you do something for me?"

"Anything. Whatever you want, Meg."

"You must take care of the children."

"I will," he promised, reaching out to stroke her cheek, still unbelievably hot from the fever. "Don't you worry about a thing. Just rest and get well."

"Elliot." Her blue eyes stared at him hard. "You must care for Richard, Kathleen, and the baby."

"*I will*," he said again. "Until you're better. And then we'll take care of them together."

"No." She smiled sadly. "I'm going to watch over Elizabeth, Jonathon and Charles. So you have to promise me-"

"No!" Elliot cried in horror, grasping her shoulders. "We need you here, Meg."

"I can't stay." She was overcome with a fit of coughing, curling into a ball as the spasms shook her, leaving her gasping for air.

Elliot felt panic filling him as he saw the pink froth trickling from the corner of her mouth. The same thing had happened with the children, shortly before death stole them from him. His lungs began to burn and tears filled his eyes. She was slipping away and he was powerless to stop it.

"We've lost too much, Meg. You have to fight this. *Please!* I can't lose you, too."

"I watched them, Elliot. It won't be long now. And then I'll be with my babies again."

His throat was closing, cutting off his air and yet, somehow, he continued to breathe.

"No."

"Promise me, Elliot."

"You have babies *here* that need you. *I* need you!"

"Promise me. Promise me you'll take care of them." The stern tone of her voice meant she expected his compliance, that his Meg meant business.

"I promise," he whispered, the tears spilling over and streaming down his cheeks. She reached up weakly, her hand trembling, and touched his face.

"I love you, Elliot Owens. I have since the first day I saw you. You have made me happier than I ever dreamed. And it hurts to know that our time together must come to an end."

"Meg-" His shoulders began to shake as the sobs he'd tried so hard to hold back escaped.

"As much as I want to stay here, I want you to live a good, long life even more. To be happy."

"Not without you. I can't go on without you." He had to force the words past the lump that had lodged in his throat, and he cupped her cheek with his hand. "You're my life, Meg."

"You *will* go on, Elliot," she said firmly. "You *will* finish raising Richard and the girls the way we planned. You'll make sure they grow up to be fine adults. You'll welcome each of our grandchildren, and you'll tell them, someday, of the uncles and aunt they never got a chance to know. Of the grandmother who wanted to hold and spoil each one of them. And one day, Elliot, when you've done all of this for me, the four of us will be waiting to welcome you into heaven."

Elliot took her hand and pressed its palm against his lips, weeping uncontrollably.

"Shh. It's all right my dear. I'm not afraid of dying. I don't want you to be afraid either. You're a strong man. I know it will be hard for a while, but you're a strong, good-hearted man. You'll be fine.

Just fine."

"No, Meg. I can't do it."

"You will. I have to go care for part of our family. We need you here to take care of the rest." Another bout of coughing tore at his heart as she writhed in pain. But she managed to continue, breathlessly. "Someday, Elliot. Someday we'll all be together again. Forever."

"Meg-" How was it possible to reach the limit of grief time and again, only to have it climb ever higher?

"Please. Call the children in so I can tell them goodbye."

"Oh, God. Meg, *please!* I need you. *They* need you."

"Call them, Elliot. *Hurry.*"

She didn't say it. But then she didn't need to. Her time on earth was all but finished. His heart was breaking. Shattering into millions of tiny fragments as he forced himself to leave her side and walk out to the landing.

"Richard. Come up here and bring Kathleen with you," he called, his voice thick with the sorrow he couldn't hide.

A long silence followed but, finally, he heard slow footsteps on the stairs and hurried back to his wife's side.

"They're coming, Meg," he told her quietly. She smiled at him gratefully.

It was clear by the guarded expression on Richard's face that he thought his mother had already died. Kathleen, who had begun to realize the significance of the past few days hid behind her brother, clutching his leg in fear. Elliot motioned them to the bedside.

"Your mother wants to talk to you," he said, almost inaudibly.

Richard's shoulders sagged in relief and he pulled Kathleen with him to where his mother lay. Margaret looked up at them with the tender love only a mother could feel, and held her hand out to Kathleen. With a muffled cry she flung herself into Margaret's arms, burying her face against her neck.

"My sweet, beautiful baby," she murmured, stroking the soft hair she'd spent countless hours brushing. "You'll always be a good girl for your papa, won't you?"

"Yes, Mama."

"Look at me, Darling." Gently she raised Kathleen's face and looked at her with such hunger that Elliot knew she was trying to commit the image of it to mind, long enough to last for the duration of Kathleen's long, happy lifetime. "Mama must go away, Kathleen."

"Can I come, too?" came the eager response.

"Oh no, Sweetheart! No. You must stay and help take care of Papa and Richard and your new baby sister."

"Where are you going, Mama?" Curious eyes regarded her mother.

"I have to go to Elizabeth, Jonathon and Charles."

"In the ground?" Fat tears welled in her big blue eyes because she knew that 'in the ground' was a bad thing. A very bad thing.

From behind a low, agonized sob came from

Richard.

"In heaven, baby," Margaret said softly.

Heaven? Her face cleared a bit. Heaven was a good place. She laid her head back against her mother's breast.

"Why can't I come?"

"Because your father is going to need you here. So will your brother and your sister."

"They could come, too," she suggested hopefully. Margaret shook her head, kissing the soft brown hair resting against her chin.

"It's not time for any of you to come. But I told your papa that we will all be together again someday."

"Promise?"

"With all my heart. I love you, Kathleen. I want you to remember that. Always."

She looked up at Richard then. His sobs were quiet, though he trembled almost violently. Margaret stretched her hand out to his.

"Come here, son." She tugged him with what little strength she had left and he eased down beside his sister. "Let me hold you."

Crying harder, he laid his head on her shoulder. Elliot watched the scene, his heart twisting painfully in his chest.

"Richard." She stroked his hair with her free hand. "Things won't be easy for a while. But I have faith in you. You're a strong young man and you're going to do very well."

"Mama, no!" The high pitch to his voice sounded everything but strong.

"Shh. Shh. I'm sorry. So very sorry. Shh."

Elliot wished he could ease some of his son's pain but didn't even know what to do about his own.

~~~

"Here, let me help you," Daniel said softly, sitting on the edge of the bed and helping to arrange the tray on Nina's lap.

"I'm fine," she assured him, but though the dark shadows beneath her eyes were disappearing, she still looked tired. He wasn't taking any chances with her.

"I know you are. But I still want to help." And he did, spooning small bites of oatmeal for her. The doctor had warned him to feed her soft foods for about a week, to give her throat a chance to heal from the violent coughing.

"That's good. You're spoiling me, Daniel."

"I hope so, because that's my plan." He leaned forward and kissed her brow. "I really thought I lost you, Nina. I've never felt so scared or alone in my life." He watched at tears filled her eyes and she reached up to stroke his cheek.

"I'm sorry. I wish I could have spared you that."

"As long as you're here now. That's all that matters," he said fervently. "I don't know what I would have done if you'd really died."

"Don't laugh at me but- I- I think I might have," she admitted slowly, looking at him through her lashes.

"What?"

"I think I might have died."
~~~

"No, you're here, Sweetheart. You didn't die."

"It didn't feel like a dream."

"What didn't? Here, eat this." He fed her another bite of the cereal.

"I think I was in heaven, Daniel. Not for very long. But there was a light. It was so bright and so warm. There was a voice that told me it wasn't time yet, that I had to go back to you. I – didn't really want to leave because I'd never felt anything like that before. But I wanted to be with you, too, because I love you so much." She'd been looking intently at the tray but peeked up at him. "Do you think I've lost my mind?"

"I do not."

"Do you think it was real? Or a dream?"

Daniel hesitated before answering her, his mind reliving the moment when he thought she'd died. Her chest had rattled with the effort it cost her to breathe. She'd been coughing harshly. And then she'd simply stopped. Long enough that he'd known she was gone. And then she'd taken that oh so welcome breath. No more rattling. No more coughing. The fever gone.

"I don't think it was a dream, Nina. I think you were in the presence of God and that He, in His mercy, gave you back to me."

Chapter 19

"Marcus! Marcus, I know you're in there. Open up!" Colby shouted, pounding on the door of the darkened house. No one had seen Marcus since the day of Charles Owens' funeral. If he hadn't known it to be five days ago, the pile of papers on the walk would have told him as much. Hopefully he hadn't fallen ill, too.

"Wait here," he said absently, turning around and hurrying down the steps, and around to the back porch. Marcus had never before locked this door and it seemed he hadn't changed his habits now.

A slightly sour smell assaulted his nostrils as he crept into the kitchen. In the dim light of evening, he could see a pile of dishes in the sink, which meant that his friend had been eating. If he were ill, he'd have been too weak to fend for himself

A quick tour of the main floor led to the second

in his search for Marcus. He didn't have far to look. He was sitting in an arm chair in his almost dark bedroom. Colby walked to the gas lamp on the far wall, turned the switch and light filled the room.

From the looks of things, Marcus hadn't shaved in days. Nor slept much either. What little he had gotten must have been in the wrinkled dressing gown he wore. Other than a brief glance, he ignored Colby's presence entirely. Colby went and knelt in front of him. Taking a hand in his he said,

"I know things have been hard, my friend, but you can't run away from life."

"It's too much," he said tonelessly. "They're all dying, Colby. Everyone is dying."

"Not everyone. You're still here. I'm still here. And we have to go on living."

"I don't know if I can. Or if I want to." Colby sighed. This wasn't good. He hoped the discouragement wasn't permanent because there was going to be a problem if it was.

"Marcus, I have something to show you. You need to come downstairs with me now."

"I don't want to see anything."

"Marcus, now please." He tugged on the hand he still held until Marcus rose reluctantly to his feet. Then, like a child, he led him down the stairs and into the parlor. "Wait here."

He left the room quickly, to return moments later with two young children in tow. Marcus stared at them as though they were alien beings, eyes wide, jaws slack.

"Who are they? Why are they in my house?" Colby sat the girls on the settee and walked to stand beside Marcus and whispered,

"The conductor at the train station tried to get you by telephone, then called me when you didn't answer. Your friend Derek, and most of his family, died of the influenza, Marcus. These girls are all that's left, and they came with a letter saying you had agreed to raise his children should something ever happen to him and his wife."

"Oh, Lord." Marcus closed his eyes remembering, Colby assumed, an agreement he seemed to be regretting.

~~~

Shaking his head in disbelief and sadness, Marcus tried to accept the fact that his best friend in the world was gone. Along with his wife and two sons. Then he opened panic filled eyes and focused on the objects on before him. "But- Colby, they're- They're *girls!*"

"Little girls who have lost *everything* they've ever known," he reminded him gently. "Their parents, their brothers and grandparents, and Lord knows who else. Their home is gone. You promised to take care of them, Marcus."

"I know I did. But – *little girls*, Colby?" He could feel what little color that remained in his face drain. Probably all the way down to his toes. "I don't know what to do with little girls."

"Feed them, clothe them. Love them. I don't think it's terribly hard, my friend."

Marcus closed his eyes and rubbed a hand over them, peeked out and closed them yet again when
~~~

the girls remained seated across the room.

"Their names are Rebecca and Rachael. They're five years old."

"They're twins." It wasn't a question. He'd gotten an excited phone call from Derek the day they'd been born.

"They most certainly are," Colby said with a smile. "You're going to have a little trouble telling them apart, I suspect."

"Could you – could you and the missus take them? I'd pay you-"

"Anna died a few days ago. I'd be in the same position you are. Marcus, they're *your* responsibility now. You're not going to let Derek down, are you?"

It took a few moments before Marcus reluctantly shook his head no. He wondered if Colby could tell what a difficult decision this was. But no one could ever accuse Marcus of not fulfilling his responsibilities.

"No. I won't let him down."

"Have you ever met the girls before?"

"No."

"Maybe you should introduce yourself then."

~~~

For a moment Colby was expecting a complete disaster. That maybe he would just stand there and say, 'I'm Marcus," and nothing more. But Colby's jaw fell open when Marcus McClelland walked slowly – very slowly – across the room and knelt down before the tiny girls with long blonde curls and said very gently,
~~~

"Hello. My name is Marcus. Your father was my best friend and I'm going to be taking care of you from now on." He swallowed so hard that Colby heard him clear across the room. "I guess you're my little girls now."

~~~

Though the sun was up Elliot saw no reason why he, too, should be. More than half his family had been taken from him in one short week. His beloved wife. A beautiful daughter. Two wonderful sons. More than he could bear. More than anyone should have to bear.

The future, once so bright and filled with hope was now bleak and empty. Forever filled with the agony of these losses. Places in his heart that would never cease aching for the sight and touch of them. Places that could never be filled with anything but pain.

He felt a tear tickle his temple as he lay on his back staring at the ceiling. In the bed Margaret would never share with him again. The bed he never wanted to leave because he didn't want to face this new, lonely and frightening life. So different than what it should have been.

'Take care of them, Elliot. *Promise me*.'

"I can't," he wept softly, curling onto his side and holding her pillow close.

'Take care of them.'

"Not without you, Meg. It's too hard. I can't do it alone."

'Promise me.'
~~~

He saw her face again, her eyes pleading with him to go on and make a life for Richard, Kathleen and the baby. And he had promised. Anything to ease her unbearable sorrow. But she hadn't known what she'd asked of him. The utter impossibility of the task she'd set before him.

What would she say if she knew he was too weak and spineless to keep that promise? His lips trembled with a little smile. He knew full well what his Meg would say.

'Bad things happen to everyone, Elliot Owens, and you are no exception. But that's no excuse to give up and hide. Now get yourself out of that bed and go take care of our children.'

"I'll try, Sweetheart," he whispered, placing a soft kiss against her pillow. Reluctantly he put it back beside his, stroking it softly before letting it go. It felt like he would have to let her go.

It took every ounce of strength he could muster but Elliot did get out of bed. It was Sunday, after all, and his wife would have his head on a platter if he didn't get this family, what was left of it, into their pew on time.

It wasn't long before he was dressed in a suit and glancing at his pocket watch. They had about ninety minutes before they had to leave. Of course Sara Elizabeth was soaked, and he had to take a few minutes to change her. Then he lifted her into his arms, holding her close and wishing Meg could see the beautiful child they'd made.

His first stop was Kathleen's room. He rapped lightly on her door and stepped inside. She still slept, with every 'baby' she possessed tucked in with her. She had also managed to get hold of her mother's dressing gown and it was clutched tightly to her breast. A lump formed in his throat, making it difficult to swallow as he knelt beside the bed. He brushed her hair, so much like Margaret's, away from her face saying thickly,

"Hey, Darlin,' it's time to get up." He forced as much cheerfulness into his voice as possible. It wasn't much. "Come on, Kathleen. It's time to get ready for church. Up and at 'em."

Her eyes fluttered open and, for a moment, she looked happy to see him. As she'd been in the not so distant past. Then, as had happened every morning since her mother and brothers' funeral, she remembered and her eyes filled with sorrow.

"Good morning," he said, pasting a smile on his face for her.

"Good morning, Papa," she answered quietly, her voice still sleepy.

"Do you think you can get yourself dressed for church today?" he asked, stoking her cheek.

"We're going to church?" She obviously didn't want to go any more than he did.

"We sure are. We all promised your mother that we'd take care of each other, and you know how she felt about us going to church." He leaned close and whispered, "I don't think I'd want her frowning down us from heaven because we stayed home again, do you?"

"Oh no, Papa!" At her utterly serious tone, Elliot smiled his first real smile since before their lives had been torn apart.

"That's my girl! Now get dressed so I can go

wake Richard. I need to get downstairs to fix our breakfast." He got to his feet and winked at her. "I don't think Reverend Thornton would be pleased with us if we didn't eat something and our stomachs grumbled all through the service."

Her giggles filed his ears as he walked down the hall as she was imagining, he was sure, the good reverends message being drowned out by four hungry bellies.

As he'd done at Kathleen's door, Elliot knocked once and pushed the door open, to find that Richard was not sleeping. Rather he stood by the window, turning as his father entered.

"Good morning, Pop."

"Good morning, son."

Even though he was eight years older than his sister, Richard looked every bit as lost as she did, unsure of how to live life now that it had changed so dramatically. Why that should come as a surprise to him, Elliot didn't know. He wasn't sure how to go on either, and he'd had a lot more experience than either of his children.

"Why don't you get dressed while I make breakfast," he said, again trying to force some cheerfulness into his voice.

"Pop?"

"We're going to church. That was a hard and fast rule of your mother's. And we have missed the past few Sundays." He smiled at his son and turned to leave saying, "I'll see you downstairs in a few minutes."

Elliot tried to recall who had sent what as he rummaged through the icebox. He would have to send notes of appreciation to the ladies in the church who had been sending meals and groceries since the funerals. He sent up a prayer of gratitude as he pulled a slab of bacon, wrapped in brown paper, out and headed for the stove.

Before he realized what he'd done, he'd filled the pan with it, then had to remove more than half. It hurt to know that he would be cooking for three and not seven. One of the endless new things he would have to get used to. He glanced at the bottle, sitting in a bowl of warm water on the counter. He'd have to get used to that, too. Meg had nursed the other children, but feeding Sara was going to be up to him now.

And maybe someday doing things for just four would begin to feel normal. Because surely they would have to find a new sense of normalcy. Soon. This was simply too hard.

Richard was the first to join him and, wordlessly, he took a stack of plates from the cupboard. Like Elliot had done, he had to put four back when he realized he'd taken out seven. Elliot's heart ached at his wounded expression when he hesitated at the table. The last time it had been set, it had been for everyone.

"Why don't we sit at my end?" he suggested gently and watched as Richard slowly put one plate at the head, the others on either side. Napkins, glasses and silverware followed, but it didn't look right. Instead it looked vast and empty. Only the baby, lying on a folded quilt on the other end kept it from looking worse than it did.

"Can I help with anything, Pop?"

"I don't suppose you know how to make biscuits?" Elliot asked helplessly. That had been Meg's specialty. In the past, when his wife had still been asleep, he'd just gone ahead and made toast. This morning it would have been nice to have something of her with them.

But it wasn't to be. Though he scoured the kitchen, Richard couldn't find a recipe. So toast it would have to be.

By the time Kathleen entered the kitchen, everything was nearly ready. He saw that she was near tears, the back of her dress gaping open.

"I tried, Papa, but I can't fasten the buttons," she whispered.

"I'll do it," Richard volunteered, sitting in one of the chairs and pulling his sister between his knees.

It stuck Elliot then how difficult it was going to be for two men to raise these girls. For him especially. Things that Meg would have dealt were now going to fall to him, and he had to admit that they just might be more than he could manage. How was a father supposed to discuss with his daughters the changes that would come as they grew from children to women? He rubbed his chin as he stirred the eggs, not looking forward to the conversations that would come. Conversations sure to embarrass all of them.

After grace was said, the meal was a relatively silent affair. Only an occasional, "Please pass the bacon," broke the oppressing silence. So different from the meals eaten before. It was a relief when it was over, and they all rushed to clear the table, putting the dishes in the sink to soak while they were at church.

In the hall they bundled up in coats and scarves to protect them from the brisk November winds, Sara wrapped snugly in a small quilt, and the blanket her mother had knitted before the influenza. Elliot surveyed their sad little group and, unable to help himself, drew both children to him and held them close.

"This isn't going to be easy," he said softly. "Everything is going to be strange and different for a long time to come. But we're all we have now and we'll get through this. I promise."

"I know we will, Pop," Richard told him, his voice muffled against his father's neck.

"We have to remember that they're safe in heaven. They'll never be hurt, or suffer ever again. And they're waiting for us to join them someday. We must remember that when it gets hard and we don't know if we can go on. And we have to try to be happy again. That's what your mother wished for the most. That we would have long, happy lives." As he said the words, Elliot couldn't imagine ever coming to a place of happiness again.

He kissed each of their cheeks and set them away from him. "I love you both. Very much. You know that, don't you?"

"Yes, Papa."

"Yes, sir. We love you, too, Pop."

"All right then. Are we ready to go?"

At their nods, they left the house, Kathleen walking between her father and brother, holding their hands tightly. Sara was so light, even with the blankets, that he hardly felt her weight in his other arm.

As they strolled down the sidewalk Elliot saw Mr. Mertz approaching them, heading in the other direction. If he remembered correctly, Mr. Mertz attended the Catholic church. His steps slowed as he neared them, faltering to a stop. For a long moment they just stood there, staring at each other.

"I knew what he was doing," the old man said thickly, his faint German accent more pronounced today. "Sometimes I would do things because it made him happy. I once buried a ham bone in my backyard. He was watching me from a tree." He stopped to take a shaky breath, then his eyes filled with tears and he whispered, "He was a good boy, your Jonathon."

Elliot tried to thank him but could only nod his head, unable to speak past the lump in his throat. When Mr. Mertz patted his shoulder, he just nodded again and tried to blink his own tears away.

Epilogue

Colby turned the collar of his coat up in an effort to stop some of the cold wind from turning his neck into a solid block of ice. He was trying to hurry to get downtown for the parade that would celebrate the official end of the war. Just yesterday word had reached them. According to the newspaper, communities around the world were celebrating.

Or pretending to.

In his opinion the influenza had taken too big a toll for any honest celebrating to be going on. Some estimated that the loss of life from it numbered around twenty million while others thought the number to be closer to forty. Charlotte had only lost a small portion of that but he'd yet to see a face over the past couple of weeks that hadn't looked haunted.

Most people had buried at least one family member, and those few who were fortunate enough to have not lost someone close had known many of those who had died. The parade today was nothing more than an effort to keep living. Part of the charade they would play at until life returned to normal. Or something close to it.

It wasn't as though they had a choice. Life would always march on, and it would drag each and every one of them along with it, no matter how much they might hurt right now. Time would help to heal their pain, though it would never erase it completely.

He only wished he could feel some of that pain. Anna had been his wife after all. But the only sadness he felt was in knowing where she would be spending eternity. The same as he felt for anyone who had rejected God's precious gift. Grief over a lost soul, no more, no less. Mostly what he felt was gratitude, for which he continued to ask forgiveness several times a day.

As he neared Main Street, he was astounded at the size of the crowd. Perhaps he'd gotten used to the empty streets during the worst of the epidemic because the crowd seemed overwhelming. There had been days when he feared he was the only living being on the earth, so quiet and deserted was the town.

Not so today. It appeared as though anyone who could walk or hobble lined both sides of the two blocks. People talking and smiling, hoping that others wouldn't notice that their cheerfulness was forced, or that their eyes reflected the same misery they saw in eyes of everyone around them.

He stopped for a moment, fairly near the street

but behind a small group of children. They were short enough that it allowed him to see who was standing across from him.

Daniel and Nina Pullman, holding hands and looking radiantly happy over in front of the druggists. And why shouldn't they be? He'd heard the story of Nina's 'death' and found that he agreed with the young couple. He, too, believed she'd seen the glory of God and that He, in His mercy, had given her back to her husband.

A little to the north, in the next block up, he saw Marcus kneeling between Rachael and Rebecca, who were each chattering and gesturing toward the corner where the parade would begin. Marcus looked a bit overwhelmed but he was, for the first time in all the years Colby had known him, smiling the only genuine smile he'd ever seen. So big and so contagious that he found himself grinning, too.

He'd been a bit nervous upon leaving Marcus that first morning, but it was obvious he was keeping his word to his friend. The girls were clean and looked happy, even if their braids were slightly crooked and off center. Even more obvious was the fact that they were very, *very* good for his friend. He'd have to stop in soon, just to reassure himself that all was finally well in Marcus' world.

Smiling again, he continued down the street. When he reached the corner of Main and Lawrence, he looked down the line of people again, his eyes coming to rest on Elliot Owens and his children. What was left of them anyway. Their family, more than any other in town, had suffered the greatest loss. Exactly half of them gone now.

Elliot had brought Richard, Kathleen and little Sara to church the past two Sundays and his heart had broken each time. They had once taken up most of one pew because there had been so many of them. But not anymore. Colby missed Jonathon's fidgeting throughout the service. Missed the tales of his spying and other adventures. Missed them all so terribly he felt tears come to his eyes.

They spilled over and ran down his cheeks when, as the small marching band rounded the corner, Elliot lifted Kathleen to his hip so she could see everything. He'd never known a better, more loving father than Elliot Owens. Regardless of his overwhelming loss he was still that, and so much more to the ones that survived.

His eyes moved to Richard, who was holding the baby close. The poor boy looked so lost that Colby longed to comfort him. So much like his father, he'd guarded the brood like a mother hen. With only two sisters to watch out for now, he seemed to be at a loss, not sure what to do anymore.

Time. It would take more time for them than for the others but they, too, would find their way again. And he'd be there to help them in whatever he could. Someday they would discover that life still held joy for them. Perhaps not to the same degree as before, but still there nonetheless.

"Oh, Reverend Thornton! There you are!" Betsy Montgomery said, grasping his arm, her smile wide with enthusiasm. "I was hoping to find you here. I baked you a pie and wondered if it would be all right to drop it off this afternoon."

And maybe, just possibly, he might find some joy of his own.

Estimates of the actual death toll from the 1918 influenza pandemic range between 40 and 100 million people, worldwide. Conservative estimates for the United States alone are 550,000. That's more than the total number of American soldiers who died in *all* of the wars during the twentieth century.

I don't remember ever reading about this in any school history class. In fact, I don't remember hearing about this at all until I happened to catch a documentary on PBS. But if Enza has piqued your interest about this tragic event, I encourage you to browse around PBS.org. They have a fair number of videos and transcripts that you might find interesting.

~~~

If you enjoyed reading Enza, and even if you didn't, please take a moment to leave a review at www.amazon.com.

You can check out Kristy's other books at:
www.amazon.com
www.kristykjames.com

Kristy loves to hear from her readers. Please drop her an email at: kristykjames@gmail.com
~~~

I'd like to say a special thank you to:

Shineka, Katrina, Michelle, Lee, and last but not least, Jaki. Your help was invaluable. Also, thanks so much to Donna Casey, from Digital Donna, for the *fabulous* job on the cover. You made my vision a reality!

Made in the USA
Columbia, SC
19 April 2020